THE SECOND MISSION

A RETURN TO 1775

By Richard Scott

Winter Island Press

Salem, Massachusetts

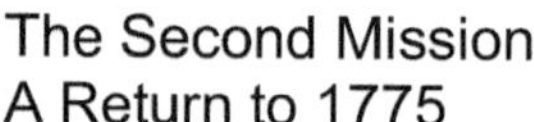

The Second Mission:
A Return to 1775

Special thanks to Jeanne Scott, Kim Scott and Mort Harrison for reading my manuscript and providing me with many helpful suggestions.

If you like

THE SECOND MISSION

You might also like the following novels by Richard Scott (Available in Kindle and Paperback)

Time Travel Novels
Mission in Time   https://amzn.to/3fHBejn

Tony Dantry Thrillers
The Reluctant Assassin   https://amzn.to/310bPxp
The Eager Assassin   https://amzn.to/2Nj1xA8
The Assassin Chip   https://amzn.to/2zSiMW8
Assassin on Main Street   https://amzn.to/3dloNs7
Revenge of the Rising Sun   https://amzn.to/3fDdo8k
The Rail Trail Murders   https://amzn.to/2CkHD5G

Other books by Richard Scott
Salem, the Novel   https://amzn.to/3dklWPS
The Second Assassination   https://amzn.to/2YjH0ln
Jefferson and the Barbary Pirates https://amzn.to/2NeVSv1
Murder on Third Avenue   https://amzn.to/3hNZB0E

Major Characters

Fictional

Arne, Timothy: Social Library trustee
Blair, Matthew (Matt): Chrononaut
Carver, Christopher (Chris): Chrononaut
Cabot, Samuel: Social Library trustee
Crockett, Mrs.: Innkeeper
Ellis, Nathaniel: Social Library trustee
English, Joshua: Wealthy ship owner in Beverly Farms
Farnsworth, Jason: Hi-tech billionaire who helped fund the mission
Fields, Simon: Nathaniel Ellis's lawyer
Gray, William: Salem Constable
Halliday, Madison: Employee of the CAE Center for Advanced
   Exploration
Howard, Thomas (Tom): Former chrononaut and now *Essex Gazette*
   employee
Lee, Gilbert (Gil): Former chrononaut and now *Essex Gazette*
   employee
Martin, Elihu: Social Library trustee
Parker, Robert: Lieutenant in Provincial militia
Purdy, Ebenezer: Member of the Anti-Witch Society
   Pynchon, Thomas: President of the Social Library Board of Trustees
Talbot, Jedediah: Schoolteacher from Lynn
Taliaferro, Obadiah: Leader of Amesbury Committee of Safety
Weeks, Jeremiah: Librarian at the Social Library in Salem

Actual Historical Figures

Burgoyne, William: British General
Gage, Governor Thomas: 1719-1787. General in British army
   and Governor of
Massachusetts Bay Colony
Hall, Samuel (Sam): Publisher of the *Essex Gazette*
Howe, William: British General
Mason, Colonel David: Leader of Salem Committee of Safety
   and Colonel in Massachusetts Committee of Safety
Pigot, Robert: British General
Pitcairn, Major John: British officer killed at Bunker Hill
Prescott, William: Colonel in the Provincial Militia
Putnam, Israel: General, serving under General Ward

—

Russell, Ezekial: Publisher of the *Salem Gazette*
Salem, Peter: Freed slave who fought for the Provincial side
    at Bunker Hill
Ward, Artemas: Major General and Commander of the
    Provincial militia
Warren, Dr. Joseph: President of the Massachusetts Provincial
    Congress and Chairman of Massachusetts
Committee of Safety. Also commissioned as a major general just
    before Bunker Hill

—

vii

Language Note:
I have tried to avoid using any words, terms, or expressions in the conversations of my characters that were not in use at the time. As a writer it is often tempting to use expressions and phrases common in the 21st century, but I tried to avoid them. When a word or expression was in doubt I researched it to be sure it was a word or expression people would have used in America in 1775.

THE SECOND MISSION

Prologue: Retrieving the Package

September 2019

MY NAME IS MADISON HALLIDAY. I work at a remote Nellis Air Force Base test facility in Nevada. Many call it Area 51. The people who work here call it Groom Lake. Whatever you call it, it's acknowledged to be a test site for secret weapons and secret aircraft. Over the years there have been numerous claims of UFO sightings in this area. Some even claim that the Air Force has built advanced aircraft based on technology derived from downed or captured alien spaceships.

The facility is quite large, and there are many projects underway at any given time. The project I work on was at one time super-secret. Then, four years ago the cat was let out of the bag to a select few people. It's still unknown to the general public.   Our project leaders aren't sure whether public knowledge of our project is desirable. I've heard both the pros and cons, and both arguments are convincing. Fortunately, that's not my decision to make.

Today I flew commercial from Las Vegas to Boston. When I arrived at Logan Airport I was greeted by pleasantly cool New England weather, a welcome contrast to the 100-plus heat I'd left back in Nevada. I immediately took an Uber to Salem, about 15 miles north of the airport. As soon as I got there I checked into the Salem Waterfront Hotel.

You no doubt wonder why someone from a Nevada Air Force test facility would be in Salem, a town known for its Witch Trials and festive Halloween celebrations. The reason is this: The Salem Athenaeum. The Salem Athenaeum is an old and highly respected membership library dating back to 1760. In the 18th and 19th centuries there were many such membership libraries. Now they only number in the teens. I'm sure you're thinking that's interesting, but why would an employee of a top-secret Nevada test facility be interested in an historic old library in Massachusetts? Why would I come all the way from Nevada to visit an old library.

Obviously there's a good reason or I wouldn't be doing it. It comes down to this: The Athenaeum has a package that we scientists back in Nevada need to get our hands on and we can't get access to it unless we go to the Athenaeum and pick it up in person. For reasons you'll soon discover, the Athenaeum people wouldn't send it to us by mail or Fed Ex or any other means. We have to pick it up in person. I had called the Athenaeum from my office in Nevada and knew that the people I needed to see would be waiting for me this evening at the library. It was a big deal for them, too.

Oh, by the way, this was not the first package we'd gotten from the Athenaeum. Back in 2015 we'd retrieved the first package and that package proved that Einstein's theory of relativity had been wrong (at least part of the theory). While that first package made those of us on the project ecstatic, at the same time it was unsettling and disturbing to those of us who thought about the implications of what we learned. It meant that some of what scientists had long believed about the laws of the universe was no longer true. The package I will retrieve today almost certainly will add more fuel to that fire.

Creating the Second Package

I wrote this journal with the hope that my mission partner, Matthew Blair, and I will successfully get it to the people in charge of this second and even more ambitious project than the one carried out four years ago by Gilbert Lee and Thomas Howard. —Christopher Carver

Chapter 1

2019

WE LEFT EARTH in early August. Our instruments tell us we are already more than one light year from Earth. A light year is the distance light travels in one year, which is about 5.9 trillion miles, in case you're wondering.

Before liftoff from the Nevada desert I agreed to write a journal covering the mission from liftoff to landing and everything that happens once we arrive at our destination.

Now here's where it gets really interesting. We're not sure what our destination is. Oh we know what we want it to be, but when you're dealing with time travel it's not so easy to get to where you want to go or when you want to get there. On the first mission four years ago our predecessors, Gilbert Lee and Thomas Howard, thought they were going two years into the future. They ended up 240 years in the past. How's that for accuracy? A two-and-a-half-century error. As a matter of fact, Gil and Tom are still living in the past right smack in the middle of the American Revolution.

The people in charge of our project decided that this new mission would attempt to drop my partner and me in the same place and in the same time period that the first mission finds itself. This makes a great deal of sense if we can do it successfully. Hopefully we will meet up with Gil and Tom and give them some 21st century company. It will also make the adjustment easier for us, since we're going to have to adapt to an entirely new lifestyle. You see, the problem with time travel is that you can't return to where or when you started. Time travel is a marvel, but so far, we don't have the ability to make it a round-trip marvel. Once you arrive there, you stay there.

No doubt you wonder what sane person would be willing to go on such a one-way trip. Not a lot of people volunteer, but believe it or not, the project did have some volunteers. My partner Matthew Blair and I volunteered for a number of reasons. Oh, by the way, I'm Chris Carver. Both of us were intimately involved in designing the first mission. We both know Gil Lee and Tom Howard, the chrononauts who went on that historic first mission and are still living back in the 18th century. So why did we volunteer for a one-way trip 240 years back in time? Gil and Tom didn't think they were going back in time, so that wasn't a choice for them when they started their mission. They thought they were going two years forward and figured they would not be that far out of touch with their friends. They had no living close relatives, so it was an easy decision to make. Matthew and I knew from the journal Gil wrote that after the initial shock of finding themselves back in time more than two centuries, both he and Thomas gradually adapted to life in the 18th century and were quite happy there. I kid you not.

For Matthew and me, it was a lot tougher decision because, despite the good reports from Gil and Tom, the thought of living in the 1700s without the conveniences and technology of the 21st century was not easy to accept. Some of the other candidates who qualified for the mission bowed out because they were unwilling to leave the 21st century behind them. I totally understand their decision. Both Matthew and I still hope we've made the right decision because we're stuck with it.

You probably also wonder what qualifies someone for a time-travel mission. For one thing you have to have a scientific degree—preferably in physics or biology. Matthew has one in physics and mine is in the biological sciences. Secondly you need a good knowledge of 18th century American history. We both minored in history. Thirdly you have to have mastered at least one skill or trade that would stand you in good stead in 18th century America. You could be trained as a farrier or blacksmith. You could train as a baker. You could train as a carpenter. Better yet you could train as a printer using historic presses and historic typesetting. You could also hone your skills as a writer. These latter skills or trades made good sense to us because working for a printer or newspaper would put us in the mainstream of 18th century thinking. It would help us establish ourselves among the movers and thinkers of the time. Matthew and I trained in two trades each in order to give us the best possible chance of fitting into the 18th century when we got there. Most importantly of all, to qualify we could not have any immediate family members. Matthew was brought up in a variety of foster homes and my parents both perished in the 911 disaster in the Twin Towers. Believe it or not they both worked there.

—

Still, despite meeting those qualifications on paper, the CAE or Center for Advanced Exploration in Nevada wanted to be sure we knew what we were doing when we volunteered to live 240 years in the past. We were young and they knew that young people often make decisions in haste that they regretted years later. As one more precaution they had us spend some time with a shrink. I remember the first time I met with Dr. Sturgis. She said, "How can you be so sure that you'll be happy in the 18th century? It's a big change," she said. Then she added ominously, "And it's irreversible."

I'd asked myself this many times since I stepped up and volunteered for the mission. I had to be sure I gave her an answer that made sense to her. "I don't have any close relatives, and I'm not married. While I obviously find the prospect of living back when our colony was fighting the Revolutionary War exciting, I also know the change will be hard to get used to, and I'm sure I will miss the conveniences of 21st century America. Still, I think the mission is important for the country, for the world, for science. It's possible that I'll regret my decision, but if I don't do this, someone else will. Nothing worthwhile ever comes easy or without sacrifice."

Dr. Sturgis nodded soberly and said, "Do you have a girlfriend?"

"I did, but we were incompatible and split up six months ago."

"Whose fault was that?" she asked.

"That's a strange question. Why do you need to know that?"

"You used the term incompatible. Compatibility is going to be extremely important on this mission. Both with your fellow chrononaut and when you get to your destination."

"Yeah, I get it. Quite honestly as we got to know each other better, we found that we didn't have enough interests in common to make for a very good long-lasting relationship. The sex was great, but that was about it."

She dipped her head an inch or so in acknowledgement and said, "If you get to your destination and find the lack of plumbing facilities that are everyday conveniences for us, you can't afford to complain to the locals or even show how disappointed or unhappy you are. You know that, don't you?"

"You mean if I miss flush toilets or running water?"

"Yes, and there will be a thousand other things that you'll be impatient with. If you have to deal with lack of conveniences in a third-world country, you know in the back of your mind that you can always go home. It won't be like that in 1776 or whatever date you land in. I'm sure you know that, but are you sure you can handle it?"

"How can I be absolutely sure? I think I can."

—

She pursed her lips and nodded ever so slightly before saying, "You said you want to do this because it will help science and help the country in some as yet unknown way. That's all very noble, but why personally are you so eager to go back in time more than two centuries? I know from your record that you've apparently been a fairly content, even occasionally happy person up till now. Are you willing to sacrifice that happiness and comfort for a scientific cause of uncertain value? I lot of people would think you were crazy to even consider it."

Sturgis knew how to get to the heart of a matter. It must have been a full minute before I answered. "How many people get to be part of the history they read about in school? Gil and Tom's account makes it fairly clear that, after the initial shock and adjustment to their new environment, they not only adapted, but adapted quite happily. Tom even fell in love. I'm sure you've read their account. You remember that, while they missed modern conveniences such as plumbing and electricity, they soon found they no longer missed TVs, cell phones, airplanes and cars. Oh, at times they knew these conveniences would be helpful, but since the other people at the time didn't have them, they never felt at a disadvantage. They were competing on a level playing field, to use a modern expression."

She didn't challenge that. She just leaned back in thought and finally said, "I understand what you're saying. Let's leave this for a few days. We'll meet again on, let's say, Thursday. In the meantime, I want you to think about our conversation."

"We did meet again on that Thursday, and my views on the subject hadn't changed, as I assumed she expected they would. Well, maybe she didn't expect them to change. Maybe she was just doing her due diligence."

You may wonder why no woman has been chosen for one of these trans-temporal missions. It's pretty simple really. The project directors early on determined that sending a male and a female off in the same time ship would very likely create hormonal tensions that could very easily turn an already stressful mission into a disastrous mission. Why not two women then? Sending two women into the middle of an 18th century culture without any male companions would almost certainly create its own disastrous scenario.

I've mentioned how we in the project believe the mission is important for the country, the world and for science. Not everyone felt that way, though. Some very important people were not convinced that a second mission was worth the investment. The project directors were unable to persuade key members of Congress to fund this second mission. The Congressional committee members agreed that what we'd accomplished was fascinating and even amazing, but they saw very little benefit for the billions of dollars they'd have to authorize to make this second mission possible. In my opinion and the opinion of the project honchos, this lack of vision on the part of politicians was disappointing in the extreme, though not surprising. They were, after all, politicians.

The mission almost didn't happen until Jason Farnsworth, the founder of the social media giant, Dream, came to our rescue. Farnsworth, like so many recent hi-tech innovators, has made billions, and he's only 39. When he learned that the second mission was not going to be funded, he came to Nevada and met with our key people and told them he'd put up the money if he could share in any scientific gains that resulted from the mission. The government would have first option, but he'd also be able to utilize anything that he felt was of value to him and any of his enterprises so long as they would not endanger American interests.

At first we feared that Farnsworth might want to change the destination of the mission by altering either the location or the year because in so doing he might be able to personally benefit from such a change. How might a change in destination help someone, you might wonder? What if a person's parent or spouse had died say three years earlier? A mission to visit that deceased person's community four years in the past when they were still alive would enable someone to see their relative once again, not just because they loved them, but also because they could learn something from that relative that they had forgotten to ask or never got the chance to ask when they were alive. Fortunately, Farnsworth made no such demands. He was totally in sync with our project goals.

But back to the flight. Our spaceship, or time-craft if you prefer, is now traveling at nearly the speed of light. We've been traveling for almost five months. The scientists back at the CAE in Nevada believe that as we approach the speed of light we will age more slowly, and we will begin to go forward in time. The plan for the first mission four years ago was to reach 90 percent of the speed of light after traveling out from Earth for four months. Supposedly that would have put them two years into the future when they turned around and returned to Earth. Due to a major glitch in the spaceship's computers they continued on past that point and actually exceeded the speed of light—contrary to what most scientists believed possible.

Most scientists believe that you cannot go faster than light. They base that belief on Einstein's Theory of Relativity that says that as you approach the speed of light your mass increases so that it approaches infinite size and you come to a stop altogether. Well, the first mission by CAE people proved that wrong. They did exceed the speed of light. The

—

Theory of Relativity is, after all, just a theory. Finally, after exceeding the speed of light, mission one was able to turn around and head back to Earth. By exceeding the speed of light for as long as they did, Gil and Tom actually went 240 years back in time instead of ahead by two years as they'd intended.

The engineers back at the CAE believe this time they have built enough safety measures into the software to prevent any variance from the intended mission destinations of both time and place. This time our intended destination is to go back in time 240 years. This time there are two backup computers so that the kind of glitches that altered the first mission can't happen again. At least that's what they've assured us.

From time to time Matthew, my fellow chrononaut, and I alternately put ourselves into hibernation so that in our minds, at least, the time passes faster, and we have a better chance of maintaining our sanity. Hibernation slows down your metabolism and also your aging process. Both desirable conditions on such a long flight. Our round trip is expected to take about 12 months. A year in an enclosed rocket cabin is enough to drive anyone crazy. Despite the hibernation there are long wake periods where time seems to stand still. You look outside your capsule and all you see is dark and millions of stars off in the distance. The view changes, but ever so slowly—so slowly that it seems the same, day after day. The feeling is that you're motionless in the vast cosmos and have been motionless for months. Obviously, that's not true. Quite the contrary. You're moving at close to the speed of light, but the stars are so distant that it feels as if you're standing still—that you're not moving at all. For the most part the scenery doesn't seem to change. Most of the time the sky you see through your portholes looks very much as it did from Earth. Beautiful, but nothing changes. Most of the time.

There are dramatic exceptions, though, and those exceptions make the trip the great adventure it is. Every once in a while, among the distant stars, nebulae and galaxies, you see a star close up. By close up, I mean maybe only100 million miles away. At one point in our flight the brightest light we'd ever experienced in our lives coruscated through our portholes illuminating the module with a brightness beyond anything you could imagine. In order to sleep we had to wear eye masks and even they couldn't block out 100 percent of this light. Over the next several days, that blazing light grew brighter and brighter, and unfortunately, our capsule grew hotter and hotter. We were passing Sirius, a star that is roughly twice the size of our Sun. From Earth Sirius appears to be the biggest star in the heavens and it's 8.6 light years away. When it's as close as our Sun is to Earth, it's huge and the heat borders on the unbearable.

—

At first it was just annoying, both the unavoidable bright light and then the growing heat. Gradually, though, the heat became intolerable. At first it was like being in an apartment without air conditioning when it's 90 degrees outside. Uncomfortable, but bearable. It didn't stop at that, though. The temperature in the module kept rising. Soon it was over 90 degrees Fahrenheit. As time went by it hit 100 degrees. Then 110. Not long after, it reached 120 and we both feared we wouldn't be able to last much longer. The capsule's air conditioning couldn't handle the extreme heat. Sensors on the exterior of the module told us that the surface metal was on the verge of melting. The internal temperature reached a peak of 131 degrees and Matt and I felt certain that we were soon going to die in this outer-space hell. Matt's face was red and dripping with perspiration. I was afraid he was going to expire at any moment. He struggled to talk. "We may not make it back in time, partner. We're not even going to make it back to Earth. I don't think I can take another day of this."

"I can't last much longer either. Nevada sure miscalculated on this."

Fortunately, because we were going almost at the speed of light, we began to move farther and farther away from Sirius and the temperature slowly receded. Gradually our capsule environment returned to an acceptably comfortable 72 degrees.

At another point our flight path took us near the Alpha Centauri star system. At 4.4 light years distance, they are actually the closest stars to Earth, even though Sirius looks bigger.

Alpha Centauri A and B are so close to each other that to the naked eye from Earth they appear to be a single star. As we passed the two stars during our flight, we were so close that we could see that they were indeed two stars, each of them roughly the size of our Sun.

We're now approaching the speed of light. We still have nearly two more months to go before we reach the *terminus ad quem*, or furthermost point out in space of our trip. To reach this furthermost point we will have to exceed the speed light. To be precise we will be going at 1.4 times the speed of light. Then the computer will gradually slow our spaceship to a complete stop and slowly turn us around for the return trip to Earth. When we reach the *terminus ad quem* we will be roughly 120 years back in time. By the time we return to Earth we will be another 120 years further back in time. In other words, we will be back in the 1770s.

As we now near the speed of light this is the point in our predecessors' trip where the computers malfunctioned and instead of slowing down their space vehicle at the intended *terminus ad quem*, they continued on for 61 more days. Our CAE scientists and engineers have assured us that there will be no such malfunction this time. Matt and I have our fingers crossed.

—

Chapter 2

YOU CAN IMAGINE how boring it can be on a round trip flight of a year's duration. There are only the two of us in a cabin approximately 12 feet long and 8 feet wide—a foot wider than the cabin on the first mission. Not a lot of wiggle room and no one else to talk to for a year. Matt and I are fairly compatible, but still, after a few months of togetherness it doesn't take much to find something annoying about the other person. Fortunately, we can go into hibernation to make the time go faster. We also brought along quite a few ebooks, egames, music, movies and recordings of our favorite TV shows to occupy our time. There is enough room to get some exercise, so our muscles don't atrophy. Still, after a few months you feel more like a prisoner than an adventurer.

The robotic female voice startled us as it spoke for the first time in several months. *"The neutrino accelerator will shut down in 10 days. I repeat, de-acceleration will commence in 10 days. At that time side thrusters will be activated so that the ship can begin its return trip to Earth."*

I looked over at Matt and saw that he was smiling. We were nearing the halfway point in our long journey. Hopefully the computer will have no surprises for us ten days from now.

Our neutrino accelerator was what made this trip back in time possible. In the mid-twentieth century scientists discovered subatomic particles they called neutrinos. Scientists at CERN, or Conseil Europeen pour la Recherche Nucleaire just outside of Geneva, discovered some weird properties of Neutrinos. Neutrinos have virtually no mass and can travel through two feet of lead with no trouble. Because they have no mass it was believed that they could travel at the speed of light or possibly even faster. Our scientists back at the CAE in Nevada are brilliant and they built the neutrino accelerators that propelled both the first mission back in 2015 and this one in 2019. These neutrino accelerators have proven that neutrinos can in fact propel a space vehicle faster than light.

The thrust from a neutrino accelerator is not powerful, so we had to lift off using conventional liquid hydrogen and oxygen thrusters to overcome Earth's gravity and get us through its gaseous atmosphere. At first the weak propulsion of the neutrinos is negligible, but in outer space there is no atmosphere, which means no resistance. As the neutrino emissions continued, the ship gradually increased its speed. Each second it was going faster than the previous second. After a while we were really moving.

The reason we won't be able to return to the 21st century after we arrive at our 18th century destination is that we will no longer have our liquid hydrogen and oxygen thrusters. They dropped off when we left the Earth's atmosphere. The neutrino accelerator, while capable of propelling us trillions of miles into outer space is not nearly powerful enough to provide liftoff for a return trip from the 18th century, or any century for that matter. Besides, you need a team to help you lift off, and we weren't going to find a team of space-rocket engineers in the 1700s.

You would think that you would feel something as you moved close to the speed of light, but you don't. Our Earth moves around the Sun at 67,000 miles per hour, but we're not aware of it. Apparently you only feel speed when it comes in quick bursts of acceleration. When we lifted off from Earth we definitely felt it. When you step on the gas in your car you feel it, but when the acceleration is gradual you either don't feel it or you barely notice it. Our neutrino accelerator's increases in speed are so minimal that you don't feel the acceleration at all.

I just grabbed a bottle of water. You wouldn't believe how thirsty you can get in an enclosed space capsule. Water is heavy, so we can't store anywhere near as much water in the capsule as we'll need on a 12-month space mission. So how do we get the water we need to sustain ourselves? The capsule has a complex water system that extracts every last drop of available moisture out of our environment. It processes condensation from the surfaces inside the capsule. It processes moisture from the air in the cabin. It processes sweat and urine. Once processed, the water is as clean and pure as bottled water. You have to get past the psychological barrier if you're going to be an astronaut or chrononaut. Fortunately, Matt and I got past that back in Nevada as we forced ourselves to drink processed urine and perspiration.

The people on the International Space Station have been drinking this kind of processed water ever since the space station went up. Interestingly, the Russian cosmonauts in the ISS do not drink processed urine, but the American astronauts do. The Russians drink processed sweat and moisture from the capsule environment, but not processed urine. The Americans, therefore, have a few more liters of water available to them at any given time.

Lately, Matt has become moody as hell. A side of him I wasn't aware of back on Earth. Maybe it's the stress of the mission. Maybe it's a real side of him that's now exerting itself and will continue to exert itself in the future. I hope he snaps out of it because it's adding to my own stress. Up till now we've both bent over backward to be as agreeable as possible

---

because we're well aware of the pressure and stress we're undergoing. Suddenly my thoughts were interrupted by a report from our computer:

"You have reached terminus ad quem." The robotic female voice announced on the tenth day. *"The neutrino accelerator has shut down. In 14 minutes the side thrusters will be initiated on the port side of the ship. Your change of course to the starboard side will take 23 hours and 11 minutes to complete. At that point the ship will be heading back toward Earth."*

We were now 8.4 trillion miles from Earth. We couldn't see our Sun from our present position in space. Believe it or not we were still within our own galaxy, the Milky Way. The Milky Way is estimated to have between 100 and 400 billion stars in it, and we know that there are at the very least over 125 billion galaxies in the Universe. The Hubble telescope confirmed it. The enormity of the Universe is still too vast for me to comprehend.

I look over at Matt and see that he had big shit-eating grin on his face. Looks like he's snapped out of his mood.
"What's with the face?" I ask.

"It's just that it looks like our computer is behaving a lot better than Gil and Tom's did. It's kind of a relief to know that we're not going to continue out into space for the rest of our lives."

I grinned. "Yes, that is sort of reassuring, isn't it?"

If the computer is as accurate as it's supposed to be, we'll be back on Earth in six months. The accuracy of our guidance system is critical. If our new heading is off by even one-tenth of one percent of a degree, we could miss Earth by thousands of miles. As we near Earth the sensors are supposed to correct for any variance, but we still have to count on their precision. No sense worrying about it now. We have six months to worry. In the meantime, we'll occupy ourselves as best we can. We've already seen all of our movies at least once. We've seen a lot of the TV shows, too.

What we miss most are good meals. Most of our meals on board are frozen or canned. Most days we have the equivalent of frozen TV dinners. Not horrible, but not like a good home-cooked meal or a good restaurant meal. We miss those a lot.

Matt must have read my mind, because he said, "I was just thinking."
"About what?"

"How we complain about the meals. Wait till we get to 18th century Massachusetts. Don't you wonder what that food will be like there? I know we looked into it as best we could, but we won't really know until we've experienced it."

"I've thought about it a lot." I was the foodie in the capsule, not Matt. "Yeah, I'm sure it'll be different. My guess is there are no vegetarians in the 1700s. Certainly not many."

"I have no idea if you're right. What makes you think they're all meat eaters?

"From what I've read many of them are hunters. The ones near the coast are fishermen. Between the deer and other wildlife and the bountiful fish supply back then, I'd just assume most of them are flesh eaters. We'll find out in six months, and we'll see who's right." He grinned.

"I wasn't disagreeing with you. I just wondered how you came to your conclusion. You're probably right."

I smiled. "I don't even know why I mentioned vegetarians. Neither one of us is a vegetarian, so we should be quite happy with the colonial cuisine."

"I hope so. Food is important. Especially after a year of this stuff."

If either of us has trouble with the food when we get to our destination, it'll be me. I almost wasn't accepted for the mission because I'm a little overweight. No, that's not true. Quite a bit overweight. It's my own fault, too. I eat too much. I'm guessing I might have lost a few pounds so far since we've been out in space because the food hasn't been that appetizing. It's okay, but it's not a foodie's food. Not by a long shot. My guess is I'll put those pounds back on after we're back on Earth for a while.

Occasionally we see space dust and small asteroids, but only when we're relatively close to a star. These encounters are scary, because if you collide with asteroid material it could be fatal. This stuff only orbits stars and planets, so if you're beyond the orbital paths of stars, which we have been most of the trip, you're not at any risk of being hit. When we passed by Sirius and the Alpha Centauri star system, we were a little more vulnerable, but only a little.

I can't stress enough just how big the Universe is: Literally 125 billion or more galaxies each of which is made up of billions of stars, yet the open space between these collections of stars is so vast that you can go for trillions of miles without hitting anything. Believe me, that very safety is also what makes space travel so boring much of the time. You very seldom see anything close up.

Chapter 3

WE NOW HAVE only a week left in our year-long voyage through space. Recently, Matt and I have been reviewing the journal Gil Lee wrote during his and Tom Howard's mission that lifted off in 2015. Gil continued writing when he and Tom found themselves in the Salem, Massachusetts of 1775, so it's become almost a Bible for Matt and me. If we land anywhere near Salem, we plan to seek out Gil and Tom because almost certainly they can make our entry into the 18th century a lot easier. They'll know what we should avoid doing and how we should present ourselves to the locals. Certainly, we're going to seem as strange to the locals as they will to us. Thanks to Gil's comments in the journal we've brought along clothing that simulates what people wore in the 18th century, so our outward appearance probably won't seem so different to the locals. Changing the way we speak, though, will not be so easy.

Gil and Tom stressed how the locals immediately noticed their unfamiliar vocabulary and distinctly different speech patterns, and reacted as if the newcomers were from outer space, which, of course, they were. They told the locals they were from Halifax, Nova Scotia, and that accounted for the way they spoke. Since most people in the 18th century didn't travel more than a few miles from where they lived, citing Halifax as their place of origin apparently was believable to the locals, since Halifax was more than 500 miles northeast of Salem. Matt and I had to decide where we would say we came from, and we'd have to come up with a reason for suddenly appearing in Salem, or wherever we landed. Would we say we were from a distant city as Gil and Tom had, or would we admit that we were from the 21st century? Not an easy decision, since either choice presented big problems. If we lied and said we were from a distant city, we'd have to keep coming up with new lies to back up our original lie. If we told the truth and said we were from the future, we'd have a hard time proving it. They'd either think we were crazy or witches. Both of those designations would make more sense to the locals than believing we were from more than two centuries
in their future.

Of course our decision between lying and telling the truth was more complicated than it might seem, since Gil and Tom had eventually fessed up to a few key people in Salem and even proven their claim that they came from the future by showing them the space module that brought them to Salem. It wasn't clear how many locals knew the truth, though.

Matt and I finally decided that we'd start with a white lie and decide later on whether to tell the truth after we spoke with Gil and Tom and got their advice on the matter. We knew before we left Nevada that telling locals in the 1700s that we were from the future would not be well received. Still, the truth seemed a lot more problematic than a white lie about where we came from. After reading what Gil and Tom had gone through when they first arrived, we could easily imagine just how difficult it could be for us. Hell, if someone in the 21st century told you he was from the future, you'd either laugh or consider him fit for the loony bin. In the 1700s you'd get one of those two reactions or worse, consider us witches. Matt and I both knew what they did to witches back then.

Just two days now till we land. I won't deny that I feel a little flutter in my heart as that momentous landing grows near. I'm excited and nervous at the same time. We expect to land close to where Gil and Tom landed at the end of the first mission. Before they landed they had no idea where it would be. At least not until they were within minutes of the landing. They eventually landed in the ocean just off Great Misery Island near Salem, Massachusetts. They had hoped to land closer to Boston and no doubt would have if they could have used their GPS system, which they couldn't. If they'd landed two years into the future as the scientists had expected, the GPS would have helped them zero in on the planned landing site near Boston. We have GPS on board now just in case *our* computers fail us and we end up in the future. As I've already explained, it is now our intention to touch down more than two centuries in the past. So far it seems that we're on target for the 18th century, and if we do, our GPS won't help guide the ship toward our intended Great Misery Island splashdown site because there are no GPS satellites in the 18th century sky.

Our brilliant CAE scientists have designed an amazing system of computer-controlled sensors that should be able to recognize the coastal terrain of Massachusetts and help us zero in on our touchdown spot near Great Misery Island even without GPS satellites. I say should, since Matt and I are well aware that on the first mission the computer seemed to take on a life of its own and change the destination from the future to the distant past. This was not a minor glitch, for God's sake. Matt and I have been assured that something like that can't happen this time, but we won't feel completely comfortable until we're within a thousand feet of our destination. At a thousand feet or so, we should be able to eyeball the ground clearly enough to determine whether any villages or towns appear to be what you'd expect in the 18th century. We should also be able to see if the towns or cities are far less developed, as you'd expect in an earlier time period, —or far more developed as you'd expect in later centuries.

We'd been decelerating now for some time. We had to go much slower if we were going to enter Earth's atmosphere and not burn up or crash into the planet. At our fastest we were traveling at 1.4 times the speed of light. We are now one day out from Earth, and our speed is down to 60,000 miles per hour and slowing steadily. By the time we begin to penetrate Earth's atmosphere we need to be down to 17,500 mph, a speed that will allow us to go into orbit around the planet. Once in orbit the computer will direct our reverse thrusters to slow us down further at the appropriate time so that we can touch down near Great Misery Island off the coast of Massachusetts. Hopefully we'll enter the water within a hundred feet of where Gil and Tom touched down four years ago. Saying 'four years ago' is weird because it was four years ago in relation to when they left Nevada in 2015, but in Gil and Tom's new reality it was actually 240 years ago.

The computer voice just announced that we were now in Earth orbit and that deceleration will slow our entry speed enough so that we can touch down near Misery Island. So far, the computer has performed flawlessly. When you think about it, it is truly an amazing accomplishment if we do land within 100 feet of where the first mission touched down. We will have traveled more than eight trillion miles into outer space and another eight trillion miles on the return trip for a total of 16 trillion miles. We were now only 200 miles above the Earth. Touching down within 100 feet of where our scientists programmed the computer to take us is as close to a miracle as most people will ever experience.

"You are now leaving Earth orbit." The computer voice was a welcome interruption to my thoughts. I hoped that it signaled a successful termination of our trip. Matt and I wolfed down some food. We had no idea when our next meal would be when we were back on Earth.

"You are now 10 miles above the surface of the Earth. In 22 minutes you will be five miles above Southern New England." So far, so good.

"You are now 1,000 feet above Massachusetts. Be prepared for touchdown in 14 minutes." Matt and I scanned the horizon for something familiar. Off in the distance was the town that would one day be the Boston we were both familiar with. Now it was just a small town. How did we know it was Boston? It was located on the Shawmut Peninsula. Both Matt and I were familiar with the Eastern Massachusetts terrain. I was born and brought up in Beverly and Matt had attended BU in his college days. Before the mission launched we'd both studied the geography carefully to insure that we were extremely familiar with it when we landed.

As Gil had noted in his journal, the neck of the Peninsula was a lot skinnier than it would be in the 21st century. Over the years the part of the peninsula called the Back Bay had been filled in to provide more land for the city. So yes, I was sure it was Boston, but the Boston of an earlier time. It was a Boston I had seen on antique maps. It looked a lot like the

Boston of the 18th century. Now we just have to hope that we touched down in 1775 or within a few years after 1775, a time in which we knew Gil and Tom would be there. In just a few minutes we'd learn just how good our onboard computers have been. If we touched down 80 or so years earlier than 1775, we would be right smack in the middle of the Witch Trials. Eighty-five years after 1775 and we'd be in the Civil War period. Up till now our flight has followed the Nevada script perfectly. I crossed my fingers, hoping against hope that our splashdown would hold no surprises for us.

Chapter 4

Sometime in the 18th century
AS WE LOOKED down, we could see Great Misery Island. I knew that Great Misery Island was just a little over a half mile off the coast from Beverly Farms, a part of Beverly. Beverly was the town just to the north of Salem. Great Misery Island got its name when shipbuilder Robert Moulton was stranded there in a winter storm sometime in the late 1620s. It was the name he gave to the island when he finally made it safely to shore. Looking toward the shore we saw small settlements of houses up and down the coast. Salem appeared to be the largest town before you got to Boston just a few miles further south. I knew from my preparation for the mission that Salem was nearly as big as Boston in the late 1700s. It was now 7:01p.m. Eastern Standard Time.

"The capsule is descending now to the north side of Great Misery Island. Splashdown will occur in three minutes. Splashdown will locate 90 feet from the island."

According to our charts sundown will come at 7:04, which is exactly when we'll splashdown. This is good. We'd planned for a late-day splashdown, as we assumed it would attract less attention. We're hoping that no one will see our capsule descend or enter the water. Most people should be home at this time of day. That's the plan anyway. Even if someone is within viewing distance, we hope that the approach of darkness will hide our entry. We'll know soon enough.

We looked over at each other and pursed our lips. This was the moment we'd been waiting for. As for me, my emotions were fighting an internal struggle. I was excited and eager for what lay ahead, but equally nervous about the very same thing—what lay ahead. This was not only the next chapter in my life, but a completely different life. And as the shrink had reminded me countless times, there was no turning back.

We were now hovering over what appeared to be about the same spot in which Gil had said they'd splashed down at the end of the first mission. Our reverse thrusters said we were easing toward splashdown at about 10 miles per hour. We were now only about 200 feet above the surface of the water. There were no boats to be seen in any direction and no people on the near side of the island. Our speed continued to slow and suddenly we made contact with the water. It was about as easy a landing as you could ask for.

Matt reached over and shook my hand. A new life was about to begin. The capsule was designed to float until we opened a stopcock to allow water in when we were ready to sink the compartment we'd lived in for 365 days. We then unlocked the canopy and attempted to slide it open. Nothing! It wouldn't move! Stuck! We looked at each other, and I think we both thought, *this can't be happening after 12 months in outer space. Do we want to be locked in an hermetically sealed capsule after all we've been through? Maybe forever.* I reached for the small hammer that was part of our limited tool kit and gave the canopy a few taps. We pushed again and the canopy still didn't budge. This wasn't good. I gave it a few more taps and it finally moved a couple of inches when we gave it our best efforts. A few more taps, and it moved again. We slid the canopy off and breathed our first fresh air in a year. God that felt good. Air in the 18th century air was as good as or better than 21st century air.

We couldn't take much with us if we were going to pose as 18th century men. What we did have stashed in the capsule was a small inflatable rubber life raft, which we would need to get to shore. Once on land we would deflate it and submerge it where we hoped it wouldn't be found—at least not soon. We also had 12 ounces in small gold bars sewn into our clothes. It was estimated that the gold we had with us would be the equivalent of well over a year's annual income of a typical tradesman in the 18th century. Certainly it would enable us to get by until we could earn a living. We also had a few bills and coins dating from the late 1700s. A staff member back at the CAE had visited a few coin and stamp dealers to round up examples of both coin and paper money. Some of them looked pretty worn and some were in surprisingly good shape. We hoped that would be what we'd use until we'd established ourselves either in Salem or one of the surrounding communities.

In addition, each of us is carrying a cell phone. The phones are sealed in watertight plastic until we're securely on dry land. Obviously we can't make phone calls, do emails or surf the web in the 18th century, but after a number of discussions back in Nevada, it had been decided that, if and when we needed to prove we were from the 21st century, the camera on the cell phone alone would be convincing. The camera had not even been invented in the 18th century, so our cell phone cameras almost certainly would amaze anyone we met in the coming days. The camera will work without satellite service, as will the dictionary, the ability to type documents, the calendar, the clock and even voice recognition for certain apps. If and when the time comes when we need to prove that we've traveled through time, we figure we can wow the locals with our magic, even though we won't be able to make a phone call. How will we charge our phones if electricity isn't available? These are specially designed solar-powered phones, so that's not going to be a problem. The only other modern conveniences we brought with us are our Swiss army knives, which we assumed would be helpful in any number of situations.

Our hope is that we won't need to demonstrate that we are visitors from the future. At least not right away. Not before we become accepted and welcomed into a community. Then, when and if we are accepted as being otherwise normal, we might break it to certain people. Who? We don't know. We just know from Gil's journal that the time might come when it will make sense to reveal our origin. We'll have to feel our way along for a while, though. Here we are, two young men from the technologically advanced 21st century, and we feel like kindergartners as we're about to enter an 18th century environment. At least we hope it's the 18th century. That remains to be seen until we look around and talk to a few locals.

The life raft inflated in minutes. It wasn't easy to get out of the capsule and into the raft. Even though we'd exercised while confined to the capsule during the past year, we found that we were still a bit wobbly and not as strong as we were when we took off from Nevada. We made it, though, and telescoped two oars so we could row ourselves to shore. We'd decided back in Nevada that if we landed near Great Misery Island, we would row directly toward the mainland unless the ocean was too rough to make such a trip safe. If the sea was rough and turbulent, we'd make the shorter trip to the island until we could somehow find our way to the mainland. As it happened, the ocean was as calm as a lake, so we headed directly toward the mainland, which we knew was the part of Beverly, Massachusetts, called Beverly Farms.

Matt took the oars and I sat facing him so I could help him keep on track for land.

"How's it feel to be rowing a real boat?" I asked. One of our exercise devices in the capsule was a rowing simulator.

"It's actually different and I love it, though now I have an extra load, which makes rowing harder."

He was referring, of course, to me.

"You're pretty good at this, Matt. Maybe you can get a job here that takes advantage of your rowing skill."

After we'd gone maybe a hundred yards the ocean began to get choppy, and we found ourselves rowing up and down into deep troughs of extremely nasty water. Water was everywhere. Soon it was as if we were in a saltwater bath. We were as wet as if we'd swum to shore. Matt was now looking fatigued. Between his slightly atrophied muscles and the rough sea, the rowing was taking its toll.

"Want me to take over for a while?"

"No, I can handle it."

"You sure?"

"If we try to swap seats in this choppy sea, we'll both end up in the drink. No, I better continue."

He was right. There was no way we could exchange seats now.

Fortunately, we were more than halfway to shore. A westerly wind was helping us get there. A good thing, too, as Matt was close to exhaustion.

When we were within a couple a couple hundred yards of shore, I told Matt to veer off a bit to his port or left side. We were heading directly toward a pier. The pier had several small buildings on it. We'd be safer landing on a beach or some barren part of the shoreline. A commercial pier or wharf was more likely to have workers on it, and we didn't want to be seen. Not just yet.

Minutes later a small breaker washed us ashore. We scraped bottom on the sand as our rubber raft made contact with the beach. We were on *terra firma* for the first time in 365 days. Soaking wet, but safe. I estimated the temperature to be in the mid 70s, so we weren't going to freeze to death as we dried out.

Why did we want to go directly to the mainland instead of the shorter, safer route to Great Misery Island, which was only 90 feet away from our splashdown? There's a very good reason: We knew from Gil's account that he and Tom had made their way to the island and met up with a teenage boy who was tending a herd of cows there. They had told the boy that they'd paid for passage on a fur traders' ketch out of Halifax and later on learned that the fur traders were in fact thieves. They told the fur traders to let them off on the nearest land and give them back their money. The thieves rowed them in from their ketch to the island, but kept their money. Matt and I couldn't use the same story to explain landing on the island and any other explanation would seem very suspicious only four years after our friends landed there. To avoid unnecessary questions, it was decided that we'd make our way to the shore of the mainland, if it was at all possible. We'd then still need a story to explain our appearance.

Before we moved on to our next life we had to hide the raft. We opened the valve and squeezed the little rubber boat until most of the air was out of it. Now for a place to hide it. The easiest way to dispose of it would be to sink it in the ocean. Not here by the beach, though. Too shallow. No, we had to find a deeper place and it had to be nearby. We decided to approach the pier that we'd avoided as we neared shore. If at this darkening hour there was nobody on it, we could go out to the end and drop the raft into the deeper water there.

As we neared the pier, we saw a light in the window of the building on the pier nearest to the shore. Obviously someone was in that building. Not good. We crept onto the pier cautiously. Hopefully we could make our way past the little building without being seen carrying the deflated life raft.

Chapter 5

Sometime in the 18th century

WE WERE NOW within a few yards of the building's entrance. The door was open, and a yellow glow emanated from the interior of the building. The glow flickered warmly. A man was sitting at a table poring over some papers. We crept past the open doorway as silently as we could. He didn't look up, and we breathed a sigh of relief as we made our way toward the end of the pier. The pier must have been at least a hundred yards long. We passed three other small buildings along the pier, which fortunately appeared to be closed. When we got to the end of the pier we did a 360 to be sure no one was looking and then Matt threw the deflated raft as far out as he could. It didn't sink, though. Apparently there was still enough air in it to keep it afloat. On the beach we'd used one of our Swiss army knives to puncture the raft in a few places, so we knew that as water entered the deflated raft, it would gradually sink. We just hoped it would be sooner rather than later.

As we passed the one lighted building on our way back to shore, the warm light in the building flickered out. The employee would be leaving soon. We picked up the pace and made it to shore just as the man came through the door and headed our way.

Matt said, "Should we ask this guy where there's an inn we can stay at for the night? We have to ask somebody."

It made sense. We couldn't just wander around looking for a place to stay.

"Yeah, I suppose we should. He's as good as anyone and there doesn't seem to be a lot of people around right now."

We waited near the end of the pier for the guy to reach us. As he drew nearer he appeared to be fairly fit and in his late forties. Maybe five-seven or eight. When he set foot on land we went up to him and I said, "Pardon me, sir, we're strangers to this town. Would you be able to direct us to an inn or someplace we can stay for the night?"

"There's no inn in Beverly Farms. Closest one is in Beverly. That be four miles from here."

He must have seen the disappointment in our eyes, for he then said, "Mrs. Crocket sometimes takes in travelers. You might want to knock on her door. That's not far from here."

We knew from our research that it was common for certain homes to open their doors to travelers. You couldn't very well call ahead for a reservation, so it was not unusual for travelers to look for such places for an overnight stay.

"We'd be much obliged if you could tell us how we might find her," I said.

"Where you folks from? You don't sound like anyone from around here."

"Halifax." We'd decided Halifax was as good as any and for a number of reasons, better than any other town we might mention. "We took a packet boat down to Gloucester and then got ourselves rides with two farmers on their wagons. Been a long trip."

"God almighty, it sounds like it. Halifax must be close to 500 miles from here."

"At least that. It's a long journey, and mighty tiring."

"What brings you all this way, if you don't mind my askin'?" He hesitated for a moment, then added, "We don't get many visitors here. Certainly not from that far away."

Matt said, "We're looking for work. I'm a printer and Christopher worked as a newspaper editor up in Halifax."

"Why come all this way for work. Don't they have jobs for you up in Halifax?"

"Only two printers and one newspaper up there. The paper recently hired their own kin to replace me and the two printers They can't afford to pay a living wage so we both found ourselves looking for work. On our way to Gloucester we landed in Portland and tried to find work there, but there was nobody there looking to hire. We remembered two mates of ours who came south to Salem a few years ago, so we decided to come to this area. Beverly and Salem have a growing population, so we assumed there'd be more work in this area. Besides, you're close to Boston where we expect there's even more work in our trades."

"Well, I wish you fella's good luck. If you don't find anything, you might come back here. I can always use a couple of good lads on one of my coastal boats. We carry trade up and down the coast as far south as Charleston. By the way, name's Joshua English. I'm fairly well known around here."

"I'm Christopher Carver and my mate here is Matthew Blair. I thank you for your offer, but I think we'll try to secure something in our line of work if we can."

"Well, I hope it works out for you lads. Now let me show you how to get to Mrs. Crocket's place."

Her Federalist period house was only a few blocks away. We'd asked Joshua English for the time, but he'd been vague, saying that it was close to the supper hour. We had to get used to people not having watches and estimating time by their awareness of the position of the sun at

---

various times of the year. A few pocket watches existed in the 18th century, but the wristwatch hadn't been invented until the next century.

Mrs. Crocket's house was a rather stately Federalist-style building among a number of similar handsome structures. From the outside it looked like it would be quite comfortable if she had room for us. I used the brass knocker on the front door and waited for a response. A minute later we heard footsteps and then the door swung open revealing a woman who appeared to be in her mid to late fifties. Her graying hair was tied in a tight bun. As soon as she saw us a broad smile appeared on her pleasant face.

"Good evening, gentlemen. What can I do for you?"

I said, "We heard that you sometimes put up travelers. Would you have a room for us tonight?"

"I most certainly do. Come in, come in."

We entered and found ourselves in a spacious foyer warmly lit by candles set in sconces on the walls.

"You have a nice place here, Mrs. Crockett. Looks very comfortable."

"Thank you Mr. . .?"

"Carver, Christopher Carver. And this is Matthew Blair. We're from Halifax. Up in Nova Scotia."

"That's a long way from this part of the world. My word, what brought you all this way?"

I sketched out our story for her and she seemed to accept it.

"I hope you will be successful in your search, gentlemen. What happens if you can't find work in Beverly or Salem? You're not going all the way back to Halifax, are you?"

"I suppose we'd go on to Boston and see if there's something there." I wanted to ask her what the date was, but I had to find a different way to get that information. Asking her would make us appear ignorant beyond belief. But we had to know, and we had to know soon. It was clearly the 1700s, but that left a lot of latitude either way. If we were going to function in this new culture, we had to know what day it was and what year it was. Fortunately, she helped narrow it down with the next words that came out of her mouth.

"I would think you'd have good fortune in your search. The recent fighting in Lexington and Concord left far too many of our good young men victims of the British regulars. I suspect that there will be many employers looking to fill these unfortunate vacancies. Their misfortune may be your opportunity." Her hand flew up to her mouth and she seemed shaken. "Oh, I pray that you not be sympathetic to His Majesty's side of the conflict. I suspect you might be, considering that you come from Nova Scotia."

<hr>

"No, from what we've read, we think you folks here in Massachusetts have good reason to resent the Crown's treatment of its own citizens. For some reason most of the people back in Nova Scotia seem willing to put up with these offenses. We aren't. That's one of the reasons we were uncomfortable living there and looked for greener pastures here in this colony." As I said this I hoped it wouldn't backfire on us.

"Greener pastures. I've never heard that expression, but I think I take your meaning. If you don't mind my saying so, gentlemen, I can tell by your speech that you don't come from here."

Matt smiled and said, "No, ma'am, we don't take offense at all. The gentleman we met at the pier said much the same thing about the way we speak."

"And who might that be? I know most everyone here in Beverly Farms."

"He said he was Joshua English."

"Oh he's a good one for you to know. Owns half the village and is one of the largest coastal shipping merchants in Massachusetts. I think he's a descendant of Philip English of Salem. I'm sure you've heard of him."

"No, I'm afraid we haven't," said Matt. "Remember, we're from Halifax."

"He's before my time, but he's legendary in Salem because he and his wife Mary were accused of witchcraft back in '92. They fled to Boston and eventually made their way to New York safely. Their lives were never the same, though, as Philip had owned a great deal of property in Salem and a good many ships. He returned to Salem in 1693 and found that the sheriff had confiscated much of his property. But I've gone on much too much about a matter I'm sure you have no interest in anyway. You gentlemen must be hungry, traveling all that way. Why don't I show you to your room and then fix you up something."

This woman was easy to like.

I looked at Matt, who nodded his approval of the plan. I then said, "That would be wonderful, Mrs. Crockett. Please don't go to a lot of trouble over the food." As I said this I hoped she wouldn't take me seriously. I had a ravenous appetite at the moment and looked forward to a home-cooked meal, even though I had no idea what it would be.

"It's no trouble at all. I don't get many guests here and when I do, I like to get to know them and make them comfortable. When my husband was alive, we never had guests, but I'm alone now, so I like to have people to converse with, and quite honestly it helps me get by. My husband didn't leave me much other than this house. Oh my, here I am blathering on and I still haven't got you settled in your room."

I was surprised to hear her go on so about herself to two complete strangers. Was this openness typical of the way things were done in the 18th century, or was Mrs. Crockett just atypically transparent?

The room was comfortable, but not exactly what we would have gotten at a Holiday Inn. On a small table at the foot of the bed, which was about the size of a 21st century double bed, she showed us a large bowl for washing. Next to the bowl was a pitcher full of water and a chunk of white castile soap. At the foot of the bed she showed us a ceramic chamber pot with a floral design. No running water and no flush toilet from now on. We'd known that when we signed up, but somehow the reality of it hit home hard when faced with the actual chamber pot.

When we told her the room looked very comfortable, she said, "Then I'll let you get sorted out. Oh, there's an outhouse in the back if you prefer to use that, but I assume you'd rather use the chamber pot at night instead of going out. I should have something for your supper in a short time. Come down when you're ready."

A few minutes later we went downstairs and found that the dining room table was set beautifully—for four people. A man was already seated at the table. Mrs. Crockett noticed our surprise and said, "Mr. Carver and Mr. Blair, this is Mr. Obadiah Taliaferro. He tells me he pronounces it Toliver, but he'll accept either way of saying it. He's from Amesbury. He's also staying with me tonight." Taliaferro nodded. He was seated so I couldn't tell how tall he was, but he appeared to be rather stocky and of average height. A fringe of graying hair circled his round head. I guessed him to be in his early sixties.

We shook hands and Mrs. Crockett began bringing out the food. "I'm afraid I only have lobster this evening gentlemen. It was all I could get on short notice. Mr. Taliaferro only arrived an hour ago and I had to run out and fetch what I could.

Matt and I looked at each other. She was apologizing for lobster. Then I remembered reading that in colonial times lobster was so plentiful that it sometimes washed up on shore a foot deep. It was often served to prisoners and the poor. Some servants had agreements with prominent families they worked for stating that they would not be served lobster more than twice a week. She also served us baked potatoes and corn on the cob. She urged us to help ourselves, offering butter, salt and pepper if we wanted it. When our food was plated she said, "Would you like some cider or small beer? I'm afraid that's all I have today."

"The beer would be fine," said Matt.

I added, "Yes, please. The small beer."

The beer wasn't ice cold, but it was cool, since she kept it just outside and the evening had gotten cool.

"I hope you like the corn. We like it on the cob here. Do you eat it

—

that way in Halifax?"

"Yes, ma'am. The same way," I said.

Taliaferro had been listening to our conversation and when he heard we were from Halifax he said, "So you gentlemen are from Canadian territory. I trust then that your allegiance is to the Crown?" How we answered this was critical. We couldn't afford to alienate ourselves before we were even settled into our new century. Yet we didn't know which side of the issue Taliaferro's sentiments fell. Was he for independence or was he, like a lot of the Canadians, happy enough with the King's rule to not want to make waves. I was surprised that he'd even bring up politics with complete strangers.

Before I could reply, Matt jumped in. "We're loyal to the Crown, sir, as long as it treats us as well as it treats British citizens back in England. From our vantage point up in Nova Scotia it appeared that in recent years the King has treated you people here in Massachusetts as second-class citizens."

A trace of a smile flickered across Taliaferro's puffy face. "Indeed. I take it you gentlemen were unhappy with that thinking up in Canada?"

I still wasn't sure which way the wind was blowing, but we had to say something, so I said, "We came here for work. For some reason, the Crown has treated Nova Scotia better than it has you people here in New England. Or at least it seemed so to us. It's true, most of the people up there, while not always happy with how London treats them, find some way to justify it or at least accept it. I sense that you New Englanders are not so willing to accept this second-class treatment—especially after Leslie's ignominious retreat in Salem and the bloody battles at Lexington and Concord."

"Aye lads, you seem to know a lot about our local troubles. Makes me wonder why you would come here, knowing that things are likely to get worse, not better."

"As I said, we came here for work. Our experience is in writing for a newspaper and in printing. There's nothing available in our trades up there right now. All the troubles down here means the printing business and local newspapers are going to be mighty busy. Two of our mates came down here a few years ago, and they wrote to us to say that the opportunities are much better down here than up in Halifax."

Taliaferro frowned. "If I hear you right, it sounds as if you've come here to make personal gain from our troubles." As the words left his lips, Mrs. Crockett's brow furrowed, and she looked terribly uncomfortable. Oops. Obviously, I'd put my foot in my mouth. I'd have to fix this fast or we could be in trouble.

"No sir, that is not the case at all. The reason we could not find work up there is because our views on how shabbily the Crown has treated the colonies here in America were not in accordance with those of our employers." There, we were now on record. I hoped to God that I'd read Taliaferro right.

"I'm glad to hear you say that, lad. Glad to hear you say that. If you really mean what you said, there may be something two strappin' lads from Nova Scotia can do to show just how strongly you feel about how shabbily the Crown has treated the New England colonies."

Mrs. Crockett was clearly uncomfortable with the political way the conversation was going. She broke in by saying, "May I get you gentlemen anything else? I see you young men from Halifax have cleaned your plates, but Mr. Taliaferro, you've hardly touched yours. Is there something wrong with your supper, sir?"

Taliaferro frowned at the interruption and said, "No, no. It's quite acceptable. Quite acceptable." He then turned his attention back to us. "Would you lads be interested in helpin' the cause of liberty here in Massachusetts?"

I wasn't sure where this was heading, and I had no idea what role this Taliaferro fellow had in all of this. "I suppose it depends on what you have in mind, Mr. Taliaferro. We've just arrived here today, and our first order of business is to find a place to live and then find ourselves work in our respective trades."

"I'm on my way to see Colonel David Mason, the man in Salem who leads the Salem Committee of Safety. I, myself, command the Amesbury Committee. The Salem committee coordinates most of the militias north of Boston. We're looking for more good men who are willing to fight for the cause against the King's regulars should conflict become necessary."

I said, "Looks like it already became necessary if I understand what happened recently at Lexington and Concord here in Massachusetts."

"Yes, the regulars forced our hand and we sent them packing."

"Let me ask you this: Are your Committees of Safety looking for a fight, or are you hoping that won't be necessary?"

Taliaferro squinted and eyed me as if I were an enemy spy. "I thought you said that you weren't happy with our shabby treatment here in New England? Did I read you wrong?"

"No, you didn't sir. I believe my question was a reasonable one. If we help out, we would like to know exactly how these committees feel. Are they established to provide defense, or is their intent to provoke conflict?"

An impatient Taliaferro then said, "The Committees are not *looking for a fight* as you so bluntly suggest. The Committees, are the creation of the Provincial Congress with the express purpose of defending our rights that are gradually being eroded by an insensitive Crown." He paused to let this sink in, then added, "Since Lexington and Concord last month

---

Provincial troops have surrounded Boston with the express intent of keeping Governor Gage and His Majesty's troops contained in the town. We've had enough of their aggression. Lexington and Concord were the last straws. Before that they sent troops into Salem to confiscate our means of protecting ourselves."

"You mean the cannons they went after and were denied access to when Salem citizens forced Colonel Leslie and 300 regulars to retreat earlier this year?"

"Yes. That was the most blatant offense, but there have been others, too. We have to keep the regulars contained in Boston." He thought for a moment, then said, "Recently we have gotten word that Gage plans to occupy the hills surrounding Boston with regular forces. He feels he is under siege and needs to make a show of strength to demonstrate who is in control by expanding his influence. The Provincial Congress believes that we cannot let him get away with that. He and the Crown have already eroded our rights with excessive taxation without any representation in Parliament. We cannot let him make further incursions on the province. I could go on, but that is merely typical of the oppression we are faced with here in Massachusetts. But back to your question. The Massachusetts Committees of Safety have been given the authority by the Provincial Congress to protect the hills around Boston should Gage order the regulars to occupy them."

Lexington and Concord last month. Good, a clue to where we were on the calendar. We were narrowing it down. I nodded and said, "I understand. If I may be direct, sir, I find it somewhat strange that you would be so open about the Committees' affairs with two people you hardly know. Isn't that a bit risky?"

He smiled for the first time. "I do like your directness, sir. It must be a trait of the people up in Nova Scotia. It's a fair question. My answer is this: We're at a critical time of transition here in Massachusetts and we cannot afford the luxury of too much caution. We need to know where people stand. We need to know if they're with us or against us, for we're fighting for our very survival as a free people. I hope you haven't minded my directness."

Matt said, "No, sir, it's refreshing."

"Then may I count on you two gentlemen to join us?"

I still wasn't sure what he was expecting of us. "In what capacity, sir?"

"You seem to be well-read young men, and far better spoken than many men your age. There could be many roles for you to play in one of the Committees."

"Then you are not asking us to take up arms?" I had to know.

"Not necessarily, though we desperately need able-bodied men to do just that. Perhaps you could join me at Colonel Mason's house. If you truly want to support the cause, I'd want the Colonel to meet you."

I then remembered something I'd read in Gil Lee's account of the first mission.

"Two mates of ours from Halifax came down here a while ago and fought against the regulars at Lexington and Concord. We're of a mind with them, if that gives you any assurance as to how we feel about the cause."

"I think I heard about them. Don't recall their names, but they made a name for themselves. Sounds to me that not everyone up in Nova Scotia supports the King."

"Not everyone, but most. Most are rather tolerant of the King's treatment of his citizens here on this side of the Atlantic. I believe that many Nova Scotians are originally from Massachusetts and other parts of New England, so it's only natural that they would feel some support for your cause. Still, for various reasons most are more tolerant of the Crown's abuses than you folks are here in New England."

"Aye, many of our Tories here in Massachusetts fled to Nova Scotia because they didn't want to be tarred and feathered if they stayed here. The King has imposed more taxes and more restrictions on us here in New England than he has up in the Canadian Territory. I don't understand the mind of the Tory. Don't see how they could side with the King in spite of all that."

I then said, "There are mixed feelings in Nova Scotia. Many are sympathetic with what you here in Massachusetts are trying to do, yet many others are fed up with war and feel that loyalty to the Crown, while not perfect, is better than the likelihood of more conflict."

"I definitely want you lads to meet with Colonel Mason. You appear to be far better informed than most folks, and I think he'll want to find a place for you." He fell silent for a moment, thinking of what to say next. "I hope you lads don't take offense, but there is something strange about you that I can't quite fathom."

"It's probably our Nova Scotian way of talking.:

"No, I don't think it's that. Though you do indeed talk differently. It's something else." He waved his hands as if to change the subject. "No matter, the important thing is you want to help. If I understand you right?"

I looked at Matt who dipped his head a half inch in agreement. I then said, "Yes, I think we would like to help, but we need to get settled here first. We have only arrived here tonight. Give us a few days to find a place to live and a place to work."

"I understand your need to find a place to sleep, but these are dire times and time is against us. Can you take a few hours with me in the morn to visit with Colonel Mason in Salem. He may have some

---

suggestions about where you can find lodgings and employment. He knows Salem and Beverly far better than I do. I think you may find a brief trip to Salem profitable and at the same time find a way to help our cause in this perilous time."

How the hell could we refuse that?

Matt caught my eye and said, "I think we could do that, providing you have a way for us to get there."

"My horse is in the stable in the back of the house. I'm sure Mrs. Crockett can direct us to the local livery stable where you can rent yourselves a couple of mounts."

I looked at Matt. We'd learned from Gil's account that skill in riding was a valuable asset, so we'd taken riding lessons back in Nevada. Good thing, too, because our hastily acquired skill was going to be put to the test soon.

"Okay, then," I said. "I suppose we should rise fairly early if we are to hire horses before we set off for Salem.

"There! That's one of the strange things about you fellows."

I was puzzled. "What? I don't understand."

"What you just said. 'Okay.' I have never heard that word. What does it mean?"

I immediately realized that the word 'okay' must have come into the language sometime after the 1770s.

"It means all right, good, acceptable. It's fairly common where we come from."

"I see. Well then, yes, perhaps, Mrs. Crockett, we could have a fairly early breakfast. Maybe sometime shortly after sunrise. Then we can set out for the livery stable and get you gentlemen some horses. We can see Colonel Mason by mid-morning if all goes right. I'd expect we'd be back here shortly after midday. How does that sound to you?"

I said, "That sounds fine if it's okay, Oops. If it's all right with Mrs. Crockett?"

"That'll be fine."

"There you go again," said Taliaferro.

I was puzzled, but Matt came to the rescue. "You must mean the word 'oops.'"

"Precisely. You men have a very strange vocabulary."

"Oops is a word we use to show acknowledgement of an error or mistake."

Taliaferro shook his head in bewilderment. "It's going to take me a while to get used to the way you speak."

We had to hope that no one else showed up from Nova Scotia or we'd have more explaining to do.

Mrs. Crockett changed the subject once again. "I have a nice lemon tart if you gentlemen are interested."

It was delicious. We went to bed satisfied and excited about what lay ahead. We had also narrowed down the time frame of where we were on the calendar. It was shortly after Lexington and Concord, which happened in April of '75, and sometime before the Battle of Bunker Hill which took place on June 17th of the same year. Hopefully we'd soon learn exactly what day it was.

Chapter 6

Late spring 1775

WE KNEW the sun would rise around 6:30 a.m., though it was hard to verify the specific time now since there were no clocks to be seen in the house. Our cell phones did say it was 6:28, but we weren't sure how long they would continue to be accurate since they could no longer get the time from satellite signals. Mrs. Crockett had smilingly provided us with a modest meal of cornmeal porridge with maple syrup and hearty bread that had been browned with a coating of butter in a cast iron frying pan. She also offered us milk and coffee, apologizing that she could no longer get tea. She finished off with freshly baked sweet rolls. She must have gotten up a lot earlier than we did.

Constantly on the alert for information that could help us adjust to our new environment I took the opportunity to ask Mrs. Crockett if per chance she knew Henry Woodbury or his wife Jane. We knew from Gil Lee's account of the previous mission, that Gil and Tom Howard had stayed with the Woodburys when they first arrived in Beverly Farms.

"Yes, I know Jane quite well. Henry, too. Good family." She looked puzzled. "How do you know them if you've just come to Beverly Farms?"

"We don't know them, but friends of ours once stayed with them when they first arrived here. Our friends suggested that we look them up."

"You men from Halifax do have a way with the language. Look them up. I take the meaning, I think, but 'tis strange to my ears. But, yes, you should visit them. I can tell you how to get to their place when you're ready to go there." She hesitated a moment, then added, "I think now that you mention it that Jane did tell me that she had two young men staying with her a while back."

"I don't suppose you know where those two young men went?"

"I think she said that they found work in Salem. No doubt, that's where they're living now, though I couldn't say for certain. I wish I could be of more help."

"Please don't apologize. We should be able to contact them based on the information you just gave."

She again looked puzzled.

"Did I use more confusing Canadian language?" I smiled as I asked her this.

"Contact means to touch. I take it you have a different meaning for it. I suppose I get your intent, but 'tis a strange way to say it." She forced a weak smile. "For me that is."

"Up north it also means to be in touch with someone. To communicate with someone."

"Aye. Yes, I believe I understand your meaning. In any event, I hope you find your friends. Jane and Henry Woodbury would be a good place to start your search. As I said, when you're ready I can tell you how to find their place."

"That would be most welcome. Maybe tonight you might tell us the directions." I could see that Obadiah Taliaferro was getting impatient, so I said, "I think now we'd best be on our way to Salem."

Since we were going to be away for several hours, we made a visit to the outhouse, which was pretty much what we'd expected it to be. It was a two-holer, but Matt and I weren't ready for that kind of togetherness.

Taliaferro fetched his horse from behind Mrs. Crockett's house and the three of us followed her directions and set off at a brisk walk to the local horse livery, which was only about four blocks away. My word, not Mrs. Crockett's. In speaking with her I'd learned that the term block when it referred to a section of a street was unfamiliar to her. She gave directions in yards or houses or other landmarks familiar to her.

I wasn't familiar with livery stables, but on seeing the one in Beverly Farms I guessed it to be one of the smaller such businesses. The attendant sized us up and said it was a good thing one of us already had a horse because he only had two horses available for rental. The other four horses he had were owned by local residents. When he learned that we were visitors at Mrs. Crocketts and not residents of the area he said he'd have to ask for a security deposit in addition to the rental fee. We said we understood and asked him how much.

"That'll be 10 pence for the day for each mount, and since you lads are not from around here, I'll have to ask each of you for a security deposit of three shillings sixpence."

I did some quick recall in my head and figured that would come out to about a day's pay for the average working man in the 1700s. Maybe a little more. Now came the next test. Did I have the right currency? I knew that the colonials used pounds and shillings right up until about May or June of 1775 when the Continental Congress authorized Continental Currency. Just to make things more confusing, though, I also understood that each colony issued its own currency and that a Massachusetts pound was worth more, than a Pennsylvania pound for example. Matt and I had a hodgepodge of bills and coins, but most of them were from Massachusetts. I dug into my pockets and came up with what I thought would cover both of our fees including the deposits.

The attendant gave a quick look at what I gave him and said, "Thank you. Oh, whoever rides Stormy here, have a care. He bucks once in a while."

Whew! Money from the 1700s that had survived till the 21st century had made it back to the 18th century successfully. Matt looked over at me and we exchanged telegraphic thoughts of relief at passing another test. I then thought that this was as good a time as any to learn more about Continental Currency, so I said, "Would you have accepted currency from Connecticut or Pennsylvania? I have a few bills from those colonies."

"I never turn down money, sir, but the Pennsylvania dollars are not worth as much as our own Massachusetts Bay money. I'd have to discount you about ten percent. Connecticut dollars are as good as our own, though. Where in tarnation did you get those bills?"

"We're from Halifax. Before we left, we went to our local bank and converted some of our currency to your dollars. They didn't have enough Massachusetts money, so we had to take some of the other bills."

"I see. Well, then, I'll see thee sometime after midday then."

Taliaferro said, "Yes, my good man. That you will."

Matt and I mounted up and smiled at each other. So far, so good. Taliaferro led the way as he was familiar with the roads from Beverly Farms to Salem. He'd obviously made the trip more than once.

I asked Taliaferro how long it would take to ride into Salem.

"Less than an hour if we don't have to wait long for the ferry."

"What ferry is that?" I asked.

"Over the Danvers River. Separates Beverly from Salem."

The ride south out of Beverly Farms and into Salem was uneventful. Beverly was much larger than Beverly Farms, though that wasn't saying much. It was a rather quaint village, but it had far more houses and shops than Beverly Farms. It wasn't long before Taliaferro pointed out the river crossing up ahead. I could see the ferry, which was a flat-bottomed barge maybe 20 by 35 feet in size. No more than that. The ferry was just approaching our side of the river with two passengers standing next to their horses. No one appeared to be waiting on our side of the river, so we were next.

The ferry captain asked us to wait on the dock until his passengers and their horses had debarked. Then he told us it would be two pence for each of us. I searched my pocket for a few pence. We hadn't brought many, as the larger denominations would go farther, and a lot of pence would be very heavy to carry around in our pockets. As I withdrew the coins from my pocket, Taliaferro held up his hand and said, "Nae, gentlemen, since you are going to Salem at my request, let me pay for it."

I saw no reason to argue, so I said, "We thank you, sir."

The river was calm, though our horses seemed a bit skittish on the crossing. They probably were not accustomed to being on a somewhat unsteady platform on water. When we got to the Salem side, Taliaferro said, "Just a few minutes to Colonel Mason's house."

Matt said, "I thought Salem was an important port here in Massachusetts. I only see a few small boats here in the river."

"'Tis a very large port, sir. The river is not the harbor, which is ahead and off to your left. I'll take you there after we meet with the colonel. Salem is nearly as busy a port as Boston. Right now Salem is more important than Boston, as Gage and his regulars now have control of the city. Rumor has it that Gage now wants to take control of the hills surrounding the city, so he can control everything that goes in and out of Boston."

I asked, "Is that why we're meeting with Colonel Mason? To prevent Governor Gage from gaining more control over Provincial geography?"

"Aye. You young men are well-informed for Nova Scotians. But, yes, I think that's what he'll want to discuss with us. I'll let him talk about it, though. I probably shouldn't say more now."

As we rode further into Salem, Taliaferro said, "We're only a few hundred yards from the harbor and we've made good time, so why don't we ride over to Front Street and I'll let you see why Salem is such a large part of the commerce of Massachusetts."

As we entered Front Street the harbor lay in front of us. Piers stretched out into the harbor in every direction. At every pier were sailing ships of all sizes. A few were flying the colors of other countries, but most flew various New England banners. One I later learned was called the Massachusetts Bedford Flag, which was associated with the Minutemen. I also learned that the piers in Salem were called wharves. Most of the wharves had rough buildings on them, similar to the one on the pier in Beverly Farms. These buildings housed the business offices for various shipping merchants that made Salem such a bustling, thriving economy. The harbor was teeming with ships of all sizes. Many were tied up to the wharves, but others lay at anchor out in the harbor. Matt and I just stared. We'd been to Salem in the 21st century, and while it was an active town with a lot of things to do, the harbor was quite different. It wasn't teeming with large ships of trade, but thousands of smaller pleasure boats. It was quite a contrast, but we couldn't share our feelings about this contrast with Taliaferro. At least not yet.

I said, "I can see why Salem is such an important town."

"I thought seeing it with your own eyes was the best way for you to appreciate just how important the town is. All right, I think now we best be getting over to Colonel Mason's house."

A few minutes later we rode up to a stately house painted yellow. I'd already noticed that most houses in 18th century Massachusetts were painted in colors. Interestingly, I hadn't seen one painted white. The

Mason house was a fine-looking structure—a house that a family of above-average means would possess.

We knocked on the door with the large brass door knocker. A few seconds later we heard steps approaching. The massive door opened and we found ourselves facing a tall and rather imposing man probably in his sixties. He had a military bearing that suggested he was used to being in command.

"Obadiah, I see you've brought friends with you. Please come in." Mason's self-assured manner was balanced by an openness that made one feel comfortable in his presence.

Taliaferro said, "David, I recently met these two young men from Halifax. After we got to know each other somewhat I was certain you'd want to meet them." He then introduced us to the colonel.

Mason said, "How much did you tell them about what we're doing?"

"After I was convinced that they were of a proper mind for it I gave them as much as the general populace knows. I leave it up to you to decide just how much you want to share with them. I think you'll feel as I do about them."

"I sincerely hope I do. But before we talk seriously, let me get you some refreshments. I have coffee, no tea I'm afraid." He winked as he said this. "Also some cider and some plum pastries my girl made this morning. They're quite good." Taliaferro said some coffee would be good. Matt and I went along with him. Mason poked his head into another room and spoke briefly. Moments later a young girl, probably in her teens, came in with a tray of coffee and some pastries.

"Now then, said Mason, I'm sure you gentlemen didn't come here just for the coffee. What did my good friend Obadiah here tell you about me that brought you here?"

"He said that you head up the Salem Committee of Safety and that you've been authorized by the Provincial Committee of Safety and Provincial Congress to help build a militia large enough to prevent Governor Gage from taking control of the hills surrounding Boston. This would be done in cooperation with the Boston Committee of Safety. He also said that the Committees of Safety have gradually assumed more and more governmental powers. The more power the Provincial Congress and the Committees of Safety have, the less power Gage and the Crown have."

Mason frowned and gave Taliaferro a look of disapproval. He excused himself and stepped away with Taliaferro for a quiet conversation. "You seemed to have revealed a great deal to these lads, Obadiah. Just how well do you know them? Could you really know them that well if you just met them?"

"As I said, I told them only what's known by the general public. As you can tell they're rather quick and come to us already quite knowledgeable about political affairs."

"I fear it may be too much. Tis the knowledge I would expect spies to possess. Not that I'm accusing you gentlemen of spying, but it's a rare citizen who knows and understands as much as you do. It's even more rare that someone from as far away as Halifax would know what you know. How do you explain this?"

I knew that what I said next was critical. "Matthew worked for a printer in Nova Scotia and I worked for a newspaper. It's hard not to know a great deal about political affairs in those trades. Much of the work deals with such things."

Mason nodded slowly, processing my words carefully. "It makes sense, but we only have your word about that, don't we? You both look like the sort of men I'd like to have working for the Committee, but I need some more assurance that you are who you say you are. I'm sure you understand."

"David," said Taliaferro desperately, "We need just such men. Can't we take a chance on them in some lesser jobs until we're more certain of them?"

"I understand what you're saying Obadiah, and my heart agrees with you, but we're at a point where our very existence hinges on what we do next. Even with our best efforts, we Provincials are at a disadvantage against the mightiest army in all of Europe. I know it's a lot to ask, but. . ."

I had to speak up. "Do you really believe that we would take up musket and bayonet against the regulars and risk our lives doing so if we were spies for Gage?"

Mason looked surprised at my words. "I was not aware that Obadiah was thinking of you as troops in the militia. I suspect he thought you were too valuable for that. I doubt he would have brought you here if only to join the militia"

Taliaferro nodded and said, "Tis true, David. I see something in these young men. Something tells me they can be useful to our cause."

"I don't deny they seem well spoken, but you've only known them for a short time, and they come from afar, so there is no one about who could speak on their behalf. I'm just being careful. Having said that, I sense that you men are who you say you are, and I do not want to discourage you. Tell me why you've come all this way from Halifax?"

We told him how we'd become *persona non grata* in our respective jobs because of our verbal support of Massachusetts Provincials against the Crown's excessive taxes. Especially since the colony had no representatives in Parliament. We mentioned, too, how we found the billeting of troops in private homes particularly offensive. We then added that friends had written to us from Salem saying how welcome we would be down here. Mason seemed to find this of particular interest, and said, "You have friends here in Salem?"

I said, "Two of our good mates arrived here late last year from Halifax. I understand they served the patriot cause well in both Lexington and Concord."

Mason's eyes lit up. I do remember quite well the two lads from Halifax. Can you give me their names?"

"Gilbert Lee and Thomas Blair."

"And you say Gilbert and Thomas are good friends of yours? How do you know them?"

I had to decide whether to continue our well-intentioned lie about coming from Halifax or telling the truth. Did Mason know where Gil and Tom really came from? If so, my lying would not help us. I took guidance from Gil's written account of their experiences in Salem in which he said that only a carefully chosen few had been informed of their arrival from the 21st century. I had to hope that Colonel Mason was not among the chosen few.

"We're all from Halifax. Actually, Gilbert and Thomas were originally from Portland, but later relocated to Halifax after the war with France. We knew them because we worked with them in Halifax. A few months after they left for Massachusetts, I received a letter from Gilbert telling us of their new life in Salem and how they had joined the fighting in Lexington and Concord. They said life here in Massachusetts was much more satisfying than back in Nova Scotia, in large part because the thinking about the King and his treatment of the American colonies was more in line with their own. They immediately felt at home here in Salem and Massachusetts. In Nova Scotia they were pretty much outcasts because of their political thinking."

Mason nodded approvingly a number of times as I told him of our friendship with Gil and Tom. I sensed that his resistance was melting away.

"Gentlemen, since our men sent the regulars running after the battles in Lexington and Concord, I have met with your two friends twice to seek counsel from them. They have an uncanny sense of what Gage and his people are planning. They seem to know better than many of our experienced military men and politicians how Gage's mind works. As I'm sure you can imagine, the conflicts at Lexington and Concord did not settle things. Gage has not altered his policies or loosened his grip on the people of Boston. If anything, his grip is getting tighter and he appears to be preparing to take possession of the hills and other territory surrounding Boston. We are not going to let him get away with it. Can I count on you men to help us contain Gage if it comes to that?"

Matt said, "Exactly what do you have in mind, sir?"

———

"I'm not sure right now. I need to confer with my key Committee members and also with Dr. Warren in Boston before I can be more specific. But knowing of your inclination to help would be appreciated. Once we know what Warren and his people have in mind, I can tell you what part I'd like you to play in this next step."

I said, "Dr. Warren is the man leading the Massachusetts Committee of Safety. Is that right?"

"Yes, and a good man, too. Lost his wife a few years ago, but not his nerve or his wit. Very impressive man. He's the one who sent Revere and Dawes out to Lexington and Concord to warn Hancock and Adams that the regulars were on their way to arrest them. Then, if that weren't enough, he went and joined in the fight himself. As I say, quite an impressive man." Mason sighed and then, as if refocusing, said, "But then, back to you lads. How can I reach you? I assume you've not yet found a lodging you can call your own?"

"No, not yet," I said. "We're staying with a Mrs. Crockett in Beverly Farms for the night. I imagine we'll be there a few more nights till we find something more permanent. The next thing we need to do is get in touch with Gilbert and Thomas. We're hoping they can direct us to someplace we can live here in Salem. Then, of course, we need to look for work. Hopefully something in our respective trades."

"I might be able to help you with that. I know one of the local printers and I know the publisher of the *Essex Gazette*, Sam Hall. If you'd like, you can use my name if you visit them."

"Thank you, sir." My eyes lit up at the mention of the paper, for that, I recalled was the newspaper that Gil and Tom were working at according to their written account.

Mason then said, "When you get settled please see me so we can find a place for you in our efforts to put a stop to Gage's oppression."

When we left Mason's house I asked if we could go by the waterfront again. I couldn't get the image out of my mind, since I'd known what the Salem harbor looked like in the spring of 2019 when I'd visited to get familiar with the area. Matt and I had been advised to check out the Salem area so we'd be somewhat familiar with the geography when we visited it sometime in or around 1775.

As we approached the busy waterfront area, I saw a number of men busily loading cargo onto a ship. I also noticed that some of the men were black. These were the first blacks I'd seen since arriving in the 18th century. I asked Taliaferro about this.

"Yes, slaves. Most of them from the West Indies, though some are from Africa. Some ship owners have made a very successful fortune for themselves in the slave trade. They keep a few for themselves. Saves considerably on labor costs."

"Is everyone comfortable with this?"

"No, not at all. There's a sizable abolitionist movement growing in Salem. Most of the shipmasters have a strong distaste for the slave trade, but there's enough of them that profit from it to keep the trade very much alive."

"Are some of these shipmasters who trade in slaves also active in the fight against Gage and his poor treatment of the colony?"

"Indeed, most ship owners are against Gage."

Matt and I exchanged looks. I then said, "Don't they find that a bit hypocritical?"

Taliaferro's brow furrowed as he tried to puzzle out what I was saying.

"I don't get your meaning, Christopher."

"What I'm trying to say is that the reason people are resisting or even fighting Gage and the King is because they believe the Crown has denied them their rights. The Crown has treated them as second-class citizens, not the way it treats citizens in England. At least that's my understanding."

"Second-class citizens. An interesting expression. Yes, if I take your meaning correctly, that is fairly accurate."

"Do they not see that they are treating these black people much worse as they accuse the Crown of treating them?"

"Ah." Taliaferro pursed his lips and nodded slowly as he processed this. "These radical abolitionists see it this way, but most good people don't. Most people would not accept your analogy. Whites both here and in England are the same in mind and body. However, everyone knows that coloreds are less advanced in development than whites. Coloreds are so unlike white folk that they're a different species altogether. Many believe the coloreds are incapable of intelligent reflection or even human emotion. True, they can experience physical pain, but it is quickly forgotten, and they soon go cheerfully about their work."

"So only the abolitionists believe the black people capable of intelligent thought?"

"Oh I doubt even they would go that far. More likely they just feel a bit more compassion for the unfortunate creatures."

Matt and I shook our heads. This exchange with Taliaferro, who seemed educated and otherwise fair minded, brought home something that I suspected we were going to experience repeatedly in the 18th century: Good-spirited well-intentioned people of the time believed that black people were inferior. Consequently, it was not much of a burden on their consciences to accept the institution of slavery. Even people with empathy and an active moral sensitivity could live with slavery as long as the owners treated their slaves with some compassion.

Matt tried another angle. "Do you really believe that all of the abolitionists consider the black man inferior and incapable of intelligent thought?"

"No, I suppose not all of them. A few of these radicals actually believe we should find a way to educate the coloreds. Some claim they have even taught a few of them to read. Frankly, I have my doubts, but that's what some of the radical abolitionists claim they've accomplished. Personally, I believe that if you're going to own slaves, you should treat them kindly, but trying to educate them is probably a big waste of one's hard-earned money."

It was fairly clear that Matt and I were not going to change the thinking of the times. At first, I thought I should at least try to set the record straight, but then I realized that prejudice was still present in the 21st century with all the knowledge and science that had been accumulated over the centuries. We, as newcomers to the Salem area of 1775, were only going to run into a brick wall if we tried to buck the zeitgeist of the time. I did vow that I'd at least try to point out what a black person might be capable of, but I didn't hold out much hope for any success in changing the minds of colonial Americans. Apparently even decent people believed in the inferiority of folks who were born with a different skin color.

We had made some progress by the time America reached the 21st century, but racial discrimination had not disappeared. Not by a long shot. How many centuries would it take for America to truly treat everyone equally?

Taliaferro changed the subject. "Perhaps you lads would like to visit the offices of the *Essex Gazette*, the newspaper Colonel Mason mentioned. Might be a good place to start in your effort to find work in your respective trades. If he doesn't have anything, he might know some place that does.

As I looked at Matt and caught his affirmative nod I said, "Yes, we would like that very much. But do you want to take the time? We could come back at another time if you have other business."

"No, my good man. I can appreciate what it must feel like to be in a strange new place without work or lodgings. If I can make it easier for you, it's my pleasure. Besides," he added with a canny smile, "the sooner you lads get settled, the sooner you'll make yourselves available to the Committee of Safety and our efforts to frustrate Gage and the abuses of the Crown."

It was only a short ride to the *Essex Gazette* office in the middle of busy Salem. As we approached the door of the paper, I felt a tingle of anticipation, as very likely we would see our friends Gil and Tom for the first time in four years. Though for them it would only be a few months. Until this mission was approved, I was sure we'd never see them again. I just hoped now that they were both at work today.

Taliaferro opened the door and we followed him in. The large room contained six desks. A young man seated at the desk nearest the front door got up and met us.

"Yes, gentlemen. I'm Joshua Pringle. How can I help you?"

Taliaferro said, "Is Sam in? I'm a friend of his from Amesbury."

"Yes, he's in the back. Wait just a moment."

A minute later a short man of considerable girth with a slightly oversized roundish tonsured head came strolling toward us with his hand extended. "Obadiah! What a splendid surprise. What brings you to Salem?"

"I've had business with Mason. Fortuitously I met up with these two young gentlemen at Mrs. Crockett's, where I'm staying in Beverly Farms. They've just come down from Halifax. They tell me you might have employed two of their Nova Scotian mates."

"Good Lord, don't tell me you're friends of Gilbert and Thomas?"

I beamed as he said this. "Yes sir, we are. I'm Christopher Carver and this is Matthew Blair." We shook hands and as I did this I saw Gil Lee coming from the back room and taking a seat at one of the desks. He looked up and noticed the group of us near the door and then he recognized us. His eyes lit up like nothing I've ever seen before or since. He immediately rose and made his way toward us.

He said, "My God, I can't believe it. I never thought I'd see you guys again."

I said, "We'll fill you in when you get off from work. Does Tom work here, too?"

"Yes, he's in the back. I'll get him. I just can't believe this. It's gonna take me some time to get used to it, but it's great."

Sam Hall's expression changed from one of cheery welcoming to the face of one who knows a lot more than people think he knows. He turned to Gil with a knowing smile, "Two more fellows from 'Halifax,' eh? Shall we expect more?"

Gil whispered to me and said, "Sam knows about our true origins. He's the only one here who does, and we'd like to keep it that way."

"We understand," I said. "When do you and Tom get off from work?"

Hall said to Gil, "You and Tom finish off what you're working on and feel free to leave early. I'm sure the four of you have a lot of catching up. Don't drink too much ale tonight, though. I need you bright and early tomorrow morning."

Gil said to us, "I think we can finish up in about two hours. Where are you staying?"

"We're staying in Beverly Farms."

Hall said, "You don't want to go all the way to Beverly Farms and then back to Salem. I hope you don't mind my making a suggestion, but you might want to spend the time walking around the town getting familiar with Salem. Then stop in at the Social Library. Fascinating place. Has volumes dating back three centuries. It's only about 15 houses from here. When Tom and Gil leave here, they can fetch you at the library and you can visit one of our local taverns for some beer and a good dinner. Then you can go back to Beverly Farms. It'll be dark, but it's not a difficult journey. I think the ferry is in operation until nine or thereabouts."

Before we left, Gil went into the back room and brought Tom out to meet us. We then all agreed on the plan Sam Hall had suggested.

As we left the *Gazette* offices, I reflected on how time travel had affected the four of us. Gil and Tom had left Nevada in September of 2015 and arrived in the Salem area in September of 1774. I'd just learned from the latest copy of a newspaper that Sam Hall had given us that today was May 19th, only a month since the Battles of Lexington and Concord. What boggled my mind was that, from Gil and Tom's perspective, the last time they'd seen us was about eight months ago. Matt and I left Nevada four years after Gil and Tom lifted off, so we hadn't seen them in four years. Somehow our engineers had managed four years later to send us back to a point in time in 1775 that was only eight months after Gil and Tom had arrived there. Time travel makes your head spin.

Chapter 7

May 19, 1775

OBADIAH TALIAFERRO left us as soon as we departed from the *Essex Gazette* offices. He urged us to get back in touch with Colonel Mason as soon as we found lodgings and a job. He said he hoped this would be within the next two weeks, as the Massachusetts Committees of Safety feared that Governor Gage was planning something soon and our help would be needed in the defense of the colonials against Gage and his Redcoats.

We left our horses tied up outside the newspaper's offices and walked through Salem on our way to the Social Library. One of the first things we noticed was the absence of sidewalks. Most of the streets were packed dirt and you had to watch where you stepped to avoid horse droppings. A couple of the major streets were paved with cobblestones. I couldn't help thinking that cobblestones had to be hard on horses and probably resulted in the occasional broken leg. I know they were certainly harder to walk on than packed dirt or the concrete or tarmac of later centuries.

The walk was fascinating as we slowly took in the 18th century culture. The shops were a far cry from our supermarkets and an even farther cry from ecommerce giants such as Walmart and Amazon. The Social Library consisted of two rooms. The walls were floor-to-ceiling with books. The librarian greeted us and asked us if we were members. We said no, but that we were guests of Sam Hall, who'd written a brief note of introduction for us. The librarian, Jeremy Weeks, a tall, skinny shiny domed man with rimless spectacles, smiled and showed us around. Little did the librarian know that in the near future the Social Library would become the Philosophical Library and that a few years after that it would evolve into the Salem Athenaeum. Needless to say, Matt and I didn't tell the young man because he would have thought we were joking, or worse.

The reason I mention this is because the Social Library was the way Gil and Tom communicated to us at the CAE in Nevada from the year 1775. They persuaded the library to hold a time capsule containing Gil's hand-written account. I retrieved that account from the Salem Athenaeum, the successor to the Social Library, in the year 2015. After Matt and I have lived here for a few months, we'll try to place our own time capsule in the library so that our team back in Nevada can learn as much as possible about this time in their history and about the mission in general. They have to get some benefit from persuading Jason Farnsworth to part with the billions it took to finance this mission. In addition to getting first-hand accounts of what to them is history and to us will be real life, they will also learn that they have already successfully zeroed in on both a specific time in history and a specific location. No mean feat in either case.

While our little tour of the Social Library was quite interesting, I have to admit that my mind and I'm sure Matt's, too, was on our upcoming reunion with our friends. It was a reunion we never thought would happen. All four of us had a lot to catch up on and my thoughts were more on this than they were on the patient descriptions and commentary given by Jeremy Weeks. At times, I realized we were so distracted by our own thoughts that we bordered on being rude to the man who was being so attentive and conscientious in his proud tour of the library.

Half an hour into our tour (Without watches or clocks, we couldn't be sure) we heard voices just outside the front door. A few seconds later, the door opened and in walked Gil and Tom looking like two young men out of the 18th century, which they were.

We all hugged and grinned from ear to ear. After explaining to Weeks that we hadn't seen our friends in months, we excused ourselves and left the library. Gil and Tom had come on horseback and suggested that they take us to a nearby tavern so we could catch up. Ten minutes later we found ourselves in a fairly secluded booth in Pierce's Tavern on Front Street overlooking the busy waterfront.

Gil lifted his tankard of ale and said, "Cheers." We all took a ceremonial drink and then Gil said, "You guys are dressed like locals. Did you plan this before you lifted off or did you buy these duds when you got here?"

"The techies in Nevada were pretty sure they could get us here around the time you guys were here so we brought some of this colonial garb with us. As you can see, the folks back at CAE are getting pretty good at this. We just landed yesterday."

Tom said, "I can't tell you how great it is to see someone from the 21st century to bring us up to date on what's happening back there. He shook his head and then said, "I suppose I should have said up there."
We talked about colleagues at the CAE and then Gil asked, "How've the Patriots and the Sox done in the last few years?"

I couldn't help smiling. "Let's see. The Red Sox were terrible in 2015, but came back the next two years and did okay. They won the series in '18. As for the Pats, they won the Super Bowl in 16 and 18. So your teams are doing fine. Don't you want to know how the country's doing?"

Gil said, "Yes. Who's President now?"

"You're not gonna believe this?"

"Try us," said Tom, who was always interested in politics.

"Donald Trump."

"No, seriously. Who is it?"

"I'm not kidding. Trump got elected. People thought he was doing it sort of as a lark, but the more he campaigned the more the country realized that he was serious. Now that he's been in office for three years, he's become very controversial. Hell, he was controversial when he ran, but since he's been in office even more so. We can tell you more about him later if you want, but let's catch up on what you guys have been doing here in 1775."

Gil said, "Damn! I can't believe you guys are here. I can't believe you're as crazy as we were. Last I knew, not many volunteers were eager to go back in time. That's one of the reasons we were supposed to be going forward. Look how that worked out. I'm not sure either Tom or I would have volunteered to go back over 200 years, but now that we're here, it's not so bad. Not bad at all. I think you'll grow to like it. I hope so."

I grinned and took another sip of my beer. "Yeah, me too. What do you guys miss the most?"

Tom said, "Pizza. They never heard of pizza here."

I said, "Why don't you show someone how to make one?"

"I would, except they don't have tomatoes here. They've heard of them, but they don't have them. They think some people in southern Europe might eat them, but they have no idea how. No recipes for tomatoes here. Not in their culture. Hell, they don't have any Italian food. They have what they're ancestors brought over from England and a couple items they got from the Indians, but other than that, no ethnic cuisines at all as far as I can tell."

"Guess we'll just have to get used to that."

"Yeah, it takes some getting used to, believe me. Some folks here are very good cooks, though, so you won't starve."

Gil said, "We also miss sports."

I asked, "Do they play any sports here?"

"They occasionally have boxing matches. In Boston they play cricket. Oh, I've also heard that some places have foot races. Frankly, most people work so hard here and make so little money that they don't have a lot of time for sports—or games of any kind, for that matter." Gil paused as he thought about it. Then said, "Young kids start working when they're 12 or so, so they don't have much chance to play anything. Some start working a lot younger than that. You're going to have to get used to it. It's 1775, not 2019."

"This really will take some getting used to." I sighed and changed the subject.

—

"Do you miss TV?"

"Of course, but not as much as I thought I would. How about you, Tom. You miss TV?"

"Yes, probably more than you do, but you learn to converse, and you spend more time reading."

This got my attention. "What do you read? Certainly not Tom Clancy or David Baldacci."

"Thanks to Sam Hall we have access to the Social Library and we get to read a lot of classical stuff we never would have read in the 21st century. We also read the newspapers. Believe me, the political commentary is wild compared to what we used to read in 21st century papers. The papers provide so much background to the history we learned in school. You see why things happened and why other things didn't. Yes, I miss some of the spy novels and mysteries, but there is enough to read if you are lucky enough to have access to it, which we do thanks to Sam Hall. My guess is that the average citizen probably doesn't read much more than the newspaper and the Bible. Most people don't have access to the Social Library, and there is no public library. There are no bookstores here in Salem, either. I think there may be one in Boston, though. Of course some people can't read at all. I am surprised at how many are literate, but not all of them are."

Tom set his tankard down and said, "I miss my cell phone and of course the Internet. It's a lot harder to find information now than it was in my former life. The library or the *Gazette's* archives are the places I go to look things up, but they both have obvious limits. One of the biggest limits is what happened after 1775. There's no information about anything that came after 1775." Tom thought for a moment, then added, "It's not easy to do research in the 18th century."

Gil added, "Much of what Tom and I know happened after 1775, so none of that can be referenced except in our own minds. It's frustrating as hell when we're talking to someone and we know stuff that they couldn't possibly know. We just have to hope they'll just believe us. Many things we know from the future sounds like magic or even black magic to these colonials, so we don't bring these topics up at all. It's maddening as hell, because we know so much that we can't share."

"Still," I said knowingly, "It must also give you an edge many times."

"Yes, I suppose it does, but not as much as you'd think. Too much of our 21st century knowledge is useless in the 18th century." Gil finished off his beer and motioned to the man behind the rustic bar. When he came over, Gil said, "Will, bring us four more, please." Then he turned back to us looking serious. "Enough about us. You guys are going to need a place to stay here in Salem and a job. I don't suppose you have any ideas about either, since you just got here yesterday?"

I said, "We don't have a clue about where to stay. We'll stay in Beverly Farms for a few days until we find something. I suppose before we find a place to live we're gonna need jobs. If we don't find them in Salem we'll have to live somewhere else. Colonel Mason said he'd put in a good word for us with Sam Hall. How do you guys like working for him?"

"He's a terrific boss. Smart as a whip and respected by everyone from Boston to Portland from what I can tell."

"Does he need anybody, though?"

"I think he is looking for one person. Another typesetter. I hope you guys boned up on your typesetting and English-press skills."

I smiled. "After reading your account that I got from the Salem Athenaeum, we made it a point to get pretty good at press work and typesetting." According to Gil's written account, he and Tom were working on what's called an English press. Most of the printing presses in the colonies at the time were English presses.

"Good, why don't you guys drop in tomorrow mid-morning. I will have spoken to Sam about you and maybe he'll hire at least one of you. If he hires only one, he might refer the other to one of the two printers in town."

Matt and I exchanged nods of agreement. I then said, "We can't leave you guys without telling you how proud we are of how you fought in the Lexington and Concord battles. Hot Damn! For two guys from 2015 to fight in two historic battles just blows my mind. Weren't you scared out of your gourds?"

Tom said, "What really gets to you is how close you are to the other side. Guys coming at you with muskets drawn and bayonets attached. Men dying beside you. Others screaming in pain. Scares you shitless. Funny, before the first battle started, we were talking about how we knew we couldn't be killed because we were alive 240 years later in 2015. Made us relax a little at a time when we should have been shaking in our boots. Literally." We all smiled at this. The bizarre incongruity of what he'd said was dizzying. Tom went on, "Then, when the shooting started and the Redcoats started coming at us, I felt myself shake with fear. The idea that we couldn't be killed was farthest from my mind as I saw our fellow Continental soldiers falling and the guns of the enemy firing directly at us."

"Did either of you get injured?"

"No, we were lucky. We did get locked up, though. That's a story in itself. Tell you about it some other time, though. By the way, I know you just got here, but you both obviously know that an even bloodier battle is coming up at Bunker Hill next month. I'm still part of the militia and will most likely be called up to help out down there. If you want to be part of history, you might want to consider joining the militia. If you don't, I won't blame you. It can get really gory, but if you do, it will give you a view you don't get from a history book. Think about it."

"We will." Matt nodded his affirmation. "First things first, though. We need a job and a place to live."

"I understand. When you come to the *Gazette* tomorrow morning we'll get you started on your job search. By the way, how much do you know about Obadiah Taliaferro?"

"Not much actually. You ever heard of him? He seems sincere, but who knows. We just met him."

"I don't know him, but he's quite well known in the Massachusetts Committee of Safety. His Amesbury group is small, but he's quite vocal and seems to play a role disproportionate to the size of his local committee. Word is he's related to the Virginia Taliaferros. One of them is a general in the Virginia Continental militia. Apparently the Taliaferros came over to Virginia in the 1600s from London. One of them was a musician in the Court of Queen Elizabeth. Anyway, I think he's the real deal. I think you can trust him."

I started to chuckle, but stopped myself. "This is weird. You reminded us that the Battle of Bunker Hill is going to be fought next month. You're already planning on being part of it, yet I'm fairly certain that Colonel Mason has no idea the battle is going to be fought."

"Of course he doesn't, but he does know that Gage is planning to take possession of the hills surrounding Boston and Bunker Hill is one of them. Bunker Hill will actually be fought on the nearby Breed's Hill. I'm sure neither Mason, nor Gage know that, either. Anyway, since we know that you'll survive if you do decide to join up, what's the risk? You'll get all the excitement and still live through it. What could be better than that?"

I was extremely curious now. "How does Mason know about Gage's plans?"

"There's a teenager, a kid by the name of Jimmy Ames, who works in the house that Gage now lives in in Cambridge. Gage just assumes Jimmy is a Loyalist, and when he has visitors—usually military men or other British officials representing the Crown—he talks freely, ignoring Jimmy. It's almost as if Jimmy didn't exist. Jimmy then reports to Dr. Warren, the chairman of the Massachusetts Committee of Safety. Warren meets often to spread the word with other area Committee of Safety leaders, including Colonel Mason."

Matt said, "I'm already excited. I honestly don't know if I'd be this excited if I didn't know I'd survive the battle, but I'd still like to do my part and get a better understanding of history than I've had up to this moment."

"Amen to that," I said. "Damn! I have so many questions about so many different things, I don't know where to start."

Gil laughed. "I know exactly how you guys feel, but I'd suggest you get settled into a job and a place to live. You'll gradually get answers to a lot of your questions. Tom and I can answer a lot of the others over the next few weeks. Face it, you're not going anywhere, so you have plenty of time to get answers to your questions."

"Yes, you're right," I said. "We should get going. We have to find our way back to Beverly Farms in the dark. And we have to do it on horseback. That should be interesting." I grinned and added, "We don't have GPS, either." Then it dawned on me. "But we do have our cell phones."

Gil and Tom stared at us in disbelief. Tom said, "You do know that you can't use them here?"

"Yeah, of course," said Matt, "but we can use the cameras and a few other apps. One app we have is the Merriam-Webster dictionary. It's about 100 megabytes, but it's worth it. From what I've read, you can't find a dictionary in this century, except Dr. Johnson's."

"Unbelievable," said Gil shaking his head slowly from side to side. "I haven't run across the Johnson dictionary, though they may have one at the Social Library." Then he pointed to my phone and asked, "You have any pictures of your ship? Love to see if it's any different from ours."

"Yes, we do. And a bunch of other pictures of Nevada, New York City and Boston. Also a few shots of your friends back at the CAE."

"Damn! We didn't bother taking our phones because we expected to end up two years into the future. Figured we get ourselves some very advanced phones when we got there. You're gonna have yourselves a lot of fun here with those, but you shouldn't start showing them off right away. And if you ever do, it should be limited to a very few people."

"I know," I said. "We picked that up from what you said in your account. If we show it to just anybody, and to too many people, there's no telling how it will affect history. It's going to be awfully frustrating, though, if we can't show them to anyone."

"I know, but believe me, you'll make it a lot easier on yourselves if you do it extremely sparingly. Every time you even hint to someone that you're from the future you open yourself up to scrutiny. Scrutiny of the worse kind. At best they'll think you're a con man. At worst they'll think you're a witch. Believe me, you don't want that." Someone caught Gil's eye and he waved back. He then turned back to us and said, "That man at the bar is someone you could show your phone to. He's president of the board of trustees of the Social Library and one of the men who witnessed the raising of our spacecraft from the waters off Great Misery Island. He and his colleagues have been pledged to secrecy about us. It's not easy for them, either. As I'm sure you can understand, they would love to tell their family members and friends, but they also realize how dangerous that could be." He looked over at Tom and said, "Shall we risk it with Thomas Pynchon?"

Tom Howard smiled and said, "If anyone can keep his mouth shut, it'll be Pynchon. Yes, let's ask him over. This should be fun."

Gil said, "Okay. Hold your breath." He then got up and walked over to the bar and spoke to Pynchon. A minute later, the two men joined us at our table. The first thing I noticed was Pynchon's height. He must have been six-five or six. If he were a few years younger, he would have made a good forward on a college basketball team. He carried himself with the quiet authority of a man who was accustomed to being listened to. Gil proceeded to introduce everybody. Pynchon nodded quietly, but said nothing. It was as if he was waiting to see if coming to our table was worth his time. No one said anything for a moment, and then Gil broke the silence by saying, "Mr. Pynchon, Christopher and Matthew have just arrived from the future. We're not telling people, of course, but we thought, since you already know about our origin, you should know that we now have two more visitors from the future."

On hearing this, Pynchon's expressionless face went white. His eyes looked as if they would pop out of his head. The lines around his mouth grew tense. Finally, he said, "I suppose the proper thing to do would be to welcome you, but as you might imagine, I'm having difficulty dealing with this. I went through an unsettling time when I learned about Gilbert and Thomas. It's taken me some time, but I think I've finally come to grips with it. Now, two more of you. I can't help wondering if we are being invaded by people from the future. If that is the case, what does it forebode for us here in the year 1775?"

I had to reassure the man so I said, "I can assure you, sir, that you need not expect an invasion. I think we may be the last visitors from the future. We were sent because it was believed that Gilbert and Thomas would welcome news from 2019 and welcome us, their friends. Our scientists are attempting to perfect their science and considered it a challenge to place us in history at this specific time and place. Once they learn that they have succeeded in doing that, I believe they will wish to explore other times in their history."

Pynchon nodded slowly as he processed what I was saying. I'm sure it was a lot to process, and I can only imagine how the thought of an invasion of people from the future could be unsettling as hell. My God, they were already dealing with the abuses of the King and the likelihood of all-out war.

Gil then said, "Mr. Pynchon, you've seen our spaceship. Christopher here

—

has brought another scientific marvel from the future. We call it a cell phone."

Chapter 8

May 19, 1775

PYNCHON REACHED for his pint and took a deep draught of his beer. Then he drew in a deep breath and said, "Cell phone? Whatever is that? Good Lord, this is an evening I never could have imagined. I suppose you'd best let me see this scientific marvel so I can judge for myself just how marvelous it is."

I pulled out my phone and laid it on the table. Pynchon just stared at the black phone with the shiny Gorilla Glass display. I hadn't turned the phone on, so he appeared more puzzled than amazed. I then woke the phone up. Pynchon breathed deeply as the opening display flashed on. I watched him as he waited for the marvelous part to show itself.

I then said, "Now I'm going to show you a photo of the spaceship we flew in to arrive here."

"Photo? What, pray tell is a photo?"

"Watch and you'll see." As I said this I clicked on Photos and then on one of the shots of our spaceship at the launchpad in Nevada. It was a great shot in vivid color." His eyes lit up. He had never seen a photo and his expression showed it.

"This is truly the marvel you say it is. I have never seen such a ship. Ships are supposed to be in the sea. I have never seen such a painting, either. It is so realistic I feel as if I am right there. You have marvelous artists in your 21st century."

"It's not a painting, sir. It's a photograph. We sometimes just say photo."

"A photograph. You must tell me how you achieve such a picture."

"About 40 years from now a man in France by the name of Nicephore Niepce will invent a process called photography. It enables a person to capture an image on paper. At first his images were very crude, but over time people improved on the process and now, or I should say, in the early 21st century cameras produce extremely realistic pictures in seconds."

"Cameras? This is another word that is foreign to me. Though I am familiar with the term camera obscura. I take it there is some connection."

"Yes, yes. I believe the *camera obscura* was the inspiration for the invention of the camera, which put as simply as I can is a device used to produce photographs. Here, let me show you a few more photos." I then proceeded to click on some photos of our colleagues back in Nevada.

With each picture he shook his head in amazement. I then clicked on some photos of New York City and Boston. He pushed his chair back and breathed in deeply. It was all almost too much for him to take it when I told him that Boston would one day look like the pictures I showed him of the Prudential Tower and the John Hancock building. The skyline of New York blew him away.

"You must show these to my friends over there." He pointed to two men sitting at the nearby bar.

I didn't like the way this was heading. It was my own fault for wanting to be the one to show someone in 1775 what 2019 looked like. Hubris was going to alter the course of history if I didn't get control of this.

Gil stepped in to bail me out. "Are you sure that's wise sir? Remember our agreement. It could be dangerous to share this with anyone outside the original group. I'd be glad to show these to the other Social Library board members, but don't you think we should limit it to that?"

He recognized the wisdom of this as soon as Gil said this.

"Yes, of course. I was just so excited by what you've shown me I wanted to share it. But it probably would be a mistake. Perhaps though I will take you up on your offer to share this with our board members. If I set up a meeting would you be willing to come?"

I looked at the others and they all nodded their agreement.

Chapter 9

May 20, 1775

WHEN WE ARRIVED at the *Essex Gazette* the next morning Sam Hall took us into his personal office at my request.

Hall then said, "What is it you wanted to talk to me about, Mr. Carver?"

"My friend Matthew and I are looking for work in the newspaper or printing business. We were wondering if you might have a need for someone or, if not, knew of someone who did?"

"It so happens that I need a typesetter. Do either of you have experience in typesetting?"

"We both do."

"If you gentlemen are half as good as your friends Gilbert and Thomas, then I'd be happy to hire one of you for a trial period. I know the printers here in town so I can direct the other to them. As a matter of fact I can send one of you to my competitor, Ezekial Russell, who publishes the *Salem Gazette*. We're business competitors, but we're on the same side against the abuses of the Crown."

After a brief discussion it was agreed that I would start work for Sam at the *Essex Gazette* one week from today. The week would give Matt and me time to find a place to live and get familiar with our new environment. To be fair, Sam told me that he was thinking of moving the paper to Cambridge sometime in the future. I said I'd take my chances. Matt went to the *Salem Gazette* and met with Ezekial Russell, who happily was willing to take him on for a trial period of one month. We both counted on our ability to prove ourselves in our respective trial periods. Needless to say, Matt did not tell Russell about his time travel from the 21st century. Gil and Tom had told Sam Hall about it, but Hall was not about to share that knowledge with anyone else without discussing it with us and the Athenaeum Board members who already knew.

We'd only been in the 18th century a couple of days and I could see how hard it was going to be to keep our real origins secret. There were times where it would simplify things so much if we just told the truth. Yet if we did, it would complicate things far more than simplify them. Fortunately, if you said you came from as far away as Halifax, nobody expected you to provide references. At least not when your supposed former employers allegedly frowned on your political beliefs. Bottom line, both publishers in Salem were willing to take a chance on us. Sam based his decision on his good experience with Gil and Tom. Ezekial Russell based it on a note from Sam Hall.

In the next few days Matt and I found two rooms in a rooming house that was recommended to us by Ezekial Russell. He said he knew the owner, Mrs. Emma Thompson, and had heard that she not only ran a clean rooming house, but was considered to be a very good cook. He knew her because he had known her husband, who had passed away several years ago.

Mrs. Thompson's rooming house was not far from the center of Salem, so living there was extremely convenient for both Matt and myself. Once we were settled into Mrs. Thompson's place we felt we no longer needed horses. We figured we could rent them at any of the three livery stables in Salem that we were now aware of if we had to go any distance.

After we'd been working a few days Gil asked me if I intended to contact Colonel Mason about working with the Committee of Safety. I said that Matt and I planned to see him that evening after work. Yes, we did want to get involved in some way assuming our respective bosses had no objection. Neither Sam nor Ezekial did, providing we didn't let our involvement interfere with work unless it came down to actually fighting in some battle if it came to that. That they would both fully understand and support.

The same day that Gil asked me about seeing Colonel Mason, Sam came to me to say that Thomas Pynchon had stopped in and wanted a brief moment of my time.

We met in Sam's private office. Pynchon said, "Mr. Carver, I'm sure you remember that you agreed to come to the Athenaeum to demonstrate your amazing device, the cell phone, I believe you called it."

"Cell phone. Yes, we were going to contact you soon about speaking to the members of the Board."

Pynchon looked puzzled. Then it dawned on me. "Oh, did I say contact? What I meant to say was communicate with you."
He shook his head ever so slightly as if to indicate that he couldn't believe what he was hearing. "You use the word 'contact' in a way quite unfamiliar to me, but I think I take your meaning now. He forced a smile. "To me, when you say you were going to contact me it makes me feel somewhat uncomfortable, but now I see that is not at all what you intended. I shall have to get used to your Nova Scotian locutions. He cleared his throat and said, "I take it then that you do intend to come visit us with your shiny little device?"

"Yes, we'd like that very much. What day do you have in mind?"

"Would the day after tomorrow be acceptable? Say seven in the evening?

"That will be fine, but we don't have a clock where we live, so. . . ?"

He smiled more warmly this time. "I understand. I would guess that Sam Hall has one here at the *Gazette*, but if you don't have access to one here or where you're now staying, come shortly after sunset. We'll be awaiting your arrival."

That same day Matt and I went to Colonel Mason's house to tell him we could now devote some of our time to working with the Committee of Safety. The colonel greeted us with less reserve than he had on our first meeting.

Mason began by informing us that he'd done his homework on us. "I've spoken to a number of people who fought at both Lexington and Concord and I've gotten nothing but good reports on your friends Thomas and Gilbert. I've also spoken with both Sam Hall and Ezekial Russell about the two of you, and I've heard nothing but good things. I gather you're here to offer your services to our cause?"

"Yes, sir, we are," I said.

"Excellent. I've given some thought to how you can help and here's how I think you can be of immediate service."

I interrupted before he could proceed any further. "We'd both like to help defend the hills around Boston. We have a feeling Gates and his regulars are going to make a move soon. Is there any way we can be a part of defending the surrounding hills?"

Mason's eyes widened. He was taken by surprise at what we were offering to do.

"I suppose if you volunteered your services to Warren he'd welcome you gladly, but why do you want to risk your lives when you can serve the cause just as usefully at far less risk?"

Matt then said, "We want to do everything we can to help the cause. We're new here and I know people are suspicious of newcomers at this time. We want to eliminate any doubt in people's minds about whose side we're on. We'd also like to help you in any way we can, but we definitely want to defend the territory around Boston if Warren will have us."

"I'll write a note that you can take to Dr. Warren introducing you. I'd suggest you meet with him soon. Since you said you would also like to help the Salem Committee of Safety I would hope that when you're in Salem and the surrounding communities you could keep your eyes and ears alert for any talk that could undermine our cause or any hint about what Governor Gage might be doing. In your positions it's entirely possible that you might hear or see something that could be helpful to us."

Matt shook his head enthusiastically and I said, "We'd be more than

---

happy to keep or eyes and ears on the alert, Colonel."

After we left Mason's house Matt and I discussed how our volunteering for both committees of safety would affect our work schedules and how our respective bosses would feel about our volunteering. It clearly meant that at times we would not be able to work. We agreed that the very next thing we should each do was take up the matter with both Hall and Russell.

The next morning I went to Sam Hall and told him that I hoped to volunteer both for Colonel Mason and Dr. Warren. Sam listened patiently as I told him what my volunteering would amount to. He responded the way I hoped he would.

"Christopher, I am delighted that you wish to do what you can for both Colonel Mason and Dr. Warren. I don't see how what you'll be doing for the colonel should interfere with your work here. However, Dr. Warren may want you to train with his militia. Or the officers working with him anyway. That could become a problem if it means you will be away from work frequently. If you can come to an agreement where you train one or two days a week I will back you enthusiastically, but I'm sure you can see that if you are not here most of the work days, I will need to replace you. I don't like restricting you that way because I want to support anyone who is willing to risk his life in support of the Provincial cause."

"I understand completely, Sam. Hopefully Dr. Warren will, too, and will accept my help on those terms. Maybe I can train on the weekends only. My greater concern is that I have no musket. I wonder if that alone will disqualify me?"

Instead of answering my concern, Sam had a puzzled look on his face. "Dear God, another word from the future."

I was just as puzzled as he was. "What word did I use that that is new to you, Sam?

"I think you said 'weekend.' A curious term and I suppose I can figure its meaning. I suppose it refers to Friday or Saturday."

I grinned. "No, it refers to Saturday and Sunday, days when most working people in the future are free to do as they wish."

"Good Lord. How do they manage that? How do they get things done in only five days a week?"

"Much of the hard work is done by machines. Not only are workers limited to five days, but most of them work only 40 or fewer hours per week."

"Tis a strange new world you come from, Christopher. I sense that I will never fully understand it."

"A lot of things change over the next 240 years. Many of the changes are for the good, though I suppose not all of them."

"I could explore the future with you for hours, Christopher, but we

———

have work to do now in 1775. As to your needing a weapon, if that's your only concern, fret not. I have an old Brown Bess left over from my days fighting the French. Still a good flintlock. You can take it. Just bring it back when you've finished helping Dr. Warren."

I was relieved that Sam was willing to work with me and my desire to fight in Dr. Warren's militia. I definitely wanted to be part of the Bunker Hill battle. I hoped that Matt would get the cooperation of Ezekial Russell.

In the meantime, we had to make an appearance at the Salem Athenaeum to demonstrate our cell phones. It should be fun, but it also portended trouble. Someone was bound to talk about what they'd witnessed, and who knew what that could lead to?

Chapter 10

May 20, 1775

WHEN MATT AND I ENTERED the Social Library shortly after sundown we were greeted cordially by Jeremiah Weeks and the board members. Sam Hall was there too, as I had reminded Thomas Pynchon, the board president, that Sam had also seen Gil and Tom's spaceship at the time the board trustees had a few months ago.

Pynchon started the meeting by saying, "I see the entire board has managed to be here this evening. And on rather short notice, too. I imagine you're as eager to see what Christopher and Matthew have to show us as I am. You'll note that Sam Hall is also with us. Sam and we board members are the only people here in Salem, or for that matter, all of the Massachusetts Bay Colony, who know where Gilbert, Thomas, Matthew and Christopher have come from. I can't stress enough how important it is that we keep it that way. No matter how tempting it may be, we cannot afford to let the general public know about this. This means our spouses, families and closest friends must be kept in the dark no matter how painful it is to us. We vowed to keep this amongst ourselves back when Gilbert and Thomas showed us their spaceship off Great Misery Island. I plead with you all to continue your adherence to this most important vow." He paused dramatically, and then continued, "Does anyone here believe they have a good reason for breaking that vow? If you do, now is the time to speak up." Pynchon waited a full minute, then said, "Good, then I welcome Christopher and Matthew and their friends Gilbert and Thomas. Please show us what you call your cell phones."

I held up my phone and said, "Thank you for inviting us. It will be our pleasure to show you the cell phone, a small example of 21st century technology. The cell phone enables a person to talk to someone anywhere in the world if that person also has a phone." As I said this, I saw jaws dropping in front of me. "Phone is short for telephone. The first telephone will be invented in 1876 by Alexander Graham Bell, a Scotsman who comes to America by way of Canada. Interestingly enough, Bell makes his first telephone call from Salem to Boston."

A man in the second row raised his hand and said, "Excuse me for interrupting, but I'm already lost. You used a word unknown to me. I believe it was technology. Can you explain that before you show us your cell phone?"

I could see that it was not going to be easy demonstrating what a cell phone could do, simply because I would need to draw on so many terms that would be new to my audience. Showing was going to be much more effective than describing. Still, I had to do a minimum of describing before I could show anything.

"Technology refers to the practical application of scientific discoveries. For example, the telephone is the practical application of Bell's discovery that sound can be transmitted over great distances. I cannot demonstrate the transmission of voices over long distances for you today because there are no cell towers in this century. Cell towers will be invented in the late 20th century. These cell towers transmit radio waves through the air to cell phones. Cell towers will be placed in millions of locations around the Earth in the 21st century. Radio waves emitted from these towers will carry the voice of a person speaking into their personal cell phone."

My audience was falling behind fast. "I can already sense that the word radio is also a new term for you, and I fully understand your confusion. The word won't be introduced into the language until the early 20th century. Radio waves are electromagnetic waves that carry audio information through the air. Electromagnetic won't be introduced into the language until the next century. The word audio won't be introduced until the early 20th century." By now, most of the people in my small audience were shaking their heads and muttering to each other in utter frustration. It was the way I would react if I were listening to an astrophysicist describing the technical aspects of his work. Or a brain scientist explaining his procedures. If I didn't show them something soon, their frustration would turn to anger.

"Enough of the new terminology. Even though I can't demonstrate the transmission of voice through space, I have other things I *can* show you. I have pictures of Salem that I took yesterday. Here, let me show you."

A new hand shot up. "From whom did you take these pictures, Mr. Carver? I hope you're not saying that you stole them?"

I started to laugh, but I could see he didn't see the humor in the situation. Instead I said, "In the 21st century when we use a camera, we say that we take a picture. Here, let me show you one that I 'took' yesterday in the middle of Salem."

"Before you show me, sir, please tell me what a camera is?" More heads were shaking at this.

I stifled another smile. I'd already gone through describing a camera with Pynchon back in Pierce's Tavern a few nights ago, but I obviously had to do it again.

"A camera is a device that captures light images in the form of recognizable pictures. The first one will be invented about 40 years from now. Here, let me show you that picture of Salem that I 'took' yesterday.

I went to my photos and clicked on a shot that I'd taken of a street scene in Salem. It showed people standing, walking and horses tied up in front of buildings. I held the camera in front of the man who'd just asked what a camera was. His mouth opened in awe. After a moment he said, "This is truly amazing. No one could have painted such a clear picture. Certainly not in one day."

I then walked from person to person giving each man a chance to look carefully at the photo. I say each man because there were no women on the board. I doubt if many women were on organizational boards in 1775, since they were still a small minority in 2019." Each board member shook his head in amazement. Samuel Cabot, a heavyset man with full gray whiskers, spoke next. "I recognize one of the men in this picture. This is truly remarkable, Mr. Carver. Do you have any other pictures in this little device?" Cabot's voice was surprisingly high pitched for a man of his size.

"Absolutely. Here is a photo of Boston in the year 2019."

Before I could show anyone, Thomas Pynchon rose from his seat and said, "I think you'd best explain the word 'photo,' Christopher."

I allowed myself a smile this time. "Of course. Photo is a short form of the word photograph, which literally means drawing with light. It will first be introduced into the language about 65 years from now. A photograph is what we call a picture we take or obtain with a camera. This cell phone contains a camera. There are also stand-alone cameras." I could see people shaking their heads again at this word. "Stand-alone means what it implies. Stand-alone is what we say about something that has only one purpose or one location. The cell phone contains a telephone and a camera." More head shaking. "You'll recall that a phone is the short form of the word telephone." I surveyed the room for more questions. The men were buzzing among themselves in obvious confusion. When the buzzing subsided, I said, "Let me show you this photo of Boston in the year 2019. Matthew has one on his phone and he will move around with it also."

The shot showed the Prudential Tower and the John Hancock Building along with the other recent additions to the Boston skyline. It was a far cry from the two and three-story buildings of the town now occupying the Shawmut Peninsula.

The buzzing renewed with a new vitality. "I said, "You don't recognize it, do you? This is fairly typical of what some of the towns of this century will look like in the 21st century. They will become big cities. How many of you have been to New York?" Two hands went up. Matthew and I then showed them a photo of Manhattan. I said, "This is New York in the year 2018."

"Good grief," said Cabot. The others, too, seemed completely overwhelmed by what they were looking at.

Jeremiah Weeks said, "Dear Lord, this is unbelievable. How does this happen?"

"Those tall buildings are called skyscrapers. Some of the tallest are now over 100 stories in height." I immediately saw another look of confusion on the faces of some of the trustees so I quickly said, "Stories is another word for floors."

A trustee in the front row cleared his throat to get my attention.

"Yes sir," I said.

"You have shown us these marvelous photos as you call them. Now could you show us how you 'take' them, as you say? How do you create these wonderful pictures?"

I smiled. "It's really quite easy. I'll let Matthew show you."

Matt strode to the front of the room and stood in front of the inquiring trustee. He then held the phone in front of the man and took a picture. He checked to see what he'd gotten. He nodded approval to himself and turned the phone around so that the trustee could see the image of himself sitting in his chair. The man nearly fell off that chair as he realized that he was looking at himself.

"This is like a mirror image of myself!"

"Yes, it is," said Matt. "The difference is that I can now carry this picture around with me. If I had a printer, I could print it out on paper. If I had email and you had email, I could send it to you."

I held my hand up. "Whoa there, Matt, you're getting way ahead of our audience." Our 21st century vocabulary was preventing us from communicating as clearly as we would like. I could tell this by the confused look on most of the faces in our little audience. I had to clear things up as well as I could. "Gentlemen. Matthew just used the term email. I'm sure you're not familiar with this word. Email is short for electronic mail . . ." As soon as I got the words out I realized that I'd introduced a new word, 'electronic,' to explain the new word 'email.'

I spent the next few minutes doing my best to clarify a few of the terms we'd introduced to them in a very short time. It wasn't fair. We were asking them to assimilate some of the technical terminology we had learned in dribs and drabs over a lifetime. It was too much to absorb in one hour. To sum it up, despite the new vocabulary, they were overwhelmed with our demonstration of what a cell phone could do. Not only did we show them the camera and some photos, we also showed them a list of contacts, a calculator, the Merriam-Webster Dictionary, Microsoft Word and Excel. Suffice it to say they were blown away. When we were about to wrap things up, Matt reminded me that we hadn't shown them any video.

"Oh," I said, "I almost forgot. We haven't shown you any video.

Matthew and I will now circulate among you and show you a video of what we took in the center of Salem earlier today." As I finished this a number of hands went up and I realized that I'd introduced another new word to them.

"I assume you're wondering what a video is. It's probably best that we show you rather than try to tell you." With that, Matt and I showed video of people walking and horses trotting. We had taken the video from the street so you could hear the clop, clop of horses and an occasional voice as you viewed the video.

"Dear God," someone in our audience yelled out. "These pictures are moving. If this isn't the work of the Devil, it is truly a form of magic that no one has ever heard of. Good Lord, what can it be like living in the 21st century?"

Pynchon said, "We must never let word of this get out or you young men will never have a moment's peace. And yet, as I say this, I must admit that I will find it very difficult to hold my own tongue."

Samuel Cabot rose, and every man in the room fell silent. Obviously, he was a man who carried a lot of weight around town. Literally and figuratively. "Gentlemen, I have seen a great deal in my life, but never in all my years have I witnessed anything even remotely as amazing and I dare say wonderful as what you young gentlemen have shown us this evening. I think we all want to run out and tell our friends and family what we've just witnessed. However, I also think that, upon reflection, we'll see the wisdom of sticking to our vow. We cannot talk about this except among ourselves. Even then we must take care that no one else is within earshot."
The other men in the room nodded their somber assent.

As I was about to thank Cabot for his support, a noise was heard coming from the street. The noise got louder. It sounded like a crowd of revelers. Several trustees rose and went to the front door. As they walked out of the building the others followed. It was now clear that it wasn't revelers. It was more like a riot. One of the trustees said, "I think they're tarring and feathering some poor soul."

Thomas Pynchon said, "Can you tell who it is?"

Someone else said, "Looks like the Custom House agent, Elton Rigby."

Another trustee said, "There hasn't been a tar and feathering here in Salem in almost ten years."

Another trustee said, "True, but earlier this year the regular army tarred and feathered a fella over in Billerica when he tried to buy a musket from one of the Redcoats. Most of the tarring and feathering's been done by our fellow patriots, though. I remember back in '68 when that Tory, Robert Wood, was stripped, tarred and feathered and placed on a

———

hogshead in the Common."

Samuel Cabot said, "Well I don't like this one. Not one bit. Rigby's a good man with a bad job. True, he's paid by the Crown, but he's had this job for years. Long before the Crown began abusing us. I know him personally, and he doesn't enjoy imposing the levies he's forced to impose. He didn't make these despicable policies, but unfortunately, he does have to carry them out as much as he hates to do it. The man is just trying to make an honest living."

Another trustee said, "Then he should have quit the job and found something truly honest to do."

"It's easy for us to say that," said Cabot, "but men like Rigby have few options." Just as he said this, Rigby screamed again and Cabot winced. "The poor man must be suffering something awful. I've heard that when these poor devils try to remove the tar and feathers, some of their skin peels off."

I sprinted past the group to get a closer look at what was happening in the street. Yes, it was true. A man, probably in his mid-fifties, was slowly moving down the street as two men kept attempting to pour something on him from a steaming vat. As the screaming man tried to avoid his pursuers, people on each side of the street threw rocks and other debris at him. The man couldn't run much faster because other taunters were just ahead of him deliberately slowing him down. It was a horrible scene. Something from the Middle Ages, but unfortunately a very real part of our history.

The awful procession moved slowly out of sight and the trustees gradually filed back into the Athenaeum muttering among themselves. Within minutes their conversation turned to other things and it was almost as if the tarring and feathering had been forgotten. I was sure it wasn't forgotten, but I realized that, to these people, the cruel practice was a sorry, but not completely uncommon part of their culture. It happened and they either endorsed it or shook their heads in sadness. Either way, they knew it happened and once it was past them, they went about their business.

The trustees took their former seats and Pynchon thanked us for our presentation, pledging once again to keep any knowledge of cell phones a secret among themselves. Matt and I exchanged looks of amazement at how these intelligent men could return to business so cavalierly after just witnessing such a shocking spectacle. Matt and I sighed and then took our leave along with Gil and Tom. Five minutes later we settled ourselves into a booth at Pierce's Tavern where we agreed that we were almost as amazed at the tarring and feathering as our hosts had been about the cell phones.

As we settled in and ordered our pints, Gil said, "Lexington and

Concord were only a month and a half ago. Tom and I will never forget it. Things are happening fast in 1775. This is Wednesday, the 31st. Bunker Hill is just a little over two weeks away."

Chapter 11

May 20, 1775

TOM TOOK A HUGE SWIG of his beer. "I needed that. I've seen men kill each other in battle, and believe me, it's brutal, but this is so blatantly cruel." He let that hang in the air as if he couldn't imagine anything appropriate to say next.

I said, "Yes. It was tough to see." I'd seen action in Afghanistan, so I wasn't new to violence. Still, this was hard to take. "What's even more difficult to stomach," I added, "was how all those civilized, cultured men just took it in their stride."

Matt said, "Cabot seemed pretty shocked by it, though it seemed more that he felt Rigby didn't deserve it; not that the practice itself was inappropriate."

Gil said, "I watched some of those trustees. They may have been used to the practice, but they were clearly shocked at actually seeing it. Tarring and feathering is a known entity in 1775, but I don't think it's so common that most people have actually seen it. Or at least if they have, not that often. Kind of like murder in the 21st century. We've all heard about it, but most of us have not witnessed it."

I said, "Good point. When they actually see a tar and feathering, they see how shocking it is. Still, after the procession passed by, our hosts had no trouble going back to the business of the day."

"I suppose," said Tom, "that these patriot folks are so intent on their cause that they still justify the practice, unlike how people react to murder."

Gil then said, "Can I change the subject?" We all looked at him. He then began, "As I said when we sat down, if you want to be part of the Bunker Hill defense, you need to decide soon. I know you've been to see Mason a couple times, so I assume you're thinking about it?"

Matt said, "We're not just thinking about it—we've told Mason we want to volunteer for the militia that defends the area that surrounds Boston because we know Gage wants to expand his authority beyond the town. We're going to see Dr. Warren tomorrow to volunteer. He's not the military man in charge, but apparently all of the key military men report to him. He's the chairman of the Massachusetts Committee of Safety, which is pretty much the Provincial government now."

Tom said, "They don't know it, but we all know that Bunker Hill is going to take place in just a little over two weeks."

I said, "True, but from what we've been told they expect something to happen soon, so they're not as poorly informed as we might have thought back in the 21st century. They know Gage wants to expand his influence and in order to do that he has to take control of the hills surrounding Boston. Dr. Warren has ordered his officers to step up their recruiting. They need to have a few thousand if they're going to defend the hills. The Brits already have thousands, and since they control Boston Harbor, they can get more troops from England when they need them.

"This Dr. Warren is quite a guy. President of the Provincial Congress and Chairman of the Massachusetts Committee of Safety. Wields a lot of power. Supposed to be a helluva good doctor, too." I smiled. "Good by 1775 standards, anyway."

Gil said, "He's the one who sent Revere and Dawes out to Lexington and Concord to sound the alarm that the British regulars were coming to arrest John Hancock and Samuel Adams. Yeah, quite a guy."

—

Chapter 12

June 5, 1775

DR. WARREN HAD RELOCATED himself and his staff from Boston to Cambridge, where the Provincial army was actively training under Colonel Artemas Ward. Dr. Warren was present and overseeing recruitment policy and strategy in general. The growing army numbered 8,000 militiamen from Massachusetts and 1,000 from Connecticut. It wasn't easy getting to Cambridge, but our horses managed, though they were exhausted when we finally arrived. The directions Colonel Mason gave us were perfect.

Two sentries with muskets met us on the periphery of the training field. They weren't dressed in uniforms, but in rough civilian clothing. We soon learned that uniforms were a luxury the nascent Provincial army could not afford. One of the sentries, a tall, powerfully built man, asked us our business. We told him we were there to meet with Dr. Warren, and he asked us why. I explained that we were there to sign up and he said, "See that first tent about 50 yards straight ahead. That's where they're signing up new recruits. Welcome aboard. We're gonna need ya."

I said, "Is that where Dr. Warren is located?"

"He comes and goes. He might be in there. You don't need to see him to sign up anyway. There's a sergeant in the tent. He'll take care of ya."

"Colonel Mason up in Salem told us it was important that we see Dr. Warren. He gave us a letter for Warren's eyes only." The sentry's eyebrows raised. This was obviously important.

"Right you are, gentlemen. Warren'll want to see that letter. Peek in that first tent. If he's not in there, he'll be in the second tent. Welcome again gents. Glad to have ya."

Clearly Mason was known, even among the troops. We strode directly toward the first tent. As we neared the open flap a voice from within said, "C'mon in, lads. C'mon in." It was a middle-aged man sitting at a table with papers and what looked like some kind of a sign-up log or journal. "You men here to sign up I assume?"

"Yes, but we need to speak with Dr. Warren first. We've been sent by Colonel Mason up in Salem."

"I expect he'll be in the next tent. After you see him come back here and we'll get you signed up."

The next tent was only another 25 yards farther into the compound. As we entered the open flap of the tent a man probably in his mid-thirties was sitting at a table going over papers. A couple other men were also seated and doing paperwork. Another was moving from table to table. The thirtyish man at the table noticed us and said, "What can I do for you, gentlemen?"

I said, "Are you Dr. Warren?"

"Yes, I am. Do you have business with me?"

"We have a letter from Colonel Mason up in Salem." I then walked over to him and handed him the folded and sealed letter.

He opened and read it quickly. He then rose, looked us up and down appraisingly. I was surprised at how young he looked. He was such an important person in Massachusetts that I'd just assumed he'd be a much older man. He cut an impressive figure. He conveyed an aura of strength in a relatively compact body. He was slightly above average in height, which at that time in history made him about five nine or ten. After sizing us up he said, "The colonel apparently thinks very highly of you. He believes you have abilities that can be extremely helpful to our cause. I trust that you are here to volunteer your services to the Patriot cause? Just how do you think you can help us?"

"We're here to take up arms if you will have us," I said.

"Mason's letter suggests that he was thinking of something else. Come over here and sit down. Let's chat for a few moments."

We sat facing Warren on worn canvas-covered wooden stools.

"I appreciate your willingness to take up arms for the Patriot cause, but I sense from this letter that Colonel Mason thinks you have talents that can be more useful to us. He says you are well-versed in the issues and much aware of the temperaments of men on both sides of the dispute. Says you handle the language well, too. Do you have contacts in Boston who could be useful to us? Or would you be willing to accept officers' commissions? We need soldiers, but we also need leaders or people who can ferret out information about Gage's plans."

I said, "In other words, you're wondering if we should be spies or army officers?"

He grinned. "You are quick. But back to my question. Do either of you have Boston connections that could be useful to us?"

Matt said, "Neither of us has any connection to Boston."

"Do you have any military experience? You probably don't, as you both appear too young to have fought in the war against the French and their Indian allies." We actually did have military experience, though we couldn't very well mention it. Both Matt and I had served and seen limited action in Afghanistan.

"No, sir. We don't. We both came down to Salem from Halifax recently. We have no military experience, but we are good with a musket and in good physical condition."

"I can see that you seem fit enough for service, but I must say that I wonder why you would not prefer to serve the cause either as useful civilians or as officers in the army? I dare say that most of the men we've recruited would prefer those choices to serving as a foot soldier. Quite frankly we have done everything possible to encourage competent men to serve as officers. Just recently we reduced the number in a company from 100 to 59. Anyone who enlists at least 59 men is entitled to a captain's commission. Does that not entice you?"

"We're not qualified to serve as officers, sir. We've never led men in any sort of activity, as you have. Besides, we are new to Massachusetts and would find it difficult to recruit five men, let alone 59. We prefer to do our part alongside every other soldier. We'll leave the leading to the experienced officers." I didn't tell Dr. Warren that our bravado was rooted in our knowledge that, since we would be alive in the 21st century, we knew we couldn't be killed in the 18th century.

Warren looked somewhat disappointed as he said, "Very well, gentlemen. Foot soldiers you shall be. Colonel Ward can use you."

"Sir, since we are both new to Massachusetts and even newer to our jobs up in Salem, would it be possible for us to limit our training to weekends?" As soon as I said it, I knew he'd be confused.

"Weekends. You mean Friday or Saturday? I'm not sure I get your meaning?"

"It's a word we use up in Nova Scotia. Refers to Saturday and Sunday. I know limiting our training to only two days a week is not ideal, but we are quick learners and . . ."

"We need men badly. Many of our troops have to train on a limited basis. I cannot demand more from you. While we need foot soldiers badly, we also need leaders. I should like to propose a compromise. I will make you, Carver, a sergeant, which means you will lead five men including you, Blair. Carver, as a sergeant you will still be able to fight alongside your men. If the two of you are willing to serve under those conditions, and if you pledge that you will quickly join your company when the unit is deployed for actual military service regardless of the day of the week, we will gladly accept you into our militia. You understand that we cannot pay you much, but you will receive a modest amount at the end of an eight-month enlistment period. Upon signing, we will pay you a small bonus. If that is satisfactory, I welcome you into the Provincial Militia."

I turned to Matt and said, "You okay with that?"

He said, "Sure. Sounds reasonable."

Warren then said, "Hopefully you will be housed in one of the college buildings or some other building in the area. We do not have enough buildings for our growing army, so I cannot promise you a place in a building. You might have to sleep in the barracks that we have established

---

in the nearby Episcopal church. Not ideal, but at least not in a tent as many of our men are doing."

We left the Cambridge training camp feeling somewhat in awe of Dr. Warren. He looked even younger than his 34 years, so it was especially impressive that his fellow patriots had made him President of the Provincial Congress and the Chairman of the Provincial Committee of Safety. He was now the most powerful person in the colony.

On our return ride to Salem Matt said, "It's kind of weird and more than a little sad isn't it."

I was confused. "What's sad and weird?"

"Warren is so alive and even vibrant, yet if I recall my history correctly, within a few weeks he'll die in the Bunker Hill battle. Don't you find that creepy?"

"Yes because, even if we warn him, it won't change anything. We know from history that it will happen."

Matt couldn't suppress a grin. "You realize that that contradicts what we've been saying all along. We've been saying that anything we do could change history."

"I know. I know. Yet we already know what happens to Warren. Face it, we have no idea what effect our being here will have on history. I still think it best that we keep as low a profile as possible and not expand the already-too-large circle of people who do know about where we came from. We have to try not to affect the course of history."

|

The next morning when I went in to the *Gazette,* Sam Hall called Gil, Tom and me into his office. He didn't look happy.

"This is probably not going to be a problem, but I thought you should be aware of it. On my way in to work this morning someone I have a passing acquaintance with came up to me and said, 'I heard from a friend that you have some men working for you with questionable pasts. Just thought you should know.'"

I said, "Did he say what he meant by questionable pasts?"

"Said the word is that three of you might be possessed. The Evil One has found new hosts for himself that outwardly appear quite normal. Meaning you chaps. I asked who told him this nonsense and he refused to tell me. I wouldn't worry too much about this, as the man I was talking to is known for spreading rumors. Still, it's good to be aware of this. How this rumor started is a mystery to me as I know you've kept your past to a very small group of trusted people."

"Yes, Sam," said Gil, "but secrets bring more pleasure if you can spread them around. Obviously, someone didn't keep the secret."

73

Chapter 13

June 14, 1775

GOVERNOR THOMAS GAGE sat facing his three invited guests: General William Howe, General John Burgoyne and General Robert Pigot. They were sitting in Gage's comfortable Galloupe House headquarters in Boston.

Not only was Gage governor of the Massachusetts colony, he also served as Commander in chief of British Forces in North America. He was a general before he became a governor. Recently Galloupe House had also become his residence as, out of expedience, he and his American wife, Margaret Kemble Gage, had moved from the comfortable mansion they had occupied in Cambridge thanks to the generous patronage of wealthy Tory, William Brattle. The move had been necessitated by the presence of the growing Provincial army camp nearby.

Gage had offered coffee to his guests, and a young man had just served steaming cups to the three officers and to the governor himself.

After a few minutes of polite exchange, Gage cleared his throat and said, "Gentlemen, we are at a turning point. We have to remind the Provincials here in Massachusetts that they are still a colony of the British Empire. After 150 years here on the North American continent, many of them seem to think that they are a sovereign entity in and of themselves. Some of them act as if they are no longer subjects of His Majesty and can make and enforce laws of their own choosing. They have gone so far as to besiege their Royal Governor and the Crown's army. The most powerful army in all of Europe has now been restricted to the confines of this small town. I don't have to tell you that we are being strangled by this siege. We cannot get foodstuff unless they come by sea. We cannot get sugar, flour, tea, rum, or wine unless it comes by sea. Nor can we get a myriad of conveniences unless they come by sea. Fortunately, we have Boston Harbor, but that is our only access to the outside world. These Americans with their siege have us in a stranglehold. Worse, they no longer respect the representatives of the Crown." Gage fell silent for a moment as he considered what he was going to say next. After a tense pause, he continued.

"I do not take this next step lightly, gentlemen. As you know, I have lived much of the last 20 years on this side of the ocean. I have even married an American. Many of my friends are American. There is much to admire in the flourishing civilization these Provincials have wrought from the wilderness of these shores. There are many admirable men and women here that we could learn from. Nevertheless, I have never forgotten that this admirable culture could not have survived the Gallic threat 20 years ago if it were not for the intervention of our noble military might. Yes, the Provincials contributed to their defense, but they would all be speaking French now if it were not for the Crown's valiant forces.

"I have called you here because it is time to show these ungrateful Provincials that they are still subjects of His Majesty. Recently they have become rebels and rebellions must be put down. We must push back on this siege. We will begin by taking control of Charlestown. To do that you will need to take possession of the Charlestown hills. I would also like us to advance on the Dorchester hills. First, though, I want you to take the Charlestown hills. General Howe, what will it take to gain control of those hills and how quickly can we accomplish the task?"

"As you know, sir, I have been on these shores less than two months, but I think I understand the terrain well." Gage nodded appreciatively. Governor Gage had great respect for Howe, as the man had come from a venerable military family. His brother George was a brigadier general who had died during the British attempt to take Fort Ticonderoga from the French in 1758. His brother Richard was an admiral in the Royal navy. When Howe spoke, Gage had confidence in the man's words.

Howe continued, "We should be able to take the village of Charlestown in a day. I would take a contingent of a 1,200 or so men, which should be more than enough to do the job. As of now the Charlestown peninsula is unguarded. We should meet with little, if any, resistance. Even if the Provincials call up their ragtag militia, they are no match for trained British regulars."

As much as Gage respected Howe, he felt it imperative that he remind him that the Americans were not to be taken lightly. "We must not underestimate these locals, William. They gave us more than we could handle recently at Lexington and Concord."

Howe frowned. "Yes, yes, Governor, but bear in mind that our forces were greatly outnumbered. They fought valiantly considering the circumstances." He paused, then said, "I know these rebels feel strongly about their cause, as ill-advised and reckless as it may be. They are British subjects, but they want more than that. They want to be treated as British subjects in England are treated, yet they want to rule themselves as if they were a sovereign nation. We must teach them that they are not a nation unto themselves, but still a province of the United Kingdom."

"I think we are all agreed on that," said Gage somberly. "How soon do you think you can take Charlestown, General?"

"I will have my men ready to go in four days or less. Within a week we shall occupy Charlestown. Hopefully when the rebels see that His Majesty's best are coming, they will wisely give way and few lives will be shed."

———

Chapter 14

June 16, 1775

IT WAS AMAZING how well we both adapted to our new roles. Matt didn't seem to mind that I was a sergeant in the militia.

As for our jobs, I feel things went even better than I'd hoped. Even though I had prepared rigorously for typesetting and working an English press, there were procedures that Sam Hall was used to that I wasn't. Fortunately, I didn't have to tell him a lie about how we did things up in Halifax because he already knew that I, like Gil and Tom, had come from the future. He knew, too, that I had trained on an antique English press, and he quickly saw that I had learned well. Things on the job were progressing smoothly, and I was gradually relaxing and actually enjoying the work.

Our troop training was also progressing well. At least Matt and I thought it was. In addition to Matt, the four other men assigned to me seemed to respond well to whatever I said, which was an enormous relief.

One day, Lieutenant Robert Parker, the man I reported to, approached us. "Colonel Ward has just informed us that Gage has ordered his army to prepare for an imminent assault on the Charlestown hills and Dorchester heights. Apparently General Burgoyne has declared that his army needs elbow room and Gage has stated that he's mortified that the Americans hold the British army under siege. Both Governor Gage and General Burgoyne obviously know that we have superior numbers just three miles away in Cambridge, yet they think they can leave Boston and take both Charlestown and Dorchester despite the adverse odds. They will have to cross the Charles if they attack and that leaves them terribly exposed. With their usual arrogance they are sanguine about their chances and show their contempt by their every action. Ever since the war against the French, British officers have believed themselves superior to Provincial officers in every way. Burgoyne reportedly said that the untrained Provincial rabble are no match for their trained troops."

I said, "I hope we are going to prove them wrong. I would like to see Burgoyne eat his words."

"So would I, sergeant, so would I. But we must not get complacent. The Crown is taking our efforts seriously now. They've sent two of their best generals here to try to contain our resistance. They put Howe in charge with Burgoyne directly under him. After leaving Lexington and Concord with their tails between their legs, they know we're a force to contend with."

Parker then went on to say, "You need to know this. The Committee of Safety voted yesterday that (Here he read from a dog-eared piece of paper) 'For the good and welfare of the colony there must be an immediate augmentation of the army. Any men without arms will be supplied arms when possible. All the militia in the colony should hold themselves in readiness to march on the shortest of notice, completely equipped, having 30 rounds of cartridges per man. The hill called Bunker Hill in Charlestown will be securely kept and defended." He took a breath and said, "In other words, lads, we're going to Charlestown to set up fortifications against the regulars—if and when they attack. If Gage's army actually tries to occupy Bunker Hill and thereby all of Charlestown, this could mean you men and your boys will be doing some fighting. This could be nasty."

We learned later that musket cartridges were rationed carefully because there was a desperate need for musket balls. Parker told me that things were so desperate that the organ pipes in some churches had been melted down to make musket balls. It was rumored that there were only 87 barrels of powder in all of Massachusetts.

Matt and I knew just how nasty it was going to be, but we couldn't share that with the lieutenant. I just said, "When will we move out, sir?"

"General Ward says later today." Matt and I knew we had to move soon, as it was June 16th and the battle was going to take place tomorrow, June 17th.

Matt and I were the only ones at the camp who knew just how imminent the battle was going to be. That meant that our militia really had only a day to set up any fortifications on Bunker or Breed's Hill. Charlestown was only three miles from Cambridge, but by horse and on foot it could take us a couple of hours or more to get there, considering how much equipment and how many men we had to move.

Less than an hour after the lieutenant updated me he came back and told us that General Ward had issued orders that Colonel William Prescott and Colonel Bridge were to prepare quickly for an expedition to Charlestown in the evening to take possession of Bunker Hill and 'erect the requisite fortifications to defend it.' Prescott and Bridges were to take a few hundred men with them on their mission. They assembled early in the evening and attended a solemn prayer meeting on Cambridge Common conducted by President Langdon of Harvard College before proceeding on to Charlestown. Prescott's orders were to keep as low a profile as possible in order to keep the opposition in the dark as long as possible. As the night drew on other detachments joined the Prescott party. By early morning the troops amounted to more than a thousand men. Previously, General Ward had examined the Charlestown peninsula

—

and had decided on fortifying Prospect Hill, Bunker Hill and lastly, Breed's Hill.

The Mystic River is on the north side of the peninsula and the Charles River on the south. As Prescott's advance team surveyed Bunker Hill, they decided that it was situated too far from where the enemy would be coming to annoy them or do them much harm. Breed's Hill was on the tip of the peninsula and faced Boston where the British forces were garrisoned. It was much bettered positioned than Bunker Hill, so they scrapped the original plan and began fortifying Breed's Hill. It was decided at the same time that a defensive structure should also be erected on Bunker Hill as a point to retreat to in case the Provincial forces were driven from their primary position on Breed's Hill. It would also provide protection of their rear.

Because of these last-minute decisions, very little got done on site before midnight when the first spade finally entered the ground. It was not for lack of trying to break ground earlier, as the men had struggled to transport tools, supplies, ammunition and weapons from Cambridge under cover of night. Already exhausted, they proceeded to build an earthen redoubt, dig trenches and erect barricades throughout the remaining hours of the night. They were working for their lives and their freedom and got the job done by morning under the direction and encouragement of Colonel Prescott, General Putnam and Major Brooks. As exhausted as the men were, they were eager to take on the enemy. Prescott and the other officers shared their eagerness but wanted to restrain their forces until the optimum moment because they were acutely aware of just how limited their ammunition was. They could not afford to waste it by firing when the enemy was still out of range.

No officer in the army deserved the honor of leading the forces at Bunker Hill more than the tall and commanding Colonel William Prescott. He had enlisted when young with the Provincial army and soon received a commission. His military talents quickly earned him an excellent reputation when he served alongside the British army when they wrested Nova Scotia from French control in 1756. Prescott was so well thought of that the British officers urged him to accept a commission in the Royal army. He respectfully refused, stating that he did not want be separated from his loyal Provincial soldiers and his countrymen. Long after the French and Indian War ended, he would often welcome his former soldiers hospitably to his mansion in Pepperell, Massachusetts, where he would treat them as honored guests. To this day he was beloved by the veterans who were once under his command.

Just before dawn, Prescott and Major Brooks proceeded to the shore near the side of the peninsula facing Boston to reconnoiter the enemy forces which had assembled on the flatlands of the peninsula's southeasternmost tip near Moulton's Point. It was still too dark to make out the outlines of the frigates *Falcon, Lively, Glasgow* and *Spitfire* moored in the river a few yards off the peninsula. Nor were the Americans aware of the handful of smaller British vessels set to pin down the rebels as the British waded ashore. This small fleet of warships sat in readiness to prepare the way for the landing of the British troops.

At the moment, things were still quiet. From their vantage point Prescott and Brooks witnessed a verbal exchange between the night guard and the sentry relieving him. The unfounded words, 'All's well' could be distinctly heard and Prescott realized just how unaware the enemy was of the presence of the American forces.

Chapter 15

June 17, 1775

AS THE SUN CAME UP over Boston, the British could hardly believe their eyes at the sight of the enemy looking down on their position.

General Gage, telescope to his eye, asked his aide, "Who is that officer commanding the rebels?"

The aide took the telescope and after a moment said, "Colonel Prescott, sir."

"Will he fight?"

"Yes, sir. Depend on it to the last drop of blood in him."

"Then we'd best begin soon. I want to meet with Howe, Pigot, Clinton and Grant as quickly as you can get them here."

As soon as Gage and his four generals were assembled it was clear that they all agreed on the necessity of driving the Americans from their position, but did not agree on the method of attack. Gage and the British hierarchy often referred to the Provincial forces as "the Americans" when they were not calling them rebels. Both General Clinton and General Grant believed that an attack from the rear would catch the enemy less well defended. They felt that the men could debark from boats and land on Charlestown Neck under the cover of fire from floating batteries and frigates. Gage, however, was convinced that this approach was too risky. They would be exposed to rebel armies on either side of them. One of the rebel armies could have superior numbers. It was finally decided that they would attack the enemy from the front, where the rebels would be more formidable, but the Royal army would have the advantage of a much larger battery of ships and barges to soften up the enemy with their cannons. Additionally, they would not be squeezed between two powerful rebel forces, but instead would have the Charles River and Boston behind them.

8:00 a.m.

Dr. Warren, who had been commissioned as a general by the Provincial

Congress just three days ago and was still Chairman of the Committee of Safety, sat with General Artemas Ward and several others at Provincial headquarters in Watertown, just adjacent to Cambridge. Back in May, the Provincial Congress had made General Ward commander of the Massachusetts forces. He was a stocky man of average height. Not an impressive looking figure, for a general, but well respected in Massachusetts. John Adams had described him as *'universally esteemed.'* Earlier in the morning they had been told that British forces were seen moving rapidly through the streets of Boston. The rattling of artillery carriages and wagons could be heard by nearby observers. It was believed that Gage's forces would begin an attack soon.

Moments ago, a sweating General Putnam had arrived breathlessly on horseback with a request for food rations and reinforcements for the men at Breeds Hill. He reported, "Our men are hungry, exhausted, and needing of sleep, yet they are prepared to engage the enemy at any moment. The enemy ships and barges have begun a tremendous fire on our position. We expect the enemy infantry to begin their advance soon under protection of their cannon fire."

General Ward said, "Are your exhausted men capable of engaging the enemy? Do you want reinforcements or replacements?"

"Despite their fatigue, they are eager to fight. Colonel Prescott and I believe that the men who have built the defenses are the best qualified to defend them. Still, our reconnaissance has indicated that Gage is assembling more men than we first expected to oppose us, so we can use reinforcements as quickly as you can dispatch them."

Elbridge Gerry, a highly respected delegate to the Provincial Congress, and chairman of the Committee of Supply, having just recently learned of the American forces' plans to occupy and fortify Bunker Hill pleaded with Dr. Warren and General Ward to abandon their plan. "I fear that the plan is 'glaringly imprudent. My sources tell me that your army has not enough powder for the troops to sustain an ongoing conflict with Gage's well-supplied forces."

Warren said, "I must confess that one part of me agrees with you, but we have too much committed to this noble venture to back out now. Our men, despite their fatigue, are anxious to take on the enemy. We outnumber Gage's men, and I believe we can win. The men believe we can win. I believe you will find that General Ward and the other generals also believe we can prevail."

Seeing that he was not going to dissuade the military men, Gerry then urged Warren not to expose his own invaluable life to such personal risk.

"Joseph, you are still a young man—a man with a great future ahead of you. You are President of the Provincial Congress and Chairman of the

---

Committee of Safety for Massachusetts. You are the most important man in all of Massachusetts. One might say all of New England. Please don't risk your valuable presence by participating in this battle."

"I cannot remain home and let my fellow citizens shed blood for me. *Dulce et decorum est pro patria mori.* It is sweet and fitting to die for the homeland."

Chapter 16

June 17, 1775 - 9:00 a.m.

AS THE CANNON assault continued, Colonel Prescott was pleased that, despite the tremendous fire levied against his position, much of it was to no effect. I was not far from Prescott and couldn't help hearing what he said to his aides. Prescott conferred with Major Brooks who said, "If they remain as inaccurate as they have been, eventually their cannon balls will be expended, and we shall have the advantage."

"Yes," agreed Prescott, "unless they begin their troop advances soon while they still have an ample supply of balls."

He had just spoken these words when an aide rushed up to him saying that a man had been killed by a cannon shot. The aide inquired, "What shall we do with him?"

"Bury him," said Prescott soberly.

"Without prayers?" said the aide incredulously.

I overheard a chaplain convince the colonel to take a brief moment of prayer over the ditch in which the fallen victim was being buried. To ease the fears of his men during the brief ceremony, Prescott stood by atop one of the defense works directing their efforts. Most of the defense works were entrenchments and wood fences, but the central redoubt or fortress consisted of rocks and earthen construction above ground. I could see why his men were willing to follow Prescott to the ends of the Earth. He stood there heedless of enemy fire as he encouraged the men, approving of their efforts and interjecting occasional humor. Prescott seemed to have an innate ability to understand his men. The oppressive heat caused him to remove his officer's hat, exposing his bald head. This neglect of his personal appearance only inspired the men more. He was human just like them. His willingness to openly expose himself to enemy fire inspired the men at a time when they were burying one of their own.

The men had already suffered greatly. They had endured the long sleepless night, many of them without water. The reinforcements, food and water that General Putnam had ridden to Cambridge for had not yet arrived. Prescott sent Major Brooks to Cambridge to press General Ward for immediate help. I heard Brooks ask if he could take one of the artillery horses, but Prescott ordered him to go on foot as he feared for the safety of the valuable artillery horses as they could be needed to move guns into new positions at any time.

Chapter 17

June 17, 1775 – 10 a.m.
WHEN A SWEATING, greatly fatigued Brooks arrived at army headquarters in Cambridge at about ten, he learned that the need for reinforcements was still being debated. General Ward doubted that the enemy intended to attack immediately. Rather, he feared that Gage's forces would attempt to take control of the scanty Provincial stores of ammunition and weapons kept in depots in Cambridge and Watertown. Once they had taken control of the two supply depots, they would then make their assault on Charlestown. Ward wanted to retain a substantial contingent of men in the event of an attack on his base camp or these supply depots.

Fortunately, the Committee of Safety was headquartered in the same house in which the Provincial forces were headquartered. Committee member Richard Devens, fearing for the safety of the men fighting in Charlestown, argued in favor of immediate reinforcements and finally Ward became convinced. Orders were sent to Medford where the New Hampshire militia troops were encamped.

At eleven the 1,300 New Hampshire troops received their orders, but were unable to obey them because they had not been provided ammunition. Eventually their officers were able to give every man two flints, a gill of powder and fifteen balls. Nearly all of them lacked cartridge boxes and had to use powder horns only. Worse, hardly any of their guns agreed in caliber, meaning the men had to hammer their balls into the proper size to fit their weapons.

Noon – Long Wharf, Boston
Twenty-eight barges were loaded with the first detachment of British troops. These consisted of the 5th, 38th, 43rd and 52nd infantry battalions, ten grenadier companies, and ten light infantry companies. Each company consisted of 50 men. Each battalion consisted of from 500 to 600 men. Each battalion was led by a colonel. Cannons were in the bows of the lead barges. The barges moved slowly and steadily across the channel between Boston and the Charlestown peninsula. The troops were resplendent in their crisp red uniforms, brilliant and spectacular as they reflected the rays of the noonday sun. At about one they landed at Moulton's Point on the peninsula. As soon as they'd landed, they

discovered that the cannon balls sent over were too large for the cannons they were carrying. They immediately sent back for a new supply.

When these first troops landed they were unmolested by American fire. They took this to mean that the Provincials were hoping to avoid a fight, probably because they didn't want to engage the mighty British army. They took their time to eat from the rations they had in their knapsacks. About two o'clock the rest of Howe's forces set out from Boston in the same barges. By the time these barges landed there were about 5,000 British troops under Howe's immediate command assembled on the Moulton's Point flatlands. Under him were General Pigot, Colonels Abercrombie, Clark, Nesbit and Majors Butler, Bruce, Spendlove, Pitcairn and several other officers.

It was now past two in the afternoon and scarcely a shot had been fired by troops on either side. The barrage of cannon fire that started in the morning had let up, with only the occasional shot being heard. So far, the only victim of the day was the one Provincial soldier buried by Prescott's men.

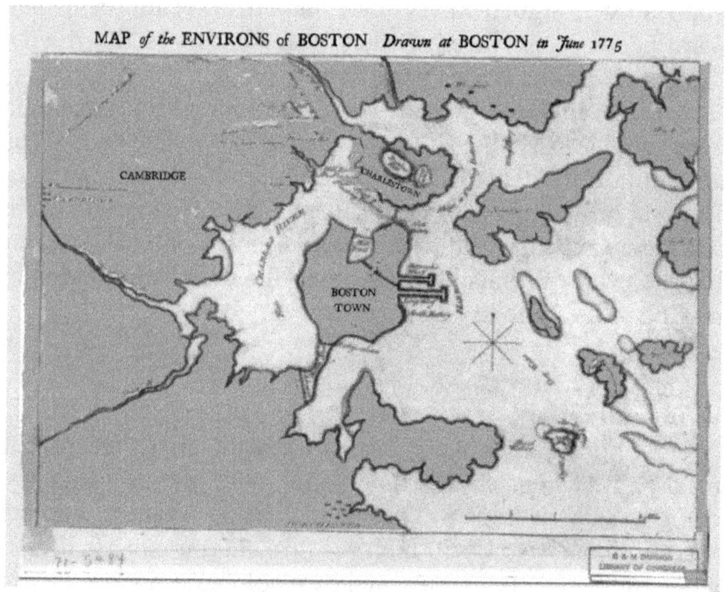

Based on a map from the Library of Congress

Suddenly a thundering cannonade erupted, and the Americans sensed that an assault was finally about to begin. The troops didn't need to be told. They quickly grabbed their weapons and flocked to their stations. The sound of the cannon barrage was so ominous that the militia from nearby Menotomy marched to General Ward in Cambridge to offer their services. The New Hampshire troops had finally arrived in Charlestown. Prescott later learned that their late arrival was deliberate, as the New Hampshire militia leader, Colonel Stark, preferred to march his men slowly, believing that "One fresh man is better than ten fatigued ones."

Chapter 18

June 17, 1775 - Noon
WE HAD ARRIVED in Charlestown about 11 o'clock last night with our Essex County detachment, the Salem militia being the largest part of the total. We had immediately been put to work helping to build the fortifications on Breed's Hill, while a few of our comrades worked industriously to build defensive works on Bunker Hill in case the enemy tried an approach from the rear. Fortunately, most of us had eaten just before we left home. Matt and I had come on our own horses with Gil and Tom, so we were not as exhausted as some of the men were who'd come on foot from considerable distances. Still, by morning Matt and I were as starved and exhausted as the rest of the troops who labored through the night. Gil and Tom had gone off with their own unit. We finished off the last of our rations and most of our water in anticipation of a long harrowing day.

When the second cannon assault began it was immediately clear that the British had adjusted or repositioned their cannons, as their fire was now more accurate. Prescott immediately ordered our forces to take cover in the redoubt and trenches and other defense works we had constructed during the night. Some of the men were slow to seek cover and not long after the second cannonade had begun Matt and I witnessed the horrible sight of a lieutenant's head being shattered by an incoming ball.

"Oh dear Jesus," said Matt.

I almost threw up.

Our lieutenant told us that a Colonel Gridley had just commandeered several men to man the six cannons we had on our side. It soon became obvious that the men he'd commandeered were barely able to operate the big guns. It takes training, practice and knowledge of gun positioning to be an effective artilleryman. It was apparent that these men had none of this experience and from what I could see, most of their efforts were ineffective.

At one point, I noticed one of the men assigned to a cannon leave his gun and fall back in the direction of Bunker Hill and away from the incoming cannon ball assault so he could prepare his ammunition in safety. General Putnam saw this and thought the man was retreating. He roared at the poor soul, threatening him with instant death if he didn't return to his cannon.

Lieutenant Parker was a good communicator. He would go from squad to squad or team to team, informing the sergeants under his command of the latest developments. He now came to me.

"Sergeant, the enemy forces are now in columns ready to advance on us. Get your men in position behind the rail fences." The rail fences were made of heavy boards, too thick for the average musket ball to penetrate, but no match for a cannon ball. Some sections of the fences had stones piled about two feet high at the base of them, but most sections were just the fence.

One of the men assigned to me was a black man named Peter Salem. He was a former slave who'd been released from slavery by his owner so he could fight for the Provincial militia. Salem told me his former owner was a Major Lawson Buckminster, who told Peter that his original owner, a man named Jeremiah Belknap, had named him Salem after the Massachusetts town of that name. Peter Salem was quite a guy. He already had considerable military experience, as he'd fought at both Lexington and Concord. He said that he knew of several other blacks who were here at Breed's Hill, ready and willing to fight for the Patriot cause. I wished that I had more time to talk with Salem about his and the other blacks' motivations, but this was not the time for long conversations. Cannons were firing at us and we expected a wave of redcoats to advance toward us at any moment.

I remember reading in Gil's account of the first mission, that he and Tom had felt intense fear when the fighting began at Lexington even though they knew that they wouldn't die in the battle since they were very much alive in the 21st century. I didn't know about Matt, but I could relate to that because I was scared shitless even though, intellectually, I knew that I couldn't die in the battle. Your mind can tell you one thing, but your reflexes and your emotions can easily take over under the pressure of a real-life battle. It also occurred to me that, even if I didn't die, I could be seriously injured. This lull before the storm was not helping my mental outlook.

Fortunately, or I should say, unfortunately, the Brits started advancing just at this moment and my focus immediately shifted to my men. I quickly went to each man, wishing them luck and reminding them to keep their heads down except when firing. The advancing columns of Redcoats were scary as hell. They were not firing yet, but clearly they would very soon.

My men and I were located not far from where General Putnam was standing. He was now joined by General Warren.

Between the cannon firings I could overhear the conversation between the two men.

Putnam said, "I'm sorry to see you here, General Warren. I wish you had left the day to us, as I expect we shall have a sharp time of it here. Since you are here, though, I'll receive your orders with pleasure."

Warren said, "I came only as a volunteer. I know nothing of your plans and will not interfere with them. Tell me where I can be most useful."

Putnam, concerned for the safety of the leader of the Massachusetts Provincial government, directed him to the redoubt, saying, "You will be covered there."

"Don't think I come here seeking a place of safety. Tell me where the fighting will be most furious."

Putnam again pointed to the redoubt, saying, "That is the enemy's object. Prescott is there, and if it can be defended, the day is ours." He then added, "From long experience and knowing the character of the enemy, I believe they will ultimately succeed and drive us from the works, though I think we shall be able to do them great injury. We must be prepared for a brave and orderly retreat when we can no longer maintain our ground."

Warren entered the redoubt and was cheered by the soldiers who recognized him. Prescott offered to turn command over to him, but Warren said, "No, I'll be happy to learn from a soldier of experience."

Prescott then pointed to a position that Warren could occupy. As Warren took that position, the enemy cannons opened fire furiously, signaling their troops to begin advancing forward. The columns of redcoats moved forward slowly, pausing periodically to give their artillery time to clear a brief passage. As I witnessed this, I couldn't help thinking, that as impressive as these redcoat columns of soldiers looked, it was also glaringly apparent that they made excellent targets for our men. The regulars were right out in the open, side by side. They made no attempt to seek cover. I wondered why, from their experience at Lexington and Concord, they hadn't learned to protect themselves more. Apparently, the vaunted British army, feared throughout the world, wasn't going to learn from a bunch of ragtag Provincials who couldn't even afford uniforms. The only Provincials with uniforms were the officers.

I knew from my reading that the recruitment practices of the British army led to an even more ragtag army than ours. The British recruiters pulled in the lowest elements of society, since the army wasn't a popular form of employment. Often vagrants and vagabonds were enticed into service by colonels leading recruiting parties on tours of villages and towns. To make up a full regiment sometimes even prisoners were brought into service. I also knew that as much as half of the British army was made up of Hanoverian, Bavarian, Hessian and Danish mercenaries hired out by their rulers under contract. With these kinds of soldiers I was amazed at how willing these men were to put their lives on the line. Their very bravery suggested a patriotism I wouldn't have expected. I suppose it speaks to the lives they must have left behind them.

Then again, maybe I was judging the British army too soon. Maybe they *had* learned something from their recent encounter with Provincial forces. They were still several hundred yards away. Maybe as they drew closer to where musket fire would be more accurate, they would disperse to avoid the slaughter that was inevitable if they continued to march toward us in tight formation. Even if they did disperse, their brilliant red uniform made them easy targets when more earth-toned uniforms would have helped them blend into the landscape.

I now wondered why our Provincial officers hadn't ordered us to fire by now, as the advancing columns of enemy soldiers were getting closer by the minute.

General Howe walked 200 yards ahead of his advancing troops reconnoitering the situation while clearly exposing himself to Provincial fire.

As the redcoats drew ever closer the American drums beat a call to arms. Putnam, who was at Bunker Hill overseeing the rear guard, left that hill and hurried to Breed's Hill where he led his men into action. As the British neared Breed's Hill, a rousing Yankee Doodle could be heard from many of the Provincial soldiers. At Lexington and Concord, the British had sung Yankee Doodle, as it was considered an insult, suggesting that the American soldiers were effeminate sissies. Since the strong performance of the colonial forces at Lexington and Concord, the Americans had adopted the song and now were using it against the British.

Now the enemy was in clear view and the Americans were chomping at the bit, wanting to fire. The enemy still hadn't dispersed. They made even better targets now because they were much closer. Putnam rode his horse through the line and ordered that no one should fire until the British were within 50 yards. He then added, *"Powder is scarce and must not be wasted. Do not fire until you see the whites of their eyes. Then fire low, take aim at their waistbands."* I had been told more than once that all of our men were excellent marksmen and could kill a squirrel at a hundred yards. Putnam then said, *"Aim at their handsome coats. Pick off the commanders."* Off in the distance I heard Prescott saying essentially the same thing.

The enemy was now within musket range of even a poor marksman. A few men disobeyed orders and opened fire on the advancing British troops. Prescott was indignant and threatened death to the next man who violated his orders. He then appealed to the men's confidence in him and promised to order them to fire at the right moment, but not sooner.

The fire from the few eager beavers drew return fire from the enemy line. When the approaching redcoats were within 50 yards, we levelled our muskets awaiting breathlessly for orders from Colonel Prescott. Prescott waited only a few seconds more before he bellowed, "Take good aim. Be sure of your mark. Fire!"

A tremendous clamor of fire decimated the front line of the enemy. Screams of pain were interspersed between the constant salvos of musket fire. When the smoke cleared as desperate troops reloaded, I saw that the ground was covered with dead and wounded. Despite their heavy losses, the enemy was as courageous as we Provincials. As one row was mowed down, the next row took its place, returning fire for fire. The odds, however, were with the Americans, as we were far better protected by our works of rail fence and our central redoubt. The red-coated enemy sustained far more casualties than the Provincials and reluctantly had to retreat under the command of General Pigot.

In a brief lull in the fighting I noticed that Warren and the rest of the officers in the redoubt were encouraging the men by setting an example with their own muskets. Practically every officer except for Putnam and Prescott had a musket and was using it.

Then a new assault was launched on the redoubt by a fresh wing of British troops. As they slowly advanced, they encountered one fence after another which they struggled to surmount or knock down. The fences were major obstacles for the advancing enemy troops, making them particularly vulnerable as they struggled to make their way over them. I had to hand it to those Brits, they kept coming even as they saw rows of men ahead of them being mowed down. So far, we were losing far fewer men than they were, though every time one of our guys fell, I felt it in my gut and wanted to run over to him to do what I could. I started to do that once and Prescott roared at me saying, "We'll tend to him when we can. Right now stay at your post. You've done well. Don't slacken off."

When he said I'd done well, I assumed he meant I'd killed my share of enemy soldiers. If you're a soldier, that's your job and I'm almost certain I had killed a few of the advancing redcoats, but I took no satisfaction from it. I'd killed a couple of men in Afghanistan too, so it wasn't a new experience for me, but you never get pleasure from killing another human being. At least I don't. You do, however, get caught up in the moment knowing it's either them or you. When you're being fired upon is no time for philosophical reflections.

—

As these thoughts passed through my mind, I heard Matt's voice off to my right. He was only a few yards away so I could easily see him. He was yelling encouragement to the men around him. When the firing slowed momentarily, he yelled over to me. "Just like Kunduz. Just like Kunduz."

He was referring to a battle we had both fought in in Afghanistan in 2015. I wish he hadn't yelled it out, though, as it would be hard to explain away if anyone picked up on it. I couldn't dwell on that, though, as the enemy was still shooting at us and cannon balls were landing much too close. We were still getting the better of the battle, and for good reason. Our men were excellent shots, as most of them had grown up shooting food for their families' next meal. But good marksmanship was only part of the reason for our success so far. We were sheltered, at least to some degree, whereas the enemy was advancing toward us in tight formation right out in the open, with nothing to protect them from our musket fire. It's also harder to shoot accurately when you're walking toward an enemy than it is when you can take careful aim from the relative safety of a rail fence or a redoubt. The only advantage the Brits had was that their soldiers had cartridges, which meant that they didn't have to take the time to pour powder into their barrels and then insert the balls. As I mentioned earlier, many of our men had no cartridges and it took two or three times as long to load their muskets before they could fire. Big disadvantage. Still, the protective cover of the rail fences and the sturdy redoubt made up for a big part of that disadvantage. As I kept my eye on the advancing enemy, I saw their dead piling up on the ground. They were suffering tremendous losses, but Howe and their other officers kept urging them on. Either those guys were brave as hell or they were more scared of running than they were of getting killed. Despite my views on killing other human beings, I was glad we were mowing them down because, as they got closer, I saw that every one of their muskets had a bayonet attached to it. We were told in training that the Provincial militia, unfortunately, was unable to provide most of us with bayonets, so we'd best dispatch the enemy before he got too close.

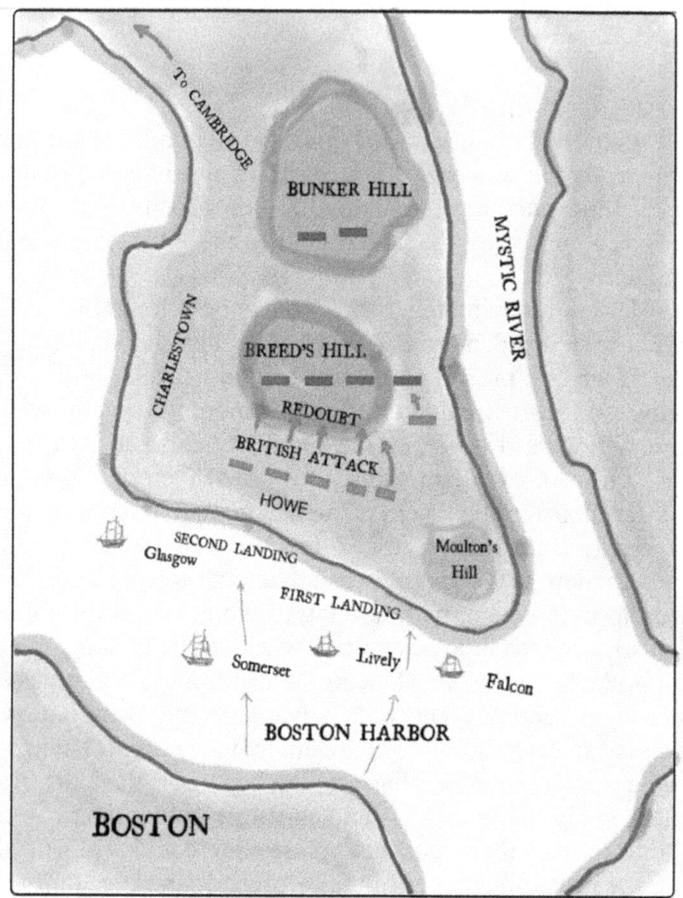

Bunker Hill Battle Site based on a map by BritishBattles.com

The British continued to fire upon us with heavy volleys, but with very poor aim. Most of their balls passed over our men. Not all of them, though. Just as I was feeling the relative satisfaction of seeing how well our guys were doing, one of my men took a ball in the chest. I quickly ran to him, but knew immediately there was nothing I could do. I didn't know the kid well, but did know that he was a likable 18-year-old farm boy from Andover. He'd told me he couldn't wait to fight for the American cause. Said his father was here, too, protecting our rear flank on Bunker Hill. When this was over I was going to have to tell his father the bad news. I dreaded that almost as much getting shot.

As the fighting continued, our men's spirits rose. We were clearly beating the celebrated and feared British army. It was an amazing feeling. Their artillery was for the most part falling short of our redoubt and barely reaching the brick kilns which some of our men were using for cover. The British were now retreating. Our men were roaring hurrahs as they sensed victory. So complete was the victory that many of the Brits hurried back to their boats. I thought at the time it was a good thing that the enemy failed to charge with their bayonets, as the ones that got through might have prevailed. Instead, they retreated giving us the apparent victory. Then I was reminded of our limited ammunition. We all had entered the battle with 15 balls. My guess was that most of the men had already used more than half of that. Maybe more.

Chapter 19

June 17

MEANWHILE, General Ward dispatched more reinforcements from the Cambridge training camp, but they had not been able to reach the battlefield because of enemy fire across the narrow neck of the Charlestown peninsula. When Putnam became aware of the situation, he made a dash to the neck with a contingent of men to clear the area briefly for the troops sent by Ward. To prove that the neck was passable, Putnam rode his horse back and forth across, lashing the animal with the flat of his sword to overcome the poor beasts' reluctance in the midst of the terrific fire coming from the enemy. As he did this, the balls from enemy muskets created clouds of dust all around him. The troops sent by Ward were convinced that Putnam was invulnerable, but were not at all convinced that they themselves were.

Eventually, as Putnam encouraged, entreated and threatened them, the new troops cautiously ventured over the neck between brief pauses in enemy fire thanks to furious bursts of fire from the troops Putnam had brought with him.

As Putnam and the reinforcements reached Bunker Hill at the rear of the peninsula, he ran into a Colonel Gerrish struggling with part of his regiment. Gerrish, who had fought with the Provincial army in '56, was struggling and exhausted. In poor condition and grossly overweight, having barely made it to Charlestown after an exhausting march in oppressive heat, he fell to the ground and lay there prostrate. His disorganized men were frantic. Having no leader, they dispersed now to the west side of the hill where they were somewhat protected from enemy fire by the hill summit.

Putnam ordered them back to the battle lines. He begged them to continue fighting. Some of the more fearful men he knocked down with his sword. Despite his efforts, it was all in vain. The men complained that they no longer had their officer. Putnam said that he'd lead them himself, the cannons were no longer being manned and no one would take on the responsibility. Without the cannons they stood no chance. The battle here on Bunker Hill was going the enemy's way, as the bombardment from the ships, batteries on barges and field cannons were landing with great accuracy on the summit of the hill.

Meanwhile, at Breed's Hill where a much bigger battle was going on, Howe had rallied his troops and with the support of a new barrage of cannon support from the batteries in the Charles River and field pieces on the flats below, launched a new assault up the sides of the hill. It wasn't easy, though, as each of Howe's infantrymen struggled in the draining heat, burdened with a 125-pound knapsack through unmown grass over half-erect fences and now the dead bodies of their comrades. As difficult as this was for the British soldiers, the sight of the bodies of their fellow soldiers spurred them on to get revenge for their fall. It was inordinately difficult as they were struggling up a hill directly into the downward fire from the Provincial marksmen. In desperation some of the troops piled up these dead bodies to create a barrier from which they could fire on the Americans.

The American troops were now gaining confidence as they witnessed for themselves how successful their efforts had been. If the enemy continued to pursue the same strategy, it seemed inevitable that that the Provincial forces would win the battle. The British couldn't afford to keep losing so many men while the American losses were far fewer. The Provincial officers, however, were aware of their dwindling ammunition and ordered their charges to minimize fire until the enemy drew even closer than before. The troops were ordered to wait until the enemy was only 35 yards away.

Chapter 20

June 17

I GLANCED OVER AT Matt to see how he was doing. His usually smiling face was grim and smeared with soot from firing his musket and grime from the dirt thrown up by balls landing much too close to him. He noticed that I was looking and forced a grin as he yelled, "Not at all like the history books, is it my friend?"

"Not at all. If we survive this, it'll be much better than a history book." As soon as I said that I realized how insensitive I'd been as I scanned the dead bodies all around me. "You know what I mean."

"Yeah, I do." The men around us seemed puzzled, but were too preoccupied with staying alive to give our brief dialogue much thought.

"Our side is looking pretty good right now, but those history books tell us that it's going to get worse fast."

Matt said, "I could go a cold Corona or Coors right now."

"Me too. Right now I'd take a room temperature beer at Pierce's." I could see that we were again drawing stares.

Just then I noticed smoke and flames coming from the small village of Charlestown on the western side of the peninsula. Apparently the British had set the town on fire, as they most likely were annoyed at the steady musket fire coming at them from village residents.

The second wave of British troops was getting much too close for comfort. My men were nervous as hell and I could see that they wanted to begin firing before it was too late. Still no word from Prescott or Putnam. I was afraid one of my men would begin firing in panic as it seemed that the Brits were way too close for comfort now. I could make out the pain, agony and anger on their sweating faces. If we didn't begin shooting soon, when we finally did, some of the lucky ones would make it through our musket fire and begin using their bayonets on us. Not a comforting thought.

The approaching second wave of British infantrymen made their advance in columns in full view of our men. When they were approximately 30 yards away Prescott and Putnam roared, "Begin your fire, men, and make every shot count."

The incoming Brits levied a tremendous volley in our direction. Fortunately for us and unfortunately for them, most of their shots were too elevated and went over us as we were mostly hidden behind our defense works. Obviously, these well-trained men, no doubt perfect in parade formation and other drill disciplines, were not that familiar with their weapons. This lack of intimate familiarity with their weapons was in time of battle a thousand times more important than perfect marching formations. Despite the generally poor aim of their troops, some of their balls did find targets in our ranks. A number of troops were hit. Two officers were hit by musket balls. One was a Colonel Nixon. I was pretty sure that Peter Salem was in Nixon's unit. Ironically, the other officer hit was Colonel Buckminster, the man who released Salem from slavery so he could fight for the American cause.

The life of Captain Balfour, Howe's aide de camp, was saved when a ball hit his canteen and passed through him without hitting any vital organs as he fought valiantly at the general's side. He was one of the fortunate British officers. At one point, as Howe surveyed the scene around him, he realized that almost every other officer serving under him had been shot. Embarrassed and discouraged at the wasted blood all around him, he seemed to prefer an honorable death to a second defeat by the peasant army he faced. Finally, he was persuaded that the odds were against him. He turned and followed his army as they retreated, yielding victory to the Americans. Behind him a Major Small was the only one standing with American muskets aimed directly at him. His death was almost a certainty when Putnam suddenly made an appearance and threw up his men's muskets with his sword. Putnam begged his men to spare the man's life as he was a personal friend of Putnam and no longer a threat to them. The general's humane chivalry gained him his men's admiration and his friend was allowed to retreat without being fired upon.

Howe was not about to give up, though. Once again he led his exhausted men into the face of our deady fire. The advancing redcoats, undeterred, kept coming at us with Howe boldly leading the advance. As I scanned down the slope at the endless wave of British troops making their way over and around their fallen comrades, I estimated that they must have already lost a thousand men either killed or wounded. Howe seemed undaunted as he made his way forward in plain sight on the field of battle. So far, the man had led a charmed life. I couldn't understand how he could remain so undaunted under such intense fire all around him. The bodies of his fellow soldiers alone would have deterred most men. It was almost as if Howe preferred an honorable death to a humiliating defeat at the hands of an enemy he despised as rebellious peasants.

I sensed that many of the men around me grudgingly respected Howe for his bravery in the face of such adverse odds. I, too, had to admire the man. I remembered reading that, after the French and Indian War in which Howe fought valiantly and won most of his battles against the French, it was known that he favored the American colonies and felt that the Crown was taking unfair advantage of them. Howe's oldest brother, General George Howe, had died fighting against the French at Ticonderoga in 1758. Admiral Richard Howe, his other brother,

———

continued to serve in the Royal Navy. The Howes had put their lives on the line more than once to defend the English colonies in North America. Obviously, General William Howe no longer believed in defending them, as he was now risking his life in a deadly battle against those very same colonials. Ultimately, his allegiances lay with the British. The fact that King George III was his first cousin had to be an influence on his thinking.

Our soldiers were now euphoric over their successes. They had not only kept the great British army at bay, they had made them pay for their advances. The Americans were well aware that the British had suffered greatly so far and were likely to suffer even more injuries as the battle continued. Knowing what I knew about the outcome of the Bunker Hill battle, I realized that this exultation was soon going to turn to disappointment.

Lieutenant Parker came over with a smile on his face. "Looks like the boys in their pretty red uniforms have learned a lesson. I don't think we'll see them again today. Probably not for a while."

I wasn't sure how to handle this, since I knew a lot more than Parker could have known. I hesitated before I said, "I sure hope you're right sir, but I have a feeling they're going to attack again, and if they do, we're going to suffer dearly."

"Good God, boy, where's your spirit? Look at that bloody field out there." He grinned and added, "And I do mean bloody. We've beat 'em good. Even the arrogant Brits are smart enough not to come back for more of the same."

"From what I can see, sir, most of our men are out of powder and balls. I know my men are, and I've heard others around me say they are, too. We can beat them if we have ammunition, but we're sitting ducks if we don't."

It seemed to suddenly dawn on him that I was right. Why he didn't see that himself is a mystery. He obviously got so caught up with the euphoria of two victories over the great British army that he failed to assess the situation the way he should have.

"Jesus, Carver, you're right. We better pray to the good Lord that they don't know and decide that retreat is the better part of valor against men who can shoot the eyes out of a raccoon. Hell, pray to God they don't know we're out of powder."

"Yes, sir. Let's pray that they don't."

Chapter 21

June 17

AS MATT AND I WATCHED THE BRITS retreat in the wake of being repelled ignominiously for the second time, our troops continued to celebrate their two well-earned victories. The second British assault had been repelled resoundingly, and I could see that most of our men assumed that the defeated Brits were licking their wounds in despair. It seemed to many of our Provincial brothers in arms that the British must now be discouraged and no doubt retiring back to Boston to think about just how tough an opponent they had faced. Our soldiers had to hope for this because most of them also had to know that they were out of ammunition. The best scenario would be for the Brits to call it a day and decide to fight another day when they had recovered from their defeats.

Matt and I both knew that that was not how the day was going to go.

Howe and his officers were indeed rethinking their next step, but it wasn't to retreat and lick their wounds. They now realized that the ungrateful American peasants were far from incompetent. The rebels knew how to fight, and they knew how to use a musket. Nevertheless, a third assault would be made, but the tactics would be different. The Provincials were going to pay for the humiliation they'd brought upon the noble British army. Howe vowed to himself that he'd either win or die an honorable death trying.

Chapter 22

June 17

IN THE LULL following the latest cessation of fire, I watched as Colonel Prescott distributed powder from a few of the remaining artillery cartridges to some of the men around him. He then urged all of the men to use their muskets as clubs against the incoming Redcoats should they make a third attempt. It was a desperate tactic, but he had nothing else. His only real hope was that the enemy would lack the fortitude to make that third attack.

A breathless messenger galloped to a stop near Prescott. He jumped down from his mount and, from what I could hear, told the colonel that General Ward had no more fully armed men to send as reinforcements from Cambridge. It sounded as if Ward was saying that Prescott and his men would have to fend for themselves and not expect any new help.

At that moment, the regiment abandoned by Colonel Gerrish marched from Ploughed Hill in the nearby Somerville section of Charlestown where they had retreated in disarray. A few of the men had eventually rallied the others and they now made their way onto the Charlestown peninsula offering their help. An adjutant, an experienced Danish soldier, assumed the command and urged the men to follow him to the lines. This was the only additional support that Prescott and Putnam were to get.

Meanwhile Howe gave his men orders to prepare for another attack. A few of his officers protested, saying it was suicide to lead the men once again into the deadly accurate fire of the Americans—especially since they were somewhat protected by their redoubt and rail fences. His generals, however, and most of the other officers, were shocked that any officer would be willing to yield victory to the rebels. They could not live with themselves knowing they were defeated by an undisciplined rabble of inferior numbers. They resolved to conquer or die.

Howe and his fellow generals had finally seen the many errors of their ways in their first two attacks on the Provincials. Their inflated confidence was set aside, and a new plan of attack was devised. The heavy knapsacks were abandoned. Some men even abandoned their heavy coats. Firing with muskets was now prohibited. Instead the men were ordered to charge forward with their bayonets. Some of his men hesitated as they were exhausted and had no heart for charging directly into musket fire to get close enough to use their bayonets. It was one thing to fire at an enemy who was shooting at you. It was quite another thing to run directly into that oncoming fire with the intention of plunging your bayonet into the man shooting at you if you got that far. Still, the men knew that if they didn't charge, they would die of humiliation or worse at the hands of their own officers. Many of the malingerers were prodded forward by the swords of their officers.

As they moved forward, unburdened by their overloaded knapsacks and in many cases, their heavy coats, their path was aided by British artillery fire. The artillery pieces had been moved closer to the enemy and their accuracy improved.

One Provincial colonel had just given his men an order to lay down their shovels where they were desperately digging trenches. He said there was no time for that and told them to man their stations in preparation for the incoming enemy. As he said this, the colonel was hit by a musket ball in his groin and fell dying in agony. At that very moment his son, a 19-year-old second lieutenant came upon him. The son was desperate to help his father off the field, but the older man pleaded with him to disregard his injury and reminded him that he was engaged in an honorable cause and should continue on and do his duty. The tearful son finally obeyed his father and proved himself worthy in the final moments of the battle.

My men and I knew the next few minutes could be deadly. If there was any doubt about a third attack, it was put to rest as a new wave of British soldiers began charging toward us in the wake of an artillery barrage that was hitting close to home. Men all around me were screaming as they were hit by debris from cannonballs landing much too close to them. In one case a cannonball landed on three men about ten yards away from me. It was an horrific scene. Body parts flew in every direction, one hand landing on my musket's barrel. Suddenly silence descended on the hill. The cannonade came to a stop. The quiet was deafening and ominous at the same time.

At first I thought they had given up their attack, but within seconds their troops began to march forward again. Not exactly a march this time. This time they kept low and advanced faster than the previous two attacks. A few of them fired their muskets, but most of them did not. They just plunged straight ahead with their bayonets directly into what little fire we could muster. We had very little powder left and had to make every shot
count. Man, if I wasn't on the receiving end, I'd admire the guts of these

Brits, knowing that some of them were not going to make it as they ran directly towards guns shooting at them. They didn't know that most of us were reduced to using our muskets as clubs. We had no other weapons.

Suddenly the enemy troops stopped in their tracks. They seemed to be looking at one of their officers. It was Howe, who appeared to have taken a ball in his leg or foot. He angrily waved his men back to their mission. One little ball in the foot was not going to stop Howe from directing his men. Just as the men turned their attention back to advancing on us, I noticed two other British officers fall. From where I was located behind a rail fence, it looked like it was fatal in both cases. They were not the first British officers I'd seen fall today, and it seemed that their army should be in complete disarray with so many fallen leaders, but the remaining officers were fearless, and the men continued to follow their lead. What an awful day this was, and it was going to get a lot worse. As I considered this, I heard yet another fallen British officer yelling to those around him, "If you take General Putnam alive, don't hang him. I know him. He's a brave fellow." The honor and high mindedness on both sides was astounding. A fascinating paradox when you consider that the goal of both armies was to kill the other side.

What shocked me the most was that after seeing so much death and agonizing injuries, I no longer turned to look when I heard a man cry out. I suppose it was partly because I'd become inured to death on the battlefield and partly because I didn't dare take my eyes off the enemy as they advanced toward me. In the heat of the battle I had completely forgotten that I couldn't be killed today. Funny how even when I was aware of that astonishing fact, I didn't feel any more secure.

Artist: Percy Moran 1909 - Library of Congress LC-USZC4-4970

The regulars were now under the eastern side of the redoubt where it was difficult for us to fire at them without exposing ourselves too much. Our forces now retired to the opposite side of the redoubt so we could take the British troops as they neared the top of the hillside and came into view. A nephew of Colonel Prescott, a young lieutenant, took a ball in his arm, which now hung broken and useless at his side. His uncle told him to take cover and do his best to encourage his men. The nephew was not about to sit back and do nothing. He did his best to reload his musket and as he was passing by an open port of the redoubt a cannon ball cut him in half.

By now many of the Americans were out of ammunition and resorted to throwing stones, but this only proved to the British just how weak the Provincials were and served to energize the dog-tired regulars. The first regular to mount the defense works was instantly shot down. The others who made it over the barrier first met the same fate. Among the brave men who made it to the top of the works was Major John Pitcairn, who cried, "The day is ours," and was immediately shot down by Peter Salem, not three yards away from me. I instantly recognized Pitcairn from the Battle of Lexington where he led a large contingent of regulars onto the common in a face-off with Captain John Parker. I also knew that Pitcairn had a jaundiced view of colonial Americans and a particularly dim view of their ability to fight. Just prior to Lexington and Concord he was reported to have said, *"I have so despicable an opinion of the people of this country that I would not hesitate to march with the men I have with me to any part...and do whatever I was inclined. I am satisfied they will never attack Regular troops."*

As if that arrogance was not enough, he had also written the following: *"Orders are anxiously expected from England to chastise those very bad people. The General had some of the Great Wigs, as they are called here, with him two days ago, when he took that opportunity of telling them, and swore to it by the living God, that if there was a single man of the King's troops killed in any of their towns he would burn it to the ground. What fools you are, said he, to pretend to resist the power of Great Britain; she maintained last war three hundred thousand men, and will do the same now rather than suffer the ungrateful people of this country to continue in their rebellion. This behaviour of the General's gives great satisfaction to the friends of the Government. I am satisfied that one active campaign, a smart action, and burning of two or three of their towns, will set everything to rights. Nothing now, I am afraid, but this will ever convince these foolish bad people that England is in earnest."*

As I said before, I don't like to see people killed, but if anyone had to die in this battle, it was fitting that it was John Pitcairn.

Chapter 23

June 17

IT WAS NOW READILY APPARENT that the British regulars were going to end the day as victors despite the terrible price they had paid. Well aware of what a hollow victory it was going to be they mounted the redoubt gaining a painfully earned satisfaction. As pyrrhic as the victory was, it was their turn to offer up hurrahs.

Warren was among the last to accept defeat. As inevitable as the defeat was, he considered retreat a disgrace and refused to leave the redoubt. Finally, at the urging of his countrymen he reluctantly followed them toward a more secure location. As he departed the besieged fortress he was recognized by his British friend, Major Small. Small ordered his men to hold fire, but a gun had already been fired and Warren took a musket ball in the head. He died instantly as a hero earning him the eternal gratitude of his country.

Meanwhile, a Colonel Scammans arrived with a partial regiment as reinforcements from Cambridge, but they were too late and soon had to retreat with the others. Slowly and with great effort the British began to occupy the redoubt. Completely drained by what they had gone through under a hot sun, they were too exhausted to use their bayonets and too much intermingled with the Americans to fire their muskets. To do so would have meant killing their own as often as they killed the enemy.

Putnam put spurs to his horse and charged to a position between his retreating men and the British. He was so close to the enemy that he could easily be taken down by a musket ball. Somehow, he remained unscathed and begged his men to turn and renew the fight. A few Provincial officers rallied with their troops and kept the enemy at bay for a while, but it wasn't for long as the first British troops that had mounted the fortress were now joined by more exhausted regulars suddenly energized by what was now becoming a victory. They soon overwhelmed the valiant last-ditch effort of the officers, killing a great many of them. The few survivors now retreated under steady fire. Putnam and his Connecticut troops covered their retreat as best they could.

Then Putnam decided to make one last stand. He threatened his men with disgrace if they failed to stand by their general. Most of his men, faced with British bayonets, left him to stand by himself against the slow, but steady advance of the regulars. Finally, with the clear threat of being bayonetted at any moment, Putnam turned and retreated.

Of the mere six Provincial cannons used in the battle, five were taken by the British. One was taken back to Cambridge. Prescott also went to

Cambridge. He was furious that Ward had not sent him reinforcements when victory was within his grasp. He had lost so many of his men and now it seemed those losses were in vain. With a little more help and with a little more powder and balls, he was convinced the day would have ended in victory.

Back in Charlestown the wounded and dead were being taken from the battlefield. The injured men of both armies were placed in boats to be taken to nearby hospitals where the surgeons were overwhelmed by the incoming wounded. It was a long time before many of the men were attended to. The British wounded waited longer as they sustained greater losses.

Chapter 24

June 17

MATT AND I FOUND OUR HORSES. Not surprisingly they were in better shape than we were. General Ward had assigned men to provide water for the hundreds of horses that were tied up in various locations behind the lines. I doubt if they'd been fed, but at least they weren't dragging like we were. We figured we'd feed them somewhere on the way home if we could find anything.

I was so tired I had trouble getting up on my horse. Just when I'd made it up on my second try, a fellow soldier with blood stains on his face and shoulders slowly dragged himself to his horse a few yards away from us. Even at that distance I could see that he was crying and could barely walk. Matt and I went over to him and asked him if we could help.

"I'm not crying in pain. This blood is from the man next to me at the fence. He took a ball to the face. Dear God, I'll never forget it. I liked the fellow, too. We both liked reading books. Told me he had a dozen of 'em back home in Lynn. We even knew some of the same folks up there. Oh my God. We'd both made it through the hell of the day until just a few minutes ago when we were leaving. Damn regulars kept firing, even at our backs."

I realized that, while Matt and I had traveled from Salem to Charlestown last night and had stayed awake all night helping to build the redoubt, the actual battle only lasted a couple of hours. Yet in that relatively short period of time thousands of men were killed or wounded. This guy had experienced something awful. We all had, but his friend had almost made it out of the battle zone safely until the last minute. I could see why this fellow was happy to talk to someone who wasn't shooting at him.

We approached him as fellow brothers in arms. Matt suddenly pulled out his cell phone and snapped a photo of the man. I'd snapped a couple of shots during the heat of the battle. What for? I didn't know, but I had a feeling I'd be glad I did when things quieted down. I'd even shot a few minutes of video. Still, I didn't think this was a good time to be taking pictures.

The blood-stained soldier said, "What did you just do? What is that thing in your hand?"

Matt was impulsive and this was clearly one of those times he acted before he thought. This was not the time to be showing off Matt's cell phone camera. Before Matt could respond I said "It's a camera. My friend just took a picture of you."

"What in God's name is a camera? And I don't have a picture with me so you couldn't have taken it. I'm too bloody tired for jests, lads. Seriously, what is that thing in your hand?" He was obviously suspicious of us and our motives.

I couldn't help but grin, which I quickly realized was only going to piss the guy off, so I said, "Matt, show him. It's a lot easier than trying to explain what it is." Matt then dragged himself over to the man and held the phone up so he could see the screen. The man found himself looking at a photo of himself."

He took a quick glance and said, "Ah, a clever little mirror. Where do you get the energy to play with me like this after what we've been through? I think this battle has affected your heads, if you don't mind my saying so."

I immediately realized that seeing himself like that must have indeed seemed like a mirror image, so I said, "Matt, take a shot of the man's horse."

Matt nodded knowingly and took a picture of the horse and then showed it to the exhausted soldier. He stared at the screen for a full minute. As he stared, his blood-stained jaw dropped. "Good Lord, man. How did you do that?"

"It's what we call a camera. We're visitors from the future and this is an invention that captures images of anything you aim it at."

At this, the now befuddled soldier just shook his head. He didn't know whether to be angry or curious. Finally, he said, "All right boys, I'll admit that I can't figure this out. That must be some kind of new contraption you got from London or someplace we've never heard of. Why in blazes would you put me on about coming here from the future. For the love of God, we're all too exhausted to play mind games."

He was probably right. We shouldn't be playing mind games at a time like this. We were taking advantage of his mental and physical fatigue at a time when he probably just wanted to go home, get a good meal and sleep for a day. We were just as tired as he was, but it was one of those times when we couldn't help ourselves. I looked over at Matt and he nodded as if to say, go on. Play it out. What the hell. We weren't hurting the guy and if he told his friends or relatives, they probably wouldn't believe him, so we weren't creating something that would alter history.

"Okay," I said, "let me try to explain. My friend Matt and I arrived in Salem a few months ago in a spaceship sent from the 21st century. I know you'll find that hard to believe, but it's true." I held up Matt's cell phone and continued, "This camera is part of a device we call a telephone. With it we can talk to people anywhere in the world. Science had progressed greatly by the 21st century and this is just one of many amazing things that exist in the year 2019 where we come from."

By now our new friend was smiling. He obviously thought we were playing this elaborate game with him and he'd decided to go along with it and see where it was going. That was good. Better than getting angry.

He said, "I'll give you lads this. You have some imagination. Just how do you prove that you're from the future? You surely don't expect me to take your word for it. And you used about four words I never heard of. You may not be from the future, but you must be from somewhere far from here."

Matt said, "What words did we use that were new to you?"

"I think one of 'em was 'okay.' Another was 'spaceship.'"

"Okay means the same as 'all right' where we come from. A spaceship is a ship that flies through the air."

Now the man was grinning from ear to ear. "Come on lads. Where do ye get these ideas?"

I was enjoying this. I probably shouldn't have been, but I was. "In the year 2019 ships called airplanes fly through the air carrying people from one city to another. Spaceships fly to the moon and Mars. Our spaceship was so technologically advanced that we were able to fly backward in time more than 240 years."

"Yes, you said that you flew back in time. You still haven't proven it."

"Where do you think we got this telephone and camera?"

"There's another word. What is this telephone?"

"I think I mentioned this before. It lets you talk to anyone in the world who also has a telephone. I can't show you now because we're the only ones in 1775 who have telephones and that's because we brought them from the year 2019."

The man was still smiling. "I admit, your device is remarkable, but maybe you got it from some other place in the world that has better science than we have. You still haven't proved you're from the future." By now, I could see our new friend was getting into this.

Then it dawned on me. "All right. This will prove it to you.
A few days ago the Continental Congress made George Washington the commander-in-chief of the Continental Army. In a few days he'll come to Cambridge and take charge of the army. General Ward will then be second in command. We know that because we read about it in our history books. We also know that James Warren, a distant cousin of Joseph Warren, will replace Dr. Warren as president of the Provincial Congress two days from now because of the unfortunate passing of Dr. Warren today."

The soldier squinted as he tried to reconcile what I'd just told him with his inability to believe in the very idea of time travel. While he was wrestling with the seeming inconsistencies I said, "By the way, friend, I'm Christopher and this is Matthew. What do you call yourself?"

The man said, "Confused." Then he grinned for the second time and said, "Aye. I take your meaning. Name's Jedediah. Jedediah Talbot. Friends call me Jed. I must confess, Christopher and Matthew that you have me hornswoggled. If what you tell me is going to happen in two days, does happen, I'll be even more confused. Between your little device there and your predictions, you tell a good story and I have not the wit to contradict ye, but I still have my doubts. The kind of magic you've shown me must be some form of witchcraft. You don't look like witches, but they say witches can take any form."

"We are not witches. I can assure you. In the 21st century we don't believe in witches. We understand why you find it hard to believe us. In the year 1775 it's difficult for anyone to conceive of what we're telling you. I suppose I can see why you might think it's witchcraft since it's all so new to you. Oh, I just thought of something. These new words you heard us speak. They're in our dictionary. Here, let me show you."

"Dictionary? What in God's name is a dictionary?"

"I guess you haven't heard of Dr. Johnson's Dictionary? It was published in England in 1755. In the year 2019 there are many dictionaries. A dictionary is a book that gives you the definition of a word."

"Definition?"

"The meaning. Here, look." I pulled out my phone and turned to a dictionary that I had downloaded before the flight. "Let's look up the word 'telephone.'"

He grinned again, but it was a nervous grin, as if he wasn't sure what to think. "Look up? It's as if you're speaking a new language."

"I can see how you might think so." I then showed him the definition of the word 'telephone.'" As I held up the entry on the screen it suddenly occurred to me that he might not be literate and that I might be embarrassing him. Probably not, though. I had been pleasantly surprised by the fairly high literacy I'd observed in my few months in Salem. Sam Hall told me he believed that a higher percentage of American colonials were able to read than of the British population back in England. In any event, my fears were for naught as I saw his look of amazement as he stared at the screen.

"How does that work? It's like some sort of magic. A good magic, of course. Can you look up as you call it another word for me?"

"Of course. Give me a word."

"Can you look up the word musket?"

"Sure.

"There's another example of the strange way you talk."

Now I was confused. "I'm not sure I get your meaning, Jedediah."

"You just illustrated the difference."

"What difference are you talking about?" I really was confused.

"The first time you used the word 'sure' I think you used it to mean yes. Just now, though, you used it to mean certain, which is the way we use the word 'sure.'"

Wow! This guy was no slouch. How many people would pick up on such linguistic differences?

"I'm impressed by the way you saw the difference. Do you mind if I ask you how you make your living when you're not shooting at British regulars?"

"I'm a schoolteacher. Not very lucrative, but actually quite satisfying. I teach arithmetic to youngsters in the West Lake school up in Lynn. And what may I ask do you good fellows do when you're not shooting at British soldiers?

I said, "I'm a typesetter for the *Essex Gazette* in Salem."

"And I do press work for the other paper in Salem, the *Salem Gazette*." said Matt.

"Then we all have something in common. We all work with the printed word."

I said, "I suppose that's true. If you ever get to Salem, Jed, please look us up. Both papers are easy to find."

"I will do that, Christopher. Maybe you can show me more of your witchcraft." As he said this, I winced. I just hoped he'd keep his thoughts to himself. We never should have showed off with the cell phone.

When we were finally on our way back to Salem, Matt said, "You sure you should have invited Jedediah to Salem? He may want to talk more about our cameras. It could be awkward if he does it in front of people." "I suppose that could happen, but he seems like a decent guy with a good head on his shoulders. I think it'll be fine, if he does come. He probably won't come anyway." I hesitated a moment, then said, "You probably shouldn't have brought out your cell phone. The guy was not in a mood to be entertained after seeing the guy next to him take a ball in the face." I very seldom criticized Matt, and he looked surprised at what I'd said. But only for a moment, as he then said, "He seemed to enjoy it once he got into it. I think it perked him up. Anyway, I think he'll come. Believe me, he'll come." His response indicated that he didn't take my criticism seriously. Matt had a tendency to minimize problems. It might be good for his mental health, but sometimes problems were real and not to be ignored.

I was too tired to pursue the subject more. I was honestly fearful that we might not make it back to Salem. We were so tired that I was afraid we'd fall off our mounts.

"You okay?" asked Matt.

"Better than a lot of those guys. A lot better. Pretty damn tired, though. Hungry and thirsty, too."

Chapter 25

June 18

THE NEXT MORNING I dragged myself to work. I was actually more tired than I was when I went to bed. Before I even got settled, Sam Hall came over and hugged me.

"Thank God you all made it safely. Gil and Tom just arrived. Gil suffered a ball off his thigh. Just a little flesh on the surface, but thank God, nothing more serious. How did your friend Matthew fare?"

"He's okay. Just tired like the rest of us."

"I will never get used to that word 'okay,' Christopher." He smiled and hesitated before adding, "Oh, I suppose I will if I hear it enough. Actually seems rather functional now that I think about it."

I had missed Sam. It was only a little over a day, but I'd come to like my new boss. I then said, "I'm learning to use a lot of words that I once considered archaic. Now they're becoming quite normal."

"Let's meet mid-morning and discuss what stories you lads can write for the paper. First-hand witnesses to the battle will be of great interest to our readers. I'd suggest you go see Colonel Mason. There's a good chance he's been in touch with Ward, or Putnam and will have an estimate of the number of casualties sustained by both sides. He may have other information of value, too." I was thinking as Sam spoke that who would know any more about the battle than Matt and myself, but of course that was ridiculous. We were not looking at the bigger picture as I'm sure the generals were.

Mason received us warmly.

"My contacts tell me both of you served admirably yesterday. And you seem to have survived unscathed."

"Physically," I said soberly. "I have a lot of images in my head that will not go away easily, sir. We saw some pretty awful things yesterday."

"Yes, I'm sure you did. What is your estimation of the performance of the Provincial forces yesterday?"

"We lost the battle, sir, but I believe it was a pyrrhic victory for the British. They lost a lot of men. If we'd had enough ammunition, I believe we would have won in the end."

Mason smiled. "Interesting. That is almost precisely the assessment I received this morning in a message from Ward. You lads are quite perceptive."

I looked over at Matt and said, "I think anyone who was there would have come to the same conclusion." I smiled and added, "I suspect even the regulars would have seen it that way. They were taking a helluva beating until we ran out of powder and balls. Then they had free rein.”

“I wish I had been there. This bad leg of mine keeps me from doing a lot of things I want to do. Since you're both going to be writing up your accounts of yesterday's battle, you should know this. According to Ward the British wounded came to more than a thousand and they suffered at least 226 dead including 19 officers. We Provincials lost 115 killed and suffered a little more than 300 wounded. These figures will be helpful, too: Ward estimates that about 3,500 men joined in the battle on the Provincial side and somewhat more than that on the enemy side. Let me tell you gentlemen that Gage and His Majesty will take us seriously after this. That's both good and bad. If we're lucky, His Majesty will say it's not worth it to waste good British soldiers on a lost cause.”
Matt interrupted Mason and said, “But you don't think that's how they'll react, do you, sir?”

“No, I don't. The British are too arrogant to accept this gracefully. No one beats up on the British army, because the British army is what keeps the rest of the world in line. They can't afford to live with a pyrrhic victory, especially from one of their own colonies. I may be wrong, but I think we can expect to be in conflict with our British brothers for a good long time. Probably until one side or the other decides it can't afford to go on anymore.

Chapter 26

July 3

ON JULY 3RD GENERAL GEORGE WASHINGTON took command of the Provincial forces in Cambridge. The Continental Congress had just made him Commander in Chief of the Continental Army. The Provincial militias were no more. A few days later the *Essex Gazette* in Salem published the following letter to the public from Washington:

May your warmeſt wishes be realized in the fuccefs of America at this important and interesting period, and be aſſured, that every exertion of my worthy colleagues and myself will be equally extend to the re-eſtabliſhment of peace and harmony between the Mother Country and thefe Colonies: -As to the fatal but neceſſary operation of War--------when we aſſumed the Soldier, we did not lay afide the Citizen, and we fhall moſt fincerely rejoice with you in that happy hour when the eftablifment of American Liberty on the moſt firm and folid foundations fhall enable us to return to our private ſtations in the bofom of a free, peaceful, and happy Country. G. WASHINGTON

At first the long S, which looks a lot like an F, seemed strange to Matt and myself, but we quickly got used to it, and it now seemed perfectly normal. Sam told us that he was fairly certain that it had its origin in the cursive written form of the S in Roman times.

It was clear now to most colonists that we were on a war footing and that our British brothers were now our enemies. The King and his House of Lords were not about to let the ungrateful colonists have their way.

Not all British subjects in the Old Country agreed with the King or his generals—not even all of the members of the House of Lords. In a speech before the House of Lords on March 18, a month before Lexington and Concord, Lord Camden had spoken out against a proposed Fish Act that would limit New England's fish trade to Britain and the British West Indies. Trade with other countries would be prohibited as of July 1, 1775.

"I think it a measure cruel, impracticable and unnecessary." Lord

Camden went on to say that the proposed bill was tyrannical and cruel. "A great and essential part of the subsistence of those provinces, my Lords, is fish. They cannot live without it. Is this a punishment proportioned to the guilt? A mob destroyed the cargo of a tea ship and did it in a manner highly outrageous and deserving of punishment. What did you inflict? At one stroke you shut up the port. That is, you ruined the whole town, involved the innocent with the guilty in one common decision. This might perhaps have been defended had an attempt been made to separate them. You made no requisitions to have the offenders delivered up. You inflicted your punishment without the party being heard or allowed to speak a syllable in his defence." —Lord Camden

A group of merchants from Bristol, England, wrote to King George III expressing their *"most anxious apprehensions for ourselves and posterity that we behold the growing distractions in America threaten."* They begged the King's wisdom and goodness to save them from a *"lasting and ruinous civil war."* Unfortunately, the King remained steadfast in his view that the war should continue until the colonies were subdued. The King believed the very survival of the British Empire depended on victory over the rebellious New Englanders.

Chapter 27

July 23

LORD NORTH had been summoned to the King's residence in the 775-room Buckingham Palace. Frederick North, 2nd Earl of Guilford, better known as Lord North and the British Prime Minister for the last five years. Despite his familiarity with King George III, he still honored the royal protocol that said that anyone in the presence of the monarch did not speak until the King spoke. Nor did the visitor sit until the King sat. The King motioned Lord North to sit with a wave of his hand. He stared at North for an uncomfortable moment before speaking. Finally, he spoke.

"The report you sent me, Frederick, is not encouraging. Not long ago you told me that Gage and his regiments had things well under control in America. This report tells a different story."

"I have reports from both Gage and Howe. They both say that the Americans are not as disorganized and ill-trained as they first thought. Many of their officers had fought alongside of our officers in the French War. And their troops are excellent shooters. No doubt due to their experience shooting game in the forests that surround them."

"This speaks poorly of Gage's and Howe's judgement, does it not?"

"I'm not sure I understand you, Your Majesty?"

"Surely Gage and Howe should have known that these Provincials would be prepared, since they had fought side by side with their officers. They should have known that the colonist would be good with a musket, too."

"Well they did win the battle at Charlestown, Your Majesty, so in the end they are still in control of the situation."

"The reports I have from Boston say that Howe's forces won that battle because the Americans exhausted their ammunition. Even the reports of men wounded and killed shows that the Americans came through with fewer losses than we did. I must say, Frederic, that I'm concerned. Very concerned. The very future of the Empire rests on our winning this regrettable war with our New England colonists. We must teach these Americans that despite their self-serving claims, they are still subjects of the British Empire and as such must obey our laws."

"I quite agree, Your Majesty. I have already told Gage that he has our complete support. If he needs more men, we will supply them."

"That is not so easy to do, but we shall try. The army has purchased the services of many foreigners and mercenaries at great cost to the treasury. Our allies on the continent see our need as a weakness, so they will demand even more for every man we purchase in the future. This drain on the treasury has put a great strain on the government. Nevertheless, this uprising in America must be dealt with. Do whatever it takes to teach these rebellious colonists that they cannot defy the British Empire and get away with it."

"Yes, Your Majesty. It is painful that it has come to this."

"Quite painful. I rather like the few Americans I have met."

North recalled the visit he'd received from John Derby, the Salem shipping merchant, and Gil Lee a few months ago after Lexington and Concord. They had been sent there by the Provincial Congress to present the American side of the confrontation before the Prime Minister received the British version. "I have had similar experiences with Americans. They are not the upstart country bumpkins many here think they are. The one's I've met are educated, sophisticated and well-spoken. They are men who would do quite well here in London."

The King allowed a hint of a smile as he said, "I wish they would choose careers in professions here in London instead of mouthing claptrap about not being treated as well as Englishmen here in the home country. Dear God, if they'd only see that it's reasonable that they pay for the benefits of being part of the British Empire. Can't they see how fortunate they are to be English?"

"I understand some of them do see things that way. The rebels call them Tories and treat them poorly. The rebels somehow don't seem to see that we need to tax them to pay for what we expended back in the French War and even now for the services of the government officials who help make things run in New England. Still, Your Majesty, I clearly recall my conversation with the two men the Provincial Congress sent here after those skirmishes in Lexington and Concord. They were most persuasive, and I almost sympathized with them. We're separated by 3,000 miles and that distance, I fear, has convinced the American colonists that their mother country doesn't see them the same way it sees your subjects here in England."

"I suppose great distances do influence the way these people think. It's your job, Frederick, to teach them some respect. They seem to prefer war to obedience to the law. So be it. A sound beating will teach them that they are still British subjects and cannot substitute their laws for ours."

"Yes, Your Majesty. It will be done."

"Thus far, our generals have not shown me that they are up to the task. Do you need to replace them?"

"I don't think so. Yes, they misread just how zealous these New Englanders are. And yes, they failed to recognize that the Provincial men know how to fight, but our generals will not make those mistakes again. I already have more men heading for Boston and if the treasury can find the resources, I will acquire even more foreign mercenaries. Gage tells me that even though these mercenaries have no particular loyalties, they for the most part are good soldiers. If your majesty instructs the treasury to release the funds, I will purchase more men as quickly as possible. I'd like to teach these Americans their lesson before winter comes in New England. Their winters are far harsher than ours, so a winter campaign will be much more difficult."

"I will instruct the treasury today. Make sure your generals move as quickly as they can. The sooner we end this unpleasantness, the better for all concerned and the sooner we can start building the treasury up, not draining it."

Chapter 28

July 23

SAM CALLED ME INTO his office and closed the door.

"I have an idea that I hope you'll find interesting."

"I find most of your ideas interesting, Sam."

"This is different. Sit down. This will take a few minutes."

"You've definitely got my interest now, sir."

"I thought we'd dispensed with the sir. Sam is okay." As he said this, his eyes lit up. "There! I used one of your words. The word 'okay.' It's actually rather functional."

I smiled. I couldn't have had a better boss. "Okay then, Sam. What's your idea?"

"As you know, I'm fascinated with your background. Coming from the future and all that. I also find it extremely fascinating when you demonstrate your camera and when you describe other scientific miracles that are off in our distant future. I know that our readers would be equally fascinated to read about such things."

"I'm sure they would, Sam, but we've discussed the risk in making our backgrounds public. Writing about the miracles of the future would bring about the same risk. We don't know exactly what would happen, but you and I both believe that if this got out to the public it would have a profound and perhaps harmful impact on how history evolves over the next 240 years. As tempting as it is . . . ."

"Let me stop you right there, Christopher. You know I agree with you about this. We don't know precisely what deleterious effects would come about, but we know it would change history in ways that could be damaging. It's too risky to tamper with the normal course of events. However, what I was going to suggest, would, I believe, be quite safe, yet provide our readers with exciting food for thought."

"You're good, Sam. Now you've heightened my interest even more."

"Why couldn't you write articles imagining how things will be two centuries from now? We could call them our futurist articles or maybe our futurism series. They would not be presented as fact, but merely the speculation of a farsighted newspaperman."

"I think that would work. Yes, I think we could do that with very little harm to history." I paused before adding, "You know, Sam. You just coined a word that won't come into the language for at least a hundred years."

Sam looked puzzled. "What word is that?"

"Actually two words. Futurist and futurism."

"Good Lord. Does that mean that we can't use them?"

"I think that's a risk we can take."

Sam was enjoying this. "While we're discussing the English language, you just used a locution that is unfamiliar to me, though I think I take its meaning. You said, 'I think that would work.'"

I grinned. "I suppose it is unfamiliar in 1775, but it will be quite common in 2019. But back to your idea. I like it. People would wonder how I acquired such an imagination, but I could say that even as a child I imagined what the future might be like. If I run out of ideas, maybe Gil and Tom could write some articles?"

"Perhaps, but I doubt that you will run out of ideas soon. You seem to have an endless supply of surprises. Those pictures of men in battle at Charlestown that your 'camera' captured amazed me. If only there were some way we could reproduce them in the paper."

"We would need an inkjet printer connected either by cable or WiFi to do that."

"Now I'm completely lost."

I started to explain but he held up his hand. "Don't bother to explain now. Some other time perhaps. Or maybe in one of your articles? Speaking of which, why don't you come up with a short list of possible topics for your first few articles. I imagine there are many, so don't make the list comprehensive. Just a few so we can get started as soon as possible. I think this might even bring in new readers."

Chapter 29

July 24

I LIMITED THE INITIAL LIST to the following items:
  Steam-powered boats
  Motorized carriages on rails
  Motorized carriages on roads
  Flying machines
  Vaccinations against diseases such as smallpox
  Indoor toilets
  Indoor plumbing
  Central heating
  The camera
  Color printing
  The telephone
  The cell phone
  The radio
  Television
  Supermarkets
  Computers
  The Internet

Sam thought my first one should be especially amazing, so he asked me to start with **Flying Machines**. Admittedly, he didn't understand most of the choices enough to know how to evaluate them so I went with his pick, since I figured from the perspective of an 18th century person, flying machines would be pretty amazing. We scheduled it for next week's issue. The *Essex Gazette* is a weekly, so I had time to write something up along with doing my other duties at the paper.

Two days later Sam came back to my desk and told me that a young man had just come in looking for me. Said his name was Jedediah. Sam said he had a friend with him. I immediately realized that it must be Jedediah Talbot, the schoolteacher from the Bunker Hill battle. I'd expected him to get in touch someday, but not so soon. And he'd brought a friend with him. I didn't like the sound of that. I inhaled deeply and headed for the front office.

As soon as I came through the door I heard, "Christopher. Good to see you."

"Good to see you, too, Jedediah. Who's your friend?"

"This is Charles Inglesby, a fellow teacher down in Lynn. I was hoping that we might get some time to talk while we're in Salem."

Having just committed to writing the futurist piece for the paper, I really didn't want to take too much time out of my workday, even though I liked Jedediah. I thought for a minute and said, "Why don't I meet you at Pierce's Tavern on Front Street at noon. We can get a bite to eat and talk then. I won't be able to talk long, though. Have to get the paper out for next week's edition."

Jed looked at Inglesby, who nodded his assent.

Then Jed said, "Of course. I understand. That sounds good. I can't wait to catch up, Christopher. Charles is eager to see your clever device. I told him how amazing it is."

As soon as I'd heard that Jed had brought a friend along, I feared this would happen."

"Well, Jedediah, I'm not sure we can make that happen. Anyway, let's talk about it at Pierce's Tavern."

Jed looked crestfallen and Charles didn't look too happy either, but they left without pursuing it further. I now dreaded my lunch hour.

As I walked back to my desk, Gil Lee came up to me. "What happened? You look like you've just seen a ghost."

"I wish it were a ghost." I then told him about Jedediah and how he'd brought a friend with him who was eager to see me perform with the camera on my cell phone.

"I see what you mean. As hard as it is, you have to keep the lid on this. We can't afford to go beyond the limits we've set for ourselves."

"I know that. That's why I'm struggling with how to handle this. Matt and I had this one moment of weakness in Charlestown after the battle and now we're gonna pay for it."

Gil said, "I can understand how it happened. You'd just witnessed the bloodiest, most awful event of your life and this guy who shared that experience seemed like a bit of normal. I probably would have done it, too."

"Nah, you wouldn't. I screwed up."

"Just stand your ground at lunch and in an hour or so, you'll be past it. Suck it up, my friend. You can handle it."

One of the things that struck me when I first visited Pierce's Tavern was that they didn't serve sandwiches. I happened to know that the Earl of Sandwich had invented the idea of putting slices of meat between two slices of bread back in the early 1760s, but apparently the idea hadn't reached New England. Or at least not Pierce's Tavern. I ordered a crock of baked beans with bread on the side. I knew from previous visits that the baked beans contained generous portions of bacon pieces. Jed and Charles ordered vegetable beef soup with bread. We all had a tankard of ale, which by the way, was excellent, even at room temperature.

After exchanging pleasantries Jed said, "I gather that you don't want to show Charles your camera device?"

"It's not Charles. I don't even know Charles. When we first came to Salem, Matthew and I agreed that we wouldn't show the device to anyone except maybe under extraordinary circumstances."

"But you showed it to me, a complete stranger?"

"I know. It was a moment of weakness, probably brought on by the stress of having gone through a battle in which we saw hundreds of people die. We just wanted a moment of pleasantness or relief from what we had just experienced. It was a momentary letdown, Jed. We shouldn't have done it."

Meanwhile, Charles was sitting there listening to all this, knowing he was not going to witness the exciting thing his good friend had told him about. As I observed Charles I also noticed a man in a booth on the other side of the room. He looked familiar, but I couldn't remember his name or where I'd seen him before. Maybe I was imagining it, but he seemed interested in us. Had he been listening to our conversation? Whenever I made eye contact with him, he turned away. It was probably just my overactive imagination.

Jed remained quiet for a while, then turned to his friend. "I'm sorry, Charles. I thought they'd make an exception for just one person. I told them you would be discreet and not say a word to anyone."

"Of course I wouldn't. Good Lord, Jed. What's so hush-hush about this anyway? I have a feeling your friend here was putting you on about where this secret device came from. I'm sure it's all a very clever joke. Or is it worse than that? Is it an elaborate hoax?"

This guy could be annoying, but I suppose I could see where he was coming from. The situation sure made Jed look like a chump—at least from his standpoint. I felt bad about all this, but knew that I couldn't let down again. I'd done that once and look where it got me. It would even be awkward trying to explain to Charles why I couldn't show him the cell-phone camera. The more honest I was with him, the more I would sound like a charlatan if I didn't bring out the phone as proof of what I was saying.

Not only had Matt and I brought along our cell phones, we'd also brought along our pocket translator. We could have wowed Jed and Charles with that. It still wowed me. If you are trying to converse with a French-speaking person, for example, all you have to do is speak into the hand-held device and the device will say in French what you'd just said in English. Most of these translators require WiFi or a sim card to function, but ours had the data for four languages stored in the device. It included English, French, German and Spanish. I don't know when we'll use it, but the scientists back in Nevada thought it would be a good idea to have it with us just in case.

It was only human to want to show off our 21st century toys to people in the 18th century. It's fun to see the look of amazement on their faces. However, the people back in Nevada had stressed the danger of revealing too much to too many people in our new century. The possibility of changing the course of history was a fear that not only the engineers, but the social scientists felt had to be taken very seriously. If Matt, Gil, Tom or I violated this warning there was no telling what could happen in the future. At a time like this, when other folks were present, it was so tempting to tell ourselves *'What harm could it be to tell just one more person?'* I couldn't take the chance. We had to limit the number of people who knew about our past to Sam Hall, the Social Library board, Jeremiah Weeks, the librarian and unfortunately, Jedediah Talbot. That came to a total of nine people plus Matt, Gil, Tom and myself. It wasn't going to be easy keeping to this limit, but we had to try.

Jed and Charles were still waiting for my reaction. Finally, I said, "I'm going to have to say no, Charles. Think what you will. Believe me, it's nothing personal. Jed knows what he saw and I can see why he would want you, his friend, to see it also, but we cannot afford to show it to anyone else."

Jedediah's face was red now. He looked like he was going to explode. "This is so unfair, Christopher. I have a mind to go to your superior at the *Gazette* and tell him what you've done."

Now I was getting annoyed. "And just what would you tell him?"

"That you have this clever device that you claim is from the future. That you yourself claim to be from the future."

"And how do you think he'll react?"

"I would hope that he'll chastise you for spreading such wild notions. Perhaps even terminate you if he thinks you are unstable."

I smiled, almost feeling sorry for Jed. "Think about that, Jed. There's a real possibility that my boss will think you're the unstable one. As a schoolteacher, you need the respect of the community. Telling wild stories about a respected newspaperman won't help you very much." He seemed to be considering this, so before he could say anything else, I said, "Look, Jed, I know this is probably embarrassing for you not being able to prove to your friend that what you described is not a figment of your imagination. If it helps any, let me assure you, Charles, that Jed didn't make all of this up. What he tells you he saw really exists. I would love to show you the device to prove that, but I can't."

Jed said, "That's too bad, Christopher. I was going to invite you to visit my class to demonstrate your device for my students."

I then made an on-the-spot decision that hopefully would tamp down the anger that Jed was feeling.

Chapter 30

July 25

THE NEXT DAY THOMAS PYNCHON stopped by at the *Gazette* asking for me. We met in a quiet part of the office where we could talk uninterrupted.

"Christopher, Colonel Mason tells me that you and your friends from the future acquitted yourself well in Charlestown. I'm delighted to see that you seem in good health and survived the battle uninjured. I'm equally delighted that, once you became part of our century you were willing to do your part for the Provincial cause."

"Thank you for that, sir. I appreciate it. Yes, I believe all of us now feel that your cause is our cause. This is now our century." I could see that he was pleased that I'd said that.

"I was wondering if we couldn't arrange for another meeting of you, your friends from the future and the Social Library trustees who are familiar with your background. Since the meeting in May, we have thought of so many more questions about the future that we're practically bursting with curiosity. Of course, we would continue to honor our pledge of absolute secrecy and would do so in the future. Do you suppose you could persuade your friends to make themselves available one more time for perhaps an hour and a half sometime in the next week or two? It would be in the evening so as not to interfere with anyone's work. In a very real way, those of us on the Social Library board share a bond with you four newcomers."

"I'll be happy to talk to my friends about this. I would think that they would be quite willing, but I can't speak for them. I would, however, ask one thing."

"Certainly. What is it you have in mind?"

"I would hope that Jeremiah Weeks and Sam Hall will be included once again."

"Of course. Then you think we can do this?"

"I do, but as I said, I should talk to the others before giving you a definite answer."

Pynchon started to leave, but then turned around and said, "Oh, one other thought."

"Yes?"

"It occurred to me that with your knowledge of the future you could perhaps share useful information that our generals could use in fighting against our British oppressors. You might just share any thoughts you have with Colonel Mason who could pass it on the higher command. Your knowledge of how things are going to evolve might help us prevent some loss of lives. If our military leaders knew what you know they might modify their strategy. Now that I think of it, you know how this all ends, don't you?"

I had feared that someone might ask us to do this. The four of us newcomers had discussed it and agreed that it was not an easy question to deal with. We decided that we had to decline any such requests knowing that it would sound uncaring to whomever requested it. I wrestled with Pynchon's request and finally smiled as I said, "You, too, know how this ends. The four of us from the future came here from the United States of America. That tells you that the ending is a happy one for you and those who come after you.

"As for your suggestion that we go to Colonel Mason, the four of us discussed this at great length and concluded that it would be a mistake to try to advise the people in charge of our military. For one thing, it would mean a lot more people would have to know about our origin. That in itself could open up all kinds of unfortunate situations. From a practical standpoint Colonel Mason would have to convince General Ward or General Washington that we come from the future. In itself, not an easy thing to do, as you well know. The generals would probably think Colonel Mason had taken leave of his senses. But even if he were successful in persuading them that we come from the future, there's no way of knowing how our advice would affect the success or failure of the army's efforts. As you already know, the outcome is good. If we interfere, no matter how good our intentions, things might go worse, not better. No, the four of us are willing to do our part when it comes to fighting for the Patriot cause, but we think it could be dangerous to get involved in the army's tactics or strategy."

Pynchon nodded his understanding and said, "I suppose you're right. It was just a thought."

"I hope this won't come up at the meeting at the Social Library."

"Well I certainly won't bring it up."

A week later the four of us from the future were sitting at a long table in front of a small group of men at the Social Library. Board members included Board president, Thomas Pynchon, Samuel Cabot, Nathaniel Ellis, Elihu Martin, Joseph Blaney, Timothy Arne, the Reverend Thomas Barnard, and Joseph Bowditch. Also present were Sam Hall, Jeremiah Weeks, the librarian and Jedediah Talbot. Inviting Talbot had its risks, but better to have him feel that he was a part of the inner circle than on the outside looking in.

Suddenly it hit me. The man I'd seen eyeing us in Pierce's Tavern was Nathaniel Ellis, one of the library trustees. Why had he been so interested, and why didn't he come over to our booth and say hello, since he was so obviously interested in us?

The men sitting before us were chatting among themselves. I could see they were eager to begin, hoping to get answers to questions that had been nagging at them for several months. They first learned of our background when Gil and Tom tried to persuade the Social Library to accept a time capsule containing Gil's log of their experiences since lifting off from the Nevada desert in 2015. It had been decided back in Nevada that such a time capsule was the best way to communicate Gil and Tom's experiences from the past back to the 21st century. The Social Library board was reluctant to grant them permission unless they could prove they were who they said they were. Tom and Gil then decided the best way to do that was to take them to the spot in the ocean where their spaceship had entered the water. If they could access the ship, the board had to believe them. That's what they did and now the board wanted to learn more.

Thomas Pynchon rose from his seat and addressed all 14 of us.

"Members of the Social Library Board of Trustees, Sam Hall of the *Essex Gazette*, and Jeremiah Weeks, our very own librarian, I welcome you once more to an informal meeting where I hope we shall get answers to questions that have come up in these few weeks since Gilbert, Thomas, Christopher and Matthew obliged us with a fascinating exchange of ideas. Gilbert and Thomas, we are glad that you have obliged us by coming tonight to respond to some of our inquiries. And Christopher and Matthew, welcome to the Social Library. You are now honorary members of the library along with Gilbert and Thomas whenever you wish to make use of our facilities. And now, without further chatter from me, why don't we open this meeting by asking some questions. Do I see any hands?"

Samuel Cabot lifted his heavy torso from his seat. He was the only bewhiskered man present. "Gentlemen, I ask this of any of you who wishes to answer. Can you tell us how a typical day in the 21st century differs from such a day in the 18th century? I think such an explanation would be quite edifying."

This was no quick and easy question. I could see that my friends were not volunteering so I said, "I will give it a try, Mr. Cabot. The typical day changed dramatically over 240 years. Let's see. In the morning my digital alarm clock would wake me up. I would then start my coffee maker while I was getting dressed. While eating breakfast I would check my email on my cell phone." By now several hands had shot up.

I pointed to one and said, "Yes, Mr. Orne. I have a feeling I know what you're going to ask."

"I would imagine you would. Tell us what a digital alarm clock is? I can guess at alarm, but I'm at a loss at the word digital."

"It's an electric clock that displays the time in illuminated numerals. The alarm part is a buzz or sound that is loud enough to wake you at the time you have previously set on the clock." As I explained this I realized that even my explanation needed explanation.

"Electric?"

"Yes, the clock is powered by electricity. In 2019 many things are powered by electricity. The lights in our houses, our stoves, our radios, our television sets. Even our computers."

Joseph Blaney stood up and said, "I believe you're going much too fast for us, Mr. Carver. How does one acquire this electricity in the first place? I know that Mr. Franklin observed this electric fire 25 years ago, but it is a natural phenomenon, not something you can use to light your house."

I turned to Matt and said, "You want to take this?"

Matt rose and said, "In the next century scientists will learn how to harness electricity so that it can be used to provide power for the kinds of things Chris just mentioned. Electric lights can be connected to electricity by cords we call cables. The electricity enters our houses through a larger cable. That larger cable is connected to what we call a power plant where the electricity is generated. The power plant is fueled by waterpower, coal or oil."

Blaney said, "I can see that an hour and a half is not going to be sufficient for us to understand much of what you are trying to explain. It is hard enough for us to comprehend electric lighting. It's even more difficult to understand how you can generate electricity and deliver it to a house and then deliver it to those electric lights. Then you mentioned other things that we have never even heard of. This is too much, I'm afraid. The house of the 21st century must be quite different from the houses of this century."

Matt then turned it over to Gil Lee, who said, "We have lived here in Salem for more than half a year and can tell you something about how different they are. In the 21st century houses have central heating. Heating is not provided by a fireplace or a stove. It is piped into every room and can be controlled by a switch on the wall. If you want it hotter, you turn the heat up. If you want it cooler, you turn it down. They also have air conditioning, which means that in the summer when it's hot you can cool the rooms of your house." As he said this he saw the members of his audience gasp in disbelief. He moved on before any hands were raised.

"The 21st century house also has running water. By that I mean pipes bring both hot and cold water into the kitchen and the bathrooms. There is no need for bedpans because your bathrooms have flush toilets. By that I mean you press a handle or lever, and water flushes your wastes away through pipes that take those wastes to a waste disposal plant several miles away. Another difference between 1775 and 2019 is how we get our food. In 2019 we have huge shops called supermarkets. Many of them carry more than 50,000 items. The selection is enormous. Butchered meats and fish are available in various size portions both fresh and frozen. People sometimes purchase frozen food because they have electric-powered freezers in their homes to keep them until they are ready to eat them. Other foods come in metal cans and plastic containers." When he saw eyebrows raised, Gil then tried to explain plastic.

Jeremiah Weeks, the librarian raised his hand and said, "What you've described, Gilbert, sounds like a fantasy world. I assume only the very wealthy can afford such marvelous living accommodations?"

"Actually, that's not true, Jeremiah. Every house or apartment has these facilities. The wealthy have more of them or more elaborate versions, but nearly everyone has these conveniences in the 21st century. I should correct that. Nearly everyone in the developed world. There are still countries in parts of the world that lag behind the developed nations.

"Oh, I almost forgot. There are some buildings with many floors. Some have as many as 100 or more. People get to these floors in something called an elevator. That's a small cubicle that can carry several people from one floor to another simply by pressing a button." As Gil said this a hush fell over the assemblage. It was as if all of this was too much for them to assimilate.

Jeremiah Weeks said, "I think I speak for most of us, Gilbert, when I say that you have taken our breath away. This is almost too much to believe."

Another board member, Elihu Martin, rose and said, "Yes, I agree, this is almost too much to believe. I'm not sure I do. Nevertheless, in the spirit of this mental adventure, you mentioned a number of things which are completely new to us. One of them, I believe was called a radio. Can you tell us what that is?"

"A radio is a device that brings voices into your home by way of wave energy in the air. Our radios bring us news, music, entertainment of various sorts. We can now receive radio on some of our cell phones. We can even . . ."

Martin broke in. "What do you mean wave energy through the air. How do you do that?"

"Over the centuries scientists will discover at least seven different kinds of radiation in our environment. They're all invisible, but they're quite real and they're quite important. Radio waves can carry sound through the air. X-rays can penetrate your body and give physicians clear images of what's inside you. There are also gamma rays. The sun's rays consist of ultraviolet light and they can give you sunburn. You're all aware of the rays of the sun so when I tell you there are other kinds it might help you understand what I'm saying."

"I don't know about that, Mr. Lee. I never thought about sunburn as coming from rays, as you call them. All these things you are telling us demand too much from our imaginations. Yes, they sound amazing, but we have no evidence that they are anything but figments of your over-inflated imagination."

"You were present when we took you to our spaceship off Great Misery Island several months ago. And you were present at our recent meeting where Christopher and Matthew demonstrated their cell phone cameras. What more proof do you need?"

"As fascinating as those demonstrations were, they do not prove the existence of your so-called radios or central heating or toilets that carry away human waste or buildings with a hundred floors."

"No, they don't. I don't know how I can convince you, if you don't believe us now?"

Pynchon stood and said, "I don't see why you are challenging the honesty of these young men, Elihu. Good grief, how much more evidence do you need to believe that these men are who they say they are?"

"It's just that what they've described is so fantastical that I find it too much to believe. Frankly, I can't understand why you accept such nonsense."

I stood up. We had to put a stop to this if we could. "Gentlemen. I have something here that might help convince any of you who still have doubts. Before I show you, though, I hope you bear in mind that the only reason we have told you about the wonders of the future is that you have asked us to. We have nothing to gain whether we tell you or keep this information to ourselves." At this I saw nods of understanding from half a dozen in our little audience.

"What I'm holding in my hand is what we call a pocket translator. I can select two languages, one of which is my own—English. Let's say the other language is French. Does anyone here speak French? Four hands shot up. A better percentage than you'd find in 21st century America. One of the hands belonged to Samuel Cabot. I turned to him and said, "I'm going to ask you something in English, sir. If you would respond appropriately in French, I can show you how this little device works." He shook his head indicating he understood. I approached him and held the translator within a few feet of the man.

"What day of the month is it today?"

"*C'est la vingt-cinqième du mois aujourd'hui.*"

As soon as he'd spoken the French, the translator said aloud the

English translation: *"It's the twenty-fifth of the month today."*

The look of surprise on the faces of the audience showed me that most of them needed no more convincing. Elihu Martin frowned, but said nothing. I then showed the audience that the response was also written in English on the little screen.

Thomas Pynchon shook his head in awe. "You do not have to say anything more to convince us, gentlemen. If this is just a taste of what you have in your 21st century, then it truly is a fantasy world from our perspective. I see that we still have a little time left. Would you indulge us by telling us about, I believe you called it a television?"

"Of course," I said. "Television is a remarkable invention that allows the viewer to see what's happening many miles away. Actually, anywhere in the world."

"What do you mean, Christopher when you say *'see what's happening?'*"

"Television crews use cameras. They direct their cameras at something. It could be news that is happening at that very moment. Or it could be a theatrical presentation for the entertainment of the viewer. In the year 2019 they usually record such entertainment so that the viewer can select what presentation he or she wants to see when it is convenient for them. As for news, the camera crew might direct their camera at a politician making a speech. Probably one of the most spectacular news events was when men first landed on the moon and sent moving pictures of it back to viewers on Earth."

Elihu Martin stood up. "The sort of things you're talking about, Mr. Carver, are so fantastical that I can't help wondering if they aren't the ravings one might hear from a witch?"

Witchcraft had been considered inappropriate and off limits since the Witch Trials of 1692. Yet people in Europe were still being accused of witchcraft. Eighteen people were executed in Poland in the 18th century. Three were tortured to death and 11 were burned at the stake. I couldn't believe what the man had said. If people sided with him the four of us from the 21st century could be in big trouble.

"Are you accusing my friends and me of being witches, sir? If so, that is a terrible and serious accusation."

When he heard the resounding silence that took possession of the room, I think Martin must have realized that he'd spoken recklessly. "Not necessarily. It's just that I find it hard to believe the explanation you and your friends are offering for these wild imaginative stories you're telling."

"Weren't you at the site near Great Misery Island when we brought our spaceship up from the ocean floor? Surely that alone should have convinced you that we're not making this up."

"I was not there. I believe I'm the only library trustee who wasn't, so I didn't see this bit of skillful deception you played on my over-trustful fellow trustees."

"I turned to Pynchon and said, "Why was Mr. Martin invited tonight if he was not among the trustees who viewed that ship raising? I thought we were not going to expand the group?"

"I'm afraid that is my fault, Christopher. I just invited all the trustees, forgetting that Elihu had not joined us that day near the island. I am deeply apologetic to you and to Elihu for putting him in this embarrassing situation."

I said, "Are you not embarrassed that four of us here have just been accused of witchcraft?"

"Of course I am, Christopher. Elihu, I would be obliged if you would temper your comments. There is no good reason to think that these four young men are anything but what they say they are."

Martin rose angrily. "I have been a member in good standing on this board for almost eight years. I have never been told to hold my tongue before and I will not be told that by you, Thomas! As for these four newcomers among us, we really don't know much about them other than that they have made outrageous claims about coming to us from the far distant future. It is they who should be apologizing to us for insulting us with such nonsense."

Samuel Cabot rose and said, "That is a ridiculous statement, Elihu. They have nothing to apologize for. While it is true that they have only been among us for a short time, from what I have seen and heard from others, they have been exemplary members of the community."

Martin jumped up again. I could see that he now felt the need to defend his ridiculous accusations.

"Gentlemen, if these young men are so exemplary, I suggest that we hold our own court of *oyer and terminer* to put that claim to the test. If they are as pure as you seem to think they are, they should have nothing to fear. I think my fellow Salemites of Puritan heritage would feel a lot better if these men had been examined thoroughly so as to ensure that the Demon was not in their midst."

"Dear God, Elihu. You Puritans no longer dictate policy in this colony. Your influence died when the first court of *Oyer and Terminer* was terminated after those terrible trials back in '92. I think you're living in the past, my friend."

"If you no longer believe in Puritan purity, then you are not my friend, Samuel. I suggest that we take a vote to see how many of us would feel more comfortable if these four newcomers amongst us were properly examined. What have any of us to fear if these men are truly who they say they are. But if they are not, then you must think about that. If they are not from the future, but controlled by the Evil One, all of us have much to fear." He paused to let his words sink in. After a full minute, he said, "All those in favor of having these men examined by a court of *Oyer and Terminer,* raise your hands?"

Martin instantly thrust his hand into the air. Then Nathaniel Ellis slowly raised his. I couldn't believe my eyes.

I looked at my fellow chrononauts. We were all flabbergasted at the sudden turn of events and suddenly fearful for our very safety. At least I was. We believed that we couldn't die, but what Martin was proposing could put that belief to the test. I couldn't believe that educated men would seriously consider his proposal. It was ridiculous. But then I realized that it was only 82 years since the Salem Witch Trials. My grandfather has been alive longer than that. Belief in witches was waning in the 18th century, but obviously some people still took it seriously enough to think about putting someone on trial to determine if they were witches.

Martin kept scanning the room looking for more votes. "Who else wants to examine these pretenders?"

Cabot rose and roared, "I am shocked that even one trustee would stoop so low. The fact that two of you did is appalling and makes me sick. Christopher, Matthew, Gilbert and Thomas you have my apologies for the behavior of these two disappointing trustees." As he finished saying this Martin and Ellis rose from their seats and headed for the door.

Martin turned and said, "You have not heard the last of this, I promise you. All four of you. You will rue the day you ever set foot in Salem."

Cabot shook his head in despair. "In all my years in Salem I have not seen the likes of this. This is truly an embarrassment and we owe the four of you gentlemen an apology for this insult to your integrity and reputation. I hope you understand that this is not the sentiment of this board?"

Gil rose and said, "I think I can speak for all of us when I say we do not hold the board responsible for what Mr. Martin said tonight. It was disappointing, but I would hope that only he and Mr. Ellis hold these views. I understand that it is hard for people to accept that we have come from the future. If I were you, I would find it difficult. But the fact of the matter is our scientists made it happen. I should stress that we have not flaunted our origin. Just the opposite as you in this room know. We had nothing to gain from revealing our background, and as you can see, we gain only grief when we do reveal it."

A few days later Elihu Martin left his office after work at the usual time. He lived only a few blocks from his office, so he was not using his carriage but walking home. It was a pleasant night, and he was feeling good about how he'd set those arrogant young men back a bit. Maybe more than a bit. Since the meeting at the Social Library, he'd thought a lot about how things had gone. In particular he thought about the four young men and their amazing stories. Maybe they weren't witches, but how else could one explain their magic? He certainly wasn't going to buy their absurd explanation about being sent here from the 21st century. The other trustees seemed to have fallen for it, but he'd long ago learned that most people would accept anything if someone spoke well and had a decent appearance. Face it, his fellow trustees were gullible. Well, he wasn't. Sooner or later they'd see what he was perceptive enough to see instantly: These young men were clever fraudulent tricksters. They had apparently successfully fooled his fellow trustees, but definitely not him. Despite his unpleasant departure, he felt rather good about himself.

He was so involved in his thoughts that he was completely oblivious to the man following him a few yards back. The brick sidewalk absorbed much of the sound made by the man's cautious footsteps.

As he came within a few yards of his front door the man came up from behind him and said, "Nothing personal, Mr. Martin. You're making this sacrifice for the greater good."

Before he could react, he felt a sharp pain in his back. He didn't recognize the voice and he tried to turn and see his attacker. His body didn't respond, though. He no longer had the strength to do anything. His last thought was how well he'd performed in front of both his fellow trustees and the clever deceivers.

Chapter 31

July 29

A FEW DAYS AFTER the Social Library meeting, Sam Hall rushed over to me with a pained expression on his normally cheerful face.

"Good morning, Sam. What's wrong? You don't look so happy."

"I'm not. Elihu Martin was found dead last night!"

"What happened?"

"He was murdered. Stabbed to death in front of his house."

"I don't suppose anyone knows who did it?"

No. The killer got away. I never liked the man, but now I'm concerned that this is going to lead to more trouble."

"What kind of trouble?"

"Trouble for you and your friends. You people from the future."

"Us? Why would we . . .?" Then it hit me. "Oh. I see what you're getting at. Because he accused us of being witches, people might think we killed him. That's ridiculous."

"Of course, it's ridiculous. It was ridiculous that he accused you. When people get themselves in a state, they sometimes do ridiculous things. Don't pass this off lightly, Christopher. People are going to accuse one or all of you." I started to talk, but he held his hand up and said, "Wait. There's more. There was a piece of paper found on his body."

"What did it say?"

"It was just a crude drawing of a peaked hat and a broom."

Suddenly my mood changed for the worse. "I see."

"Yes. Someone is obviously trying to blame you and your friends."

"Then we have to find out who did kill him."

"We should leave it to Constable Gray, Christopher."

"How much can the constable do? Will he really be able to track down the killer? Has he ever investigated a homicide?"

"I doubt if he has. He has three or four bellmen or town criers. I assume he'll utilize them when they're not walking the streets at night calling out the time and watching for troublemakers. I think one of them is a marshal. Let's hope that they're successful. They don't often have to deal with murders. I can't remember a murder in Salem, and I've lived here most of my adult life. If they find it difficult, they might contact Colonel Mason and ask for the aid of some of his militiamen. No one is going to take this dreadful event lightly. Salem is known as a very safe place to live. We can't afford to tarnish that reputation." Suddenly Hall realized that he'd sounded rather insensitive. "And we don't want you and your friends being accused of murder. A terrible way to treat newcomers."

"Yes, it is, Sam. I doubt if Mason's militiamen have any experience investigating murders either. Do Gil and Tom know about this?"

"Yes. It was Tom who told me. Someone he met on his way into the office this morning. Simon Fields. Elihu Martin's law partner."

"So what can we do, Sam? We can't just ignore it and hope for the best."

"We can treat it as a serious news story that needs to be investigated. I assume you and your friends will be more than willing to look into this. Just be careful. Whoever did this is obviously a dangerous person."

Before we could do anything, Constable Gray appeared at the office. He asked to see Gil, Tom and myself. Constable William Gray was a tall, powerfully built man of about 50. I immediately changed my mind about him. For some reason I'd expected him to be little more than an insignificant figurehead, not the capable law enforcement officer he appeared to be as he stood before me. I made this assessment before he even opened his mouth. When he did talk, he confirmed my first impression.

"Mr. Carver, we need to talk. Is there somewhere where we can go?"

"We have a meeting room. I'm sure Sam won't mind." The meeting room was what we called a conference room in 2019.

When we were seated in the small room, Gray said, "Tell me where you were Thursday night?"

"I was home. Here in Salem. I assume you're looking into the murder of Elihu Martin?"

"If you don't mind, I'll ask the questions, but yes, It's about Mr. Martin. Can you prove you were at home?"

"No, I don't think I can. I live alone, and I don't know if anyone saw me go home. Why are you asking me?"

"It's my understanding that you both attended a meeting at the Social Library a few nights ago and that Mr. Martin insulted you. Is that correct?"

"Yes, but that doesn't mean I killed him."

"I understand that three of your friends were present at that meeting also. Is that true?"

"Yes." I wondered how much more he knew. Did he know the truth about where the four us came from?

"And Mr. Martin insulted all of you?"

"Yes, I suppose he did."

"He called you witches. Is that right?"

"Not exactly. He suggested that we might be witches."

"And you took offense at this?"

"Of course we did. Wouldn't you?"

"This is not about me. Why did Mr. Martin suggest that you might be witches?"

I didn't want to answer this. I considered how I could answer safely without revealing too much. I went through different scenarios in my mind.

"Mr. Carver, I asked you a question."

"I suppose it was because I have started writing about my views of how things might be in the distant future. I just wrote an article about flying machines in the *Gazette*. I admit that some of the things I wrote seem somewhat fantastical, but they are only the product of my overactive imagination."

"It's one thing to talk like that in normal conversation with someone close to you, sir. It's quite another to give it credence by publishing it in a respected newspaper. Did you not realize how provocative such an article might be?"

"I didn't claim that my imaginative flying machines were real. It was just meant as something to stimulate the imaginations of readers."

"Well, in any event, I can see how an upstanding citizen might wonder about you and your friends. It was reckless of you. But back to the matter at hand. I can also see why you and your friends would take offense at being called witches. As we all know, being accused of witchcraft can be deadly. It's unfortunate that you can't account for your whereabouts last night after you left the meeting at the Social Library."

"I hope you're not accusing me and my friends of this murder. I understand that piece of paper with drawings of a peaked hat and a broom were found on his body."

"How do you know about that?"

"One of my friends met Martin's law partner this morning. He told him about it."

"I'm afraid that that little piece of paper does you no good, Mr. Carver. Can you explain it?"

"Would an intelligent person kill someone and then deliberately leave something that might incriminate himself? We're obviously being set up."

The constable looked confused. "I don't take your meaning?"

"We're being made scapegoats by the real killer. The drawings on that paper are too obvious to be believable."

"That may or may not be true. Some people can't help themselves when it comes to revenge. The murder was not the result of a robbery because his pocketbook contained a number of banknotes. We will leave it at that for now, Mr. Carver. I want to talk to each of your three friends before I make my decision."

"Are you saying that you're not even considering the possibility that someone else might be the killer?"

"All I can say now is that I may want to talk to you again, so you should not leave Salem."

After I left the meeting room, I saw Gil enter. I had to hope that he didn't say anything that might contradict what I'd told the constable. I'd said that, because of the article I wrote about flying machines, Martin might have thought I was a witch. I know it sounds crazy, but this was 1775, not 2019. I hadn't mentioned our 21st century origins. I hoped that Gil didn't go beyond that and get closer to the actual truth. I had to hope, too, that Tom and Matt didn't deviate far from what I'd said, either.

That was too much to hope for because none of the other three knew what I'd told Constable Gray. I suddenly realized that I had to tell the truth or this whole business would get out of hand. Better that the top law enforcement officer in town know the truth than feed him a pack of lies that would only be found out eventually anyway. Lies, even innocent ones, almost certainly would land me in an 18th century jail cell. I could imagine how comfy that would be. Maybe I wouldn't die, but spending my life in a Salem jail cell was not my idea of a great life.

"Constable, I need to tell you something else." He just stared at me, so I proceeded. "I didn't tell you this before, because I knew you wouldn't believe me."

"I'm not sure I believe what you've told me so far."

"Well this will only give you more doubts, but if you'll hear me out, I think I can convince you that I'm telling the truth. My three friends and I came to Salem from the 21st century."

I could see that Constable Gray wanted to laugh, but he stifled it and said, "I don't think you realize what trouble you're in, sir. How you could make jokes at a time like this makes me wonder about the soundness of your mind, sir."

"Please let me go on. If you hear me out, you will see that I'm telling you the truth."

I could see that he was losing his patience, but he said, "Speak fast and it better be good."

"Maybe if I you show you something, it will help you understand." I pulled my cell phone from my pocket and said, "This little device is what we call a cell phone where I come from. It contains both a telephone and a camera." Gray shook his head in bewilderment.

"I have no idea what you're talking about. It's a curious device, but what does it do that would make me believe your nonsensical claptrap?" As impatient as he was, I could tell that he was also just a little bit curious.

I took a selfie of myself and showed it to him.

"Dear God. How did you do that? You truly are a witch!" This was not the reaction I was looking for.

"I am not a witch. This is called a camera. Perhaps you have heard of the *camera obscura*?"

"Yes, yes. Of course. But that is much larger, and you cannot carry the image around with you like this."

I explained about the invention of the camera and how over the years the camera evolved to the point where it became a part of what we call our cell phones. I took a little more time to explain phones.

I took a picture of him and showed it to him. He was blown away. Then I said, "When I was at Bunker Hill I took some pictures of the fighting." I then showed him some of the horrendous battle scenes.

"I can't believe what I'm seeing. This is truly some sort of magic."

"It's not magic. It's science. Our scientists have created many things that would amaze you. They also created motion pictures." I showed him a video of the fighting at Bunker Hill."

"Good Lord. I can't believe what I'm seeing. Why have I not heard of this before?"

"Because we have not wanted it to become generally known. If too many people know about this and know about where we came from it could change the history as we know it in the 21st century. At first it might seem harmless to you in this century, but if you think about it, a few small changes in what occur in 1775 could have a huge effect on what we in the 21st century believe is our history. It might actually create wars that haven't happened. I can't make you, but I can beg you not to reveal what I've told you to anyone else."

"I cannot exonerate you unless I explain to others why I'm exonerating you. You see the dilemma, don't you?"

I did. "Yes, of course. Perhaps it will be easier if I tell you that nine other people here in Salem know of our origin. They are sworn to secrecy. The only reason I've told you about our origin is that there seems to be no other way to convince you that my friends and I are not witches." I went on to explain why the other nine knew it. I quickly summarized how Gil and Tom had approached the Social Library for permission to leave a time capsule containing Gil's account of their trip back in time to Salem. As I recounted this, Constable Gray shook his head slowly from side to side. Was he believing me or was he simply admiring my ability to tell a wild story?

"All right," he said. "That's quite a story. I'm going to have to

———

confirm it by talking to one or two of these nine people. Do you have a problem with that?"

"No. I suppose that's the only way you'll believe me. But let me know who you'll be talking to. Since they're honorable people, they may not want to confirm my story if I don't tell them it's all right to do so."

I could see he was wrestling with this. After a brief moment he said, "I'm not going to let you talk to them first. When I decide who to talk to you can go with me and tell them then in my presence. You can go back to work now. Don't talk to either one of you friends until I've talked to them. I'm sure I'll be seeing you again soon."

Chapter 32

July 29

WHEN I LEFT CONSTABLE GRAY Sam came over to me and asked, "How did it go?"

"It could have gone better. I had to tell him about our past. He needed to verify what I told him, so I told him that you and eight others also knew. He's going to talk to one or two of you to check to see that I was telling the truth. Quite honestly, I don't know if he believed me. I don't know what he thought. We'll see how it goes."

"It's not good that more people know about this, but I can see that you had to tell him. Listen, Christopher, I've been thinking about all this. I don't suppose you know, but Elihu Martin has long been a controversial figure here in Salem. Not many people liked him."

"Why was he so unpopular? I know from my own experience that the man could be quite unpleasant."

"That was typical of how he treated people. He had a reputation for making accusations—often unfounded accusations. He once accused a man of being an atheist or being possessed by the antichrist. He did it so often and so publicly that the man and his family had to leave Salem. One time he accused a greengrocer of being a Tory. I know the shopkeeper, and the man is definitely not a Tory. Still, many people stopped patronizing his shop after that. Martin felt strongly about witches. Nearly all of the people he accused of one thing or another, he hinted that it was because they were possessed. I fear he's not alone, either. While most people no longer fear witchcraft, a few, nay, more than a few still think that Satan takes possession of some poor souls. Some call it the Devil, some the antichrist, but whatever they call it, they fear possession as much as our grandparents did 80 years ago.

"Elihu Martin should not have been murdered, but frankly, I'm not at all surprised that he was. I know for a fact that he often beat his slave. She was a good worker and a kind person and didn't deserve to be beaten." As Sam told me this it sounded as if he believed the slave might have deserved a beating if she had not been a good worker or a kind person. Sam was one of the enlightened ones I'd come in contact with in my brief time in Salem. I knew from previous conversations that Sam hoped someday to see the end of slavery, but slavery was such a part of 18th century culture, that he accepted it as a given for the time being anyway. At times it was unpleasant, but like poverty and disease, it was a part of normal life.

Slavery wasn't as common or as big a part of the economy here in New England as it was in the southern colonies, but the occasional well-to-do homeowner had servants who were slaves, and nobody seemed to give the practice much thought. At least not openly.

I nodded repeatedly as Sam rattled off examples of Martin's nastiness. When he stopped for a moment I said, "So what you seem to be suggesting is that his killer could be any one of a number of people he inflicted pain on."

"Exactly. I'm going to give you back issues of the *Gazette* where we wrote about some of these instances. If one or more of his victims seems worthy of our attention again, maybe we could suggest to Constable Gray that he take a close look at them. I'm sure you want to help the good constable in any way you can." I definitely did. In fact, I thought maybe Gil, Tom, Matt and I might do some sniffing around ourselves. Anything to get the law off our own tails.

"Yes. Gladly. Obviously, someone out there in the community didn't like Elihu Martin. Someone out there hated him enough to kill him and tried rather awkwardly to place the blame on us. I suppose, though, it could be someone else entirely. It could be someone who feels strongly about witchcraft. . . someone who feels so strongly that they were willing to kill an unpopular member of the community as a way of getting at the witches. I know most people today don't fear witches the way they did back in '92, so the murderer must have felt that actually killing someone would get people's attention—make people believe that witches were still present and just as evil as people feared in the last century."

"Yes, Christopher. That's good reasoning. It might be something like you suggest. It could be someone we aren't considering. Still, I think these old articles might be a good place to start."

I told him I'd get right on it. I didn't have any better idea. We had to find this guy before someone else got killed. I had a feeling, though, that it wasn't one of the people Martin had had run-ins with in the past. It had to be someone who knew that we were from the future, or at least someone who knew we had a reputation for knowing what was going to happen before it actually happened. That narrowed it down to people we knew or at least had some contact with. Or maybe people who knew people we knew.

Then I said, "What about the other man who walked out of the meeting with Martin…Nathaniel Ellis? You haven't mentioned that he agreed with Martin."

Chapter 33

July 29

SO FAR, SO GOOD. Yes, the constable was investigating. Gray was a God-fearing man. He was fine with calling out the time and catching the occasional minor thief, but the good constable had never arrested a killer in his 20 years as a town crier and more recently as a constable.

He wasn't worried about himself. It was unlikely that Gray would even suspect Talbot. Talbot had been the perfect choice. He lived out of town, so no one would even think of him. The young man cared deeply about the ever-present threat of the possessed ones in the community. Talbot presented himself as an ordinary citizen. He wasn't constantly harping on the threat of witchcraft as Martin had, so no one would ever suspect him. Best of all, he obviously had no compunction about plunging a knife into the heart of someone if it was necessary. A lot of people shared his concern for the threat the possessed among us posed, but most of those same people were too squeamish to do anything about it. . . even when it served the greater good. Yes, young Jedediah had been the perfect choice.

It all started with these four new men who seemed to have magical powers. Magical powers that only Satan could possess. These four newcomers were a real threat to the peaceful community of Salem. This is why he'd persuaded Talbot to kill Martin. These evil newcomers could not be allowed to exist in Salem.

Hopefully Gray would eventually realize that Carver and the three other three newcomers were the real threats in Salem. Yes, the newcomers seemed pleasant enough. They appeared to get along with people. But wasn't that what made people possessed by the Evil One so dangerous? They could pretend to be anything they wanted to be. But the evidence was there. He had seen for himself what magic these people were capable of. Amazing things. Things that would astonish or bewilder the good citizens of Salem. He could see how these newcomers could charm and bedazzle the average citizen. Soon the entire community would come under their spell. Something had to be done, and he'd done it. Yes, he'd sacrificed one life, but it was the life of a troublesome, vexatious man, so it was a just sacrifice. It was true that philosophically he and Martin had agreed about the danger witches presented to the community, but Martin was an unpleasant man. . . a man who called anyone he disagreed with a witch. He gave those of us who know real witches when we see them a bad name. You can't recklessly accuse just anybody if you don't have a good reason. As a fellow trustee, Martin would eventually have given the library a bad name. It's good that he was gone. The hardest thing for him now was to act as if he wanted the killer of Elihu Martin to be found. Obviously, that's the last thing he wanted. He wanted the four newcomers to be openly accused of witchcraft.

Most of the people he knew pretended that they were ashamed of the Witch Trials. They considered them a terrible mistake. Yet he was convinced that many of those same people secretly knew the truth . . . they secretly wished that the Trials had finished the job. People were more enlightened today. Today most people knew that the real witches were often too clever to be caught. Clever like these four young men who claimed to be from the future. It was not easy to find the true witches because the Evil One was brilliant. He could take any form and the cleverest was when he masqueraded as likable, God-fearing citizens like these four visitors from afar. They would have gotten away with it, too, if they hadn't flaunted their magic. Fortunately, he was not taken in by their clever disguises.

Chapter 34

July 30

GIL, TOM AND I went over the old articles about Elihu Martin's conflicts with others in the community. We did it separately, and when we came together to talk about them, we all came to the same conclusion: The killer had to be somebody who knew us or at least had met us. We're the new people in town with the new technology that some would interpret as witchcraft. That excluded the men we read about in the old articles. More than likely the killer had either attended one of our meetings at the Social Library where we demonstrated some of our 21st century technology or he knew somebody who had attended. We also concluded that this person still had an abiding fear of witchcraft. We told this to Sam Hall, and I could tell that he didn't want to accept it.

"The men on the Social Library board are among the most prominent men in all of Salem. It must be someone else."

I said, "Elihu Martin was a board trustee, and you saw his performance that night just before someone killed him. He might have been prominent, but he wasn't very sensitive or very tactful."

"Yes, he was a trustee, but I never thought he belonged there. The others are solid. I assure you, Christopher."

"I'm sure they are. They certainly seem to be anyway. Still, you do see that our killer has to be someone who either knows our secret or knows someone who does?"

"Yes, your logic is impeccable."

"We've only been in Salem a short time so that can't be many people. Eight or nine at most. The board members, Jeremy Weeks and you. I suppose it could also be someone who heard about our secret, but that would mean that one of the eight or nine had betrayed their trust and spoken about us to someone when they shouldn't have. Let's say that happened. Then our eight or nine expands to ten or possibly even more. Apparently, our so-called magic has set this killer off. He or she must really be concerned about witchcraft.

"You mentioned she. You don't seriously think it could be a woman, do you?"

"No, probably not. In the 21ˢᵗ century people it could be a woman." I paused a moment, then said, "In the 21ˢᵗ century women play a much more prominent role in society. They're more involved in important roles in the culture. It's considered insensitive not to mention women when you aren't sure which gender you're talking about. You say 'he or she,' not 'he' as you're accustomed to in this century when you're not sure which gender it is.

"That should make an interesting discussion at another time. Right now we need to help the constable find who did this terrible deed. I'm finding it difficult to believe that it could be one of the seven remaining library trustees, and I can assure you, Christopher, that I am not the killer."

"Oh my gosh, Sam. That had not even crossed my mind. If it's not you or any of the trustees, that leaves Jeremy Weeks. I can't believe it's Jeremy, either."

As we went through these possibilities, it came to me that we hadn't included Jedediah Talbot, the Lynn schoolteacher, as one of our possibilities. I had never told Sam about him, as I wasn't proud that we'd included him into our exclusive little group. Jedediah had already made Matt and me regret ever sharing our secret background with him. It had been a moment of weakness. A moment of hubris, I suppose. Could Jedediah be a killer? As I thought about it, how well did Matt and I know really him? We did know that he has a temper and that he resented our unwillingness to share our secret with his friend.

How would a detective look at this? He or she would consider means, motive and opportunity. I suppose Jed had motive. Did he have opportunity or means? He could easily have had the means. All he needed was a sharp knife. But opportunity? He lived in Lynn, which was the next town south of Salem. In 2019, that would not have presented a logistical problem, but in 1775 getting to Salem took time. If he lived in the northern part of Lynn, he could have gotten to the middle of Salem in an hour or so. If he lived further south, it would take longer. But to commit the crime he'd first have to know about the meeting at the Social Library and he'd have to know who the trustees were in order to choose Martin as his victim. If he did know a lot about what was going on in Salem, he could have created the opportunity. That's a lot of ifs. Regardless of the ifs, I found it hard to believe that a schoolteacher could be a murderer. But maybe that was just my own misguided assumption that schoolteachers were more virtuous than other people. Why couldn't a schoolteacher be a killer?

If Jed had the means, motive and opportunity, so did the board trustees. The difference was that none of them had been angry at Matt and me. I decided I had to tell Sam about Jed and see if he minded if I went down to Lynn to talk to him. I didn't expect Jed to confess, but maybe he would give away some telltale signs that he was guilty. If he did, I would make sure that Constable Gray knew about him.

When I explained to Sam what I wanted to do, he said, "I hate to lose you for half a day, Christopher. Besides, I thought you were going to look into some of the old stories I gave you in those archived papers?"

"I did look into them Sam, and none of them looked like anything or anyone who could be the murderer. Maybe I missed something, but Gil and Tom also went over them, and they didn't think anything would lead us to our killer. I'm not saying this Jedediah is the killer, but he did threaten to embarrass me, and I did sort of embarrass him by pointing out in front of his friend that he would look foolish."

"All right. But don't you do anything foolish. Normally I'd say no to this kind of interview since I don't see a story coming out of it, but since you're trying to avoid the hangman's noose, go and God-speed. If you could do this tomorrow, though, it would be better than today."

That night after work I asked Matt if he wanted to go with me the next day. He said, "Definitely, but I'll have to ask Ezekiel in the morning. If he's okay with it, can we make the trip in the afternoon?"

"Of course."

The next day Matt came over to the *Gazette* at lunchtime and told me he was free to go to Lynn with me.

Jed's school was a two-story brick building about a half mile south of the Salem line. It was almost two-thirty when we arrived there. The school was still in session. We didn't want to interrupt his class, but we didn't want to wait around till the end of the school day, either. When we entered the school, we could hear voices coming from several different classrooms. As we passed one room a rather matronly woman whose hair was tied in a bun noticed us and came out into the corridor. She was almost a caricature of what I thought of as an old-fashioned schoolmarm. She greeted us with a smile though, and I soon learned that she wasn't prim or proper in her demeanor. She was actually rather pleasant.

She smiled as she asked, "How may I help you gentlemen?"

I said, "We're looking for Jedediah Talbot."

"He's teaching a class right now. He'll be finished at three. Would you like to wait in our vacant classroom?"

"Yes, thank you."

If the vacant classroom was any indication, the school didn't have many teaching supplies. There were worn wooden desks, but no blackboard and as far as I could see, no books. Apparently the kids had to supply their own books. How that worked I had no idea. From time to time we went out into the hallway to see if there was any activity. There wasn't and the thing that struck us most was how quiet it was. Occasionally we'd hear a teacher's voice and then a response from a pupil, but the building was a lot quieter than schools I'd been in in the 21st century. At three o'clock (I knew it was three because I wore a solar-powered watch) nothing happened. The classes remained in session. Then I realized that most people here didn't have watches. They relied on generally inaccurate clocks like the monster in the hallway that indicated 2:50. When that clock hit three it chimed three times and a buzz could be heard from the four classrooms on the first floor. We heard chairs moving above us so there were classrooms on the second floor, too. A minute passed and then kids started filing out of the rooms chatting among themselves. A minute or two later apparently the last kid came out of Jed's classroom. We headed for the room, hoping to talk to him before he came out.

He was stacking up books in a corner when we entered, so at least that classroom had some books. When he noticed us he gave a start. It was more than the startled expression you would see on someone who was surprised to see someone they knew. Maybe I was reading too much into it, but for a fleeting second, it sure looked like fear.

Matt said, "Afternoon, Jed. Good class?"

"Uh yes. Most of them are very good at their sums. I'm surprised to see you here though."

"We just thought we'd see how you're doing. You seemed so upset last time we saw you."

"You're here because of that man who was stabbed up in Salem aren't you?"

I said, "How do you even know about that, Jed? Very few people know about it. It hasn't been in the papers. It just happened two days ago."

I could see that my response took him off guard. It took him a few seconds before he said, "One of my neighbors was in Salem that day and heard about it from someone."

"Hmm. Would you mind giving us the name of your neighbor? We're working on an article for the *Gazette* and he could provide valuable information."

"Um . . . I don't actually know his name. We've only spoken that once."

"Then could you tell us where he lives?"

Was it my imagination or was Jed's face turning pale? He took a deep breath and said, "He lives nearby, but I don't know which house. We met on the street near my house."

Matt said, "Let me get this straight, Jed. You met your neighbor and even though you really don't know him, he told you that he heard about the murder of Elihu Martin from someone he met in Salem. Is that right?"

"Yeeess. That's right."

"Did your neighbor tell you who he heard it from?"

"No. It was just a brief conversation between us. That's all he told me. Why are you asking so many questions about this?"

I said, "It's just that we happen to know that no one actually witnessed the murder, so we don't understand how you know about it. We're especially surprised that you know that Martin was stabbed. As far as I know, the constable has not revealed that to very many people, yet you know that about the murder."

He drew in a long deep breath and then bit his lower lip. "I, I don't know how my neighbor got so much information."

"You do know, Jed, that this looks awfully suspicious, don't you?"

"I, I don't understand."

"Well, frankly, it makes it look like you might have been there when this all happened."

"I think you both should leave. I don't like the sound of this. Are you accusing me of killing that man?"

"We're just saying that what you've told us doesn't add up. You teach mathematics. I think you can do the math. You can see what we're getting at. If you had better explanations for what you've told us, we wouldn't be so suspicious."

His face suddenly transmogrified into an expression of sheer hatred. "My first impression was right. You are witches. You're not from the future. I don't know where you're from, but I don't want you around here. Please go."

"Look, Jed. If you could only give us a better explanation of how you know so much about this murder, we wouldn't have to talk to Constable Gray about this when we meet with him Monday. As it is now, we can't in good conscience ignore this."

"I told you all I know. I shouldn't have told you anything as you will no doubt concoct some new magic against me now."

"Are you admitting that you had something to do with Mr. Martin's death?"

"I most certainly am not. He was killed by someone possessed by the Evil One. I am not such a person."

"Why did you say that?"

"Say what?"

"That Martin was killed by someone who was possessed."

"My neighbor must have told me. How else would I know?"

"Isn't it obvious?"

"I am so sorry I ever met the two of you. When I told my friends about you, they warned me, and at first, I did not listen. Finally, with a little help from someone wiser than me, I saw the light and did what the Lord would want me to do. I will always do what whatever it takes to keep the Evil One from winning. I must admit, you two had me fooled at first, but I warn you, you will not win."

"What the hell are you talking about? Did you just admit to murdering a man?"

"I see that your comfort in using that word only confirms my conclusions about you. What I do in the name of the Lord is not murder. Anything I do is done as a soldier in the never-ending war against the Evil One."

"Then you do admit that you murdered Martin? Only you justify it as the Lord's work. And who is this wise advisor of yours?"

"Leave him out of this. My decisions are my own. I'll just say this. My advisor is in Salem. He will keep an eye on all of you and you will not like how things turn out. As for your other question, I do not admit to murdering anyone. What I do though, is advise you to leave Salem. As I said, I am not the only one in Salem and Lynn who sees you as you truly are. If you stay in Salem, your days are numbered. Too bad, too, because I found the outward you rather likeable. But now I know that it is only what the Evil One wants me to see."

Before I could respond, the woman we'd first met when we entered the building popped in and said, "Oh, Jedediah, I see that these gentlemen found you."

He flashed a warm smile as he said, "Yes, Ann. Do you need me?"

"It's not important. We can talk about it tomorrow morning. Good night."

"You have a good night, too." For a moment we saw the pleasant, good-hearted Jed we thought we'd met in Charlestown. Obviously, that pleasant front was his outward Jed. He kept the suspicious, witch-obsessed Jed just below the surface.

He then addressed us. "I think you'd better go now. If I were you, I'd take my advice and leave Salem immediately."

I said, "Are you saying that there are others who fear witches as much as you do?"

"Most people won't admit it, but many people know that the Evil One never stops. Surely you know that. Now go."

We were not going to accomplish any more with Jed, so we did leave. On the way back to Salem Matt said, "Either he's a fruitcake, or he's right. A lot of people still fear witches."

"Which makes them all fruitcakes?"

"I'm not sure that's fair. These are different times and people don't always have good explanations for what they don't understand. In our case, it may make more sense to believe we're witches than to believe our cell phones are the product of science and that we come from the future. Think about it. Someone coming from future. That's not easy to accept. Even in 2019 it wouldn't be easy to accept. But now, in 1775, I can understand why witches might be a more believable explanation."

I said, "Jed seems comfortable with what he's done. He all but admitted he killed Martin, and he apparently considers it God's work, so his conscience doesn't seem to bother him. Not only that, he seems to think many people will support what he's done if they find out about it."

"Worse, he seems to think that his fellow witch-obsessed local residents, once they know about us, will want to kill us, too. At least I think that's what he was hinting."

"Yeah," I agreed. "that's what I got out of it, too. I also got the feeling that Talbot is actually the pawn of someone he greatly respects. Someone who impressed him because of his position in the community. Someone who has Jed eating out of his hand. I don't think killing Martin was Jed's idea. I wish I knew just how prevalent the anti-witch thinking is in 1775. I know that not everyone still fears witches. Are they in the majority? I think so, but face it, we don't know. The library trustees seem to accept us. So does Jeremiah Weeks and Sam Hall."

"At least they all seem to. Still, when you think about it, that someone behind Jed has to be either a trustee, or Jeremiah or Sam. I'd swear it isn't Sam. I'm still leaning toward Jed as the actual killer."

"Of course, since he practically confessed. Still, we need to know who put him up to it. That's the real threat to the community."

"And us," said Matt soberly.

I'm sure many people in 1775 have a different view of witchcraft from how people saw things in 1692. These things evolve over time. Still, some people clearly still think the way folks thought in the time of the Witch Trials."

"I'm sure some of them do, which means we need to be careful."

Chapter 35

July 30

WHAT HE DID NOW WAS CRITICAL. Talbot had visited him at home last night. The nervous schoolteacher had ridden up to Salem to tell him that Carver and Blair were suspicious. They'd all but talked him into a confession. No, Talbot hadn't mentioned him, but the young man was rattled and there was no telling what a nervous person would do under pressure.

He still had the advantage, though. Yes, Carver and Blair were on to Talbot, but the young man had sworn that he had not mentioned his name. If Talbot was telling the truth and he kept his mouth shut, everything would be fine. Fine in the sense that he wouldn't have to worry about Gray. Not so fine since nobody was blaming the four newcomers. That was the whole point of doing away with Martin, but apparently it hadn't worked. He was glad that Talbot had gotten rid of Elihu, but the four newcomers were still practically worshipped by his fellow trustees. He had to find a new way to convince the community that Carver and his friends were possessed by the Evil One.

Chapter 36

July 30

AFTER MEETING WITH JEDEDIAH, I was convinced that he was the easily influenced, gullible dupe of a very persuasive man in Salem. Very likely that man, whoever he was, occupied a prominent or highly respected position in the community in order to have persuaded Jed to do his bidding. Also very likely, he was a member of the Social Library board. Matt and I had talked it over and concluded that the trustees had to be interviewed. Gray had already talked to two of them with us present, but that had been to verify that we were who we said we were. I think he now believed that we were indeed from the future. I wasn't so sure that he'd taken us off his suspects list. The interviews had not even mentioned the murder of Elihu Martin.

We assumed that the constable was going to get around to interviewing each of the trustees with regard to the murder, but Matt and I were impatient. We wanted to move things along as fast as possible to clear our names and to pin the killing on the man behind it. We had no authority to interview anyone on behalf of the constable, but it made sense to interview them for the *Gazette*, so I went to Sam to get his okay.

"You want to interview each of the trustees? Do I understand you correctly, Christopher?"

"Yes, regardless of who is eventually found guilty of Mr. Martin's murder, their views on the matter will make a good story. Frankly, I'm hoping that talking to them will make it clear that the four of us newcomers are not a threat to the community. I think we can do it without the community knowing that we came from the 21ˢᵗ century."

"From what you told me about your talk with this Talbot fellow, you're fairly certain that he's the killer, but he did it at the bidding of someone right here in Salem. Have you told this to Constable Gray?"

"No, Sam. Until we know and have some evidence to prove it, I don't think we should talk to the constable unless he asks to talk to us."

"Why do you think that, if you don't mind my asking?"

"If we just give him names without any proof, it'll look as if we're blaming someone else to move suspicion away from us. And as major suspects, that won't be very convincing. Matthew, Gilbert, Thomas and I all think that we need something more convincing before we go to the good constable. Believe me, Sam. Jedediah Talbot stuck the knife in Martin, but it wasn't his idea. He was talked into it by someone right here in town. And it's almost certain that it was someone on the board."

"I don't like that, Christopher. I don't like that at all. One member of the library board is murdered and you're saying another member is behind the killing. This is a terrible blight on the community."

"I know it is, Sam. I know it is. I'll say what you're thinking because you're too much of a gentleman to say it."

Sam looked as if he really had no idea what I was talking about, so I said, "You're thinking, '*None of this would have happened if you and your friends hadn't descended upon us.*'"

"Oh no, Christopher. That was not what I was thinking. I was thinking what a terrible way to greet you and your friends from the future. You must think you've returned to a very primitive age. If I can base it on the wonderful things you've shown me and the wonderful things you've described, I'm sure human beings behave a lot better in the 21st century."

I didn't know whether to laugh or cry. "I only wish that were true, Sam. Sadly, with all our scientific breakthroughs . . ."

"Breakthroughs?"

I couldn't help smiling. "It means advances, progress." Sam nodded his understanding, and I went on. "With all our scientific and technological progress, human behavior doesn't improve much at all in the next 240 years. We have plenty of murders and all-too-many wars in those years." As I said this I felt bad, for the look of disappointment on Sam's face was painful to behold.

"I suppose humans don't change as much as we'd like them to. But back to your request. Yes, proceed with your interviews of the Social Library board if you think you can get a good story out of it. I would ask that you tread lightly, as those trustees are pillars of the community and good patrons of the *Gazette*. If your interviews prove to be revealing, tell me and, of course, tell the constable, but please don't make accusations yourself. That is not your responsibility or your job."

"Of course. Thank you, Sam."

Chapter 37

July 30

THOMAS PYNCHON greeted me warmly in his office. Before I went there, Sam had told me that Pynchon was the managing partner in his law firm. Turns out Elihu Martin had been an active partner in the same firm.

"So you're doing a story about the death of our departed partner. I hope you'll be revealing who did the dastardly deed?"

"I spoke with Constable Gray this morning. He's being discreet about what he knows, but I distinctly sensed that he still doesn't know who's behind the killing. Maybe after our article is published in the *Gazette* someone will come forward with information leading to that person."

"Frankly, Mr. Carver, I'm surprised that Sam Hall has you making inquiries. I would have thought that the constable considered you a suspect. Not that I do, mind you, but you and your friends do have motive."

The cordial greeting didn't last. I noticed that he called me by my surname, not Christopher, as he had addressed me recently. "Sam believes that I am most familiar with the situation. Yes, I probably am a suspect in the eyes of the law, but Sam believes in me and does not consider me a suspect. If you're uncomfortable talking to me, I'm sure Sam can come up with another writer to interview you."

"No, no. I'll be happy talking to you. I note that you said Constable Gray still doesn't know who's behind the killing. That's a curious choice of words. . . *'who is behind the killing.'* What did you mean by that?"

"I think he knows who actually stabbed Mr. Martin. What he doesn't know is who instigated the killing. He's fairly certain now that someone persuaded the killer to actually do the deed." I didn't tell Pynchon that I was the one who told Gray about how Jed Talbot had more or less confessed to me, adding that someone in Salem had put him up to it. At first, Gray had been annoyed that I interviewed Jed, but when he calmed down, he said he'd follow up on what I'd told him. After he'd confirmed my background with two library trustees, he'd apparently become a believer and no longer doubted me.

"Interesting. So there were at least two people involved in the homicide. Does the constable have any idea who might have been behind the actual killer? Any suspects?"

"I don't know. One of the things Sam wants me to do in my research for this story is to look for possible suspects. If I come up with any possibilities, I'm to give them to Constable Gray. I am not to write about suspects, only about those people the constable actually accuses or arrests."

Pynchon smiled. "And if he arrests anyone you give him, you can then write a story about the successful arrests. Very clever of Sam."

"Yes, I suppose it is. But it's also done in the public interest. In a way, it's like giving the constable another deputy."

"Yes, I suppose it is, though a citizen might say that you are a deputy with a bias."

One thing about Pynchon, he spoke his mind. "Yes, I suppose people could say that too. If I give the constable any names, I will provide evidence for selecting those names. I'm well aware that accusing someone of a crime can ruin their life, so it had better be done with good reason . . . reason that would stand the test of close inquiry by unbiased people."

Pynchon held his chin between his thumb and forefinger as he considered what I'd just said. After a moment he said, "I believe you, sir. What questions do you have for me?"

"While Constable Gray wouldn't tell me who actually stabbed Elihu Martin, he does know that that person claims to have been inspired by someone in Salem who believes my three friends and I are possessed by the Devil. In other words, this unknown Salem resident believes we're witches. Now here's where it gets even more interesting. Only a few people know that my friends and I have come to Salem from the 21st century. That would be the members of the Social Library board of trustees, Jeremiah Weeks, the librarian, Sam Hall, and the constable himself. I only told him because I had to for him to believe anything else I said. Oh, and Jedediah Talbot, a schoolteacher in Lynn. Unless one or more of these people have spoken to someone outside this little circle, the killer and the one behind the killer have to be members of this small group."

"I find it very difficult to believe that any of the people you mention could be a killer. Except for this schoolteacher fellow, whom I don't know. But a schoolteacher...?"

"Yes, I know. All upstanding citizens. Yet it couldn't be anyone else unless one of these people betrayed their trust and told someone outside the group. That, of course, is possible."

"Yes, I suppose it is, though I'd be disappointed if that had happened." He fell deep in thought for another moment, then said, "I cannot believe it's one of this group."

"Suppose for the moment that it is. As disagreeable as the possibility is, if it were one of these people, who among the group feels strongly about witchcraft? Perhaps as strongly as people did back in '92?"

"Well, as you certainly know, Elihu did. He never hid the fact. He obsessed about it. Hmm. Let me think about anyone else. I hate to name anyone, for fear it could lead to trouble for them."

"I understand, but since it's likely that one of our group is involved, you could help bring a killer to justice."

"Yes, but to wrongly accuse someone. . . Well, Christopher, you know how that feels after what Elihu said at the library that night."

"Yes, I definitely know how it feels. Believe me, if you give me a name, we'll investigate thoroughly before we give it to the Constable. After talking to him, I'm convinced he'll also investigate thoroughly before he makes an arrest."

"I'll give you a name, but I must ask you not to tell Constable Gray where you got this name."

Chapter 38

July   ***30***

THE NAME PYNCHON GAVE ME was the same person I'd seen staring at us that night at Pierce's Tavern—Nathaniel Ellis. I had a feeling he might be our guy, but I couldn't very well accuse him or tell the constable about him based on my hunch or the fact that the guy hated witches.

Apparently a lot of people in Salem still feared witches.

I decided that I should interview a couple more members of the board including Ellis. Maybe I'd get lucky and learn more about him. Maybe the man himself would unwittingly reveal something. It was a longshot, but I couldn't think of anything else I could do to remove suspicion from us.

I found the Reverend Thomas Barnard at the First Church in Salem. Gil had told me that Reverend Barnard had helped mediate between the Americans and British Colonel Leslie back in February when Leslie led 300 regulars into Salem in search of a stash of cannons that the patriots had secured to protect themselves from British advances. The mediation had been successful as Leslie and his forces had been persuaded to retreat with their tail between their legs. It was hard to believe that a man like Barnard could be the motivating force behind Jed Talbot. Still, maybe he could help us find the one who was.

"Reverend Barnard, I'm a writer with the *Essex Gazette*. Would you have a few minutes for some questions?"

"Yes, of course. You didn't have to introduce yourself. Your fascinating talk at the library with your amazing devices makes you quite unforgettable. Why would I not want to talk to a man from the 21st century? It's not many of us who get that opportunity. Please sit down and make yourself comfortable. Can I get you some coffee?"

"No, thank you, Reverend."

"What in the world does the *Gazette* think I can offer?" Barnard was younger than I'd expected and had an easy, welcoming manner that could immediately put a person at ease.

"It's about the unfortunate death of Mr. Martin."

"Good Lord, that was shocking, but I don't see how I can be of any help?"

"We're trying to provide an accurate and fair report of what happened in our next edition. Do you know any of library trustees who believe my friends and I are practicing witchcraft? It would very likely be someone who does not believe us when we explain that we came from the future."

"If you don't mind my asking, why do you want to know this?"

"We have reason to believe that some influential person persuaded a very impressionable young man to plunge a knife into Elihu Martin. As much as I hate to say it, the evidence points to the library board because the trustees plus Sam Hall and Jeremiah Weeks and the schoolteacher from Lynn are the only ones who knew where we came from."

"Dear God. This is terrible. I heard about the death of Elihu, but I had no idea how he came to his end. The man had a prickly disposition, but no man deserves to die this way. After his unpleasant performance that night at the library, I would have expected you and your three friends to take umbrage, but I never would have expected anything like this." As he said this he seemed to realize something. "Please believe me, Mr. Carver, I'm not saying I think you or your friends perpetrated this vicious attack, but dear God, I can't believe anyone on the board would do it either. I do recall . . ." A pained expression clouded his face. Something was bothering him. He drew in a deep breath and went on. "I don't feel right about giving you the name of an upstanding member of our community and of my congregation. As a man of God I'm not sure I should be condemning anyone."

"I understand Reverend, but I'm sure you'd feel far worse if a man who'd committed a terrible crime was allowed to live unpunished in the community. Besides, I'm not asking you to accuse anyone. I'm just looking at people who might have resented my friends and me. Or someone who might have thought my friends and I were possessed. If you can think of any such person, we just want to talk to him. We at the *Gazette* have no power to arrest anyone."

"Yes, but you have the power to condemn. . . and to a wide audience."

I knew that he wanted to give me a name, but because he was a member of the clergy and also a member of the library board, I'm sure he felt he had a responsibility to protect Salem residents, not turn them in for questioning.

"Reverend, if you give me a name, I'll talk to him, and if I'm convinced that he had no involvement in the killing of Elihu Martin any reference to him in the story will only be as a source. If he's not involved, he may know someone who is. It's important that the person responsible be brought to trial. I'm sure you see that."

He sighed and said, "I suppose I must tell you what I know. Mind you now, I am not accusing the man, but I do recall quite clearly that Nathaniel Ellis departed with Elihu that night. I assumed it was because it was in support of Elihu, but I can't be certain of that. I do remember, though, when you and your friends were demonstrating your marvelous machines, Nathaniel was muttering his disapproval. I don't know whether it was because he didn't believe your clever machines were products of science or because he thought they were the work of the wicked one. I suspect it was the latter. Now I shouldn't be telling you this, but I suppose it's important that you know it. Both Mr. Ellis and Mr. Martin are believed to be members of a clandestine society or group dedicated to cleansing the community of witches. Most people in Salem and the surrounding communities believe in leaving the witches to themselves, as most of them are harmless. If they harm anyone, most likely it will be themselves as they will end up in Hell. The typical resident believes that there are far fewer witches in the community than Mr. Ellis and his society think there are. It's entirely possible that there are no witches in Salem. Most of us believe he exaggerates the threat and should leave people alone. Stop stirring up discord as he did the other night at the Social Library."

Chapter 39

July 30

I HAD A FEELING I was about to address a murderer. Maybe not the one who committed the physical act, but the one who orchestrated the attack. Reverend Barnard had told me that Ellis was a shipping merchant with offices on Derby wharf at the waterfront. The wharf had been built back in 1762 by Richard and Elias Hasket Derby. It was about a third of a mile in length, with a dozen or more buildings on it. I happened to know that in not too many years the wharf would be extended to a full half mile in length because the Derby business was so successful. Soon Elias Derby was to become the first millionaire in America.

The Derbys were not the only merchants operating at the wharf. Each building was the home office of a competing shipping merchant. Nathaniel Ellis was one of those shippers, and according to Barnard, a very successful one who was known for the trade he conducted up and down the East Coast.

When I entered the two-story frame building a young man at a desk said, "Yes. May I help you?"

"I'm looking for Nathaniel Ellis."

"He's occupied right now. Can you tell me what this is about?"

"I'm with the *Essex Gazette*. I would like to ask him a few questions."

"May I ask what about?"

"I'm afraid not. It'll only take a few minutes of his time."

"I'll see if he'll make time for you. He doesn't usually like to be interrupted. This better be important."

"I can assure you it is."

A minute later a man in his mid-to-late fifties appeared from a room at the rear of the building. He was well above average height. Six feet or so with flowing dark brown hair that fell just below his collar. His angular face appeared to be frowning, but it could just be his natural appearance.

"Yes, what is it at the *Gazette* that takes me away from my business? Sam knows that I don't like to be bothered by frivolous interviews." He glared at me and then added, "I know you. You're one of those . . ."

I interrupted him before he could finish. "Could we do this somewhere more private, sir? I think you'll want it that way."

"You do not know what I want."

"Could we go to your office and talk?"

He sighed impatiently. "Yes, but I don't have much time. I have a great deal of work to do."

His office wasn't very impressive. For a successful shipping merchant, I would have expected a bigger, more opulent-looking office. Still, this was 1775. Maybe this wasn't so unusual for the time. He sat behind his small desk, and with a quick wave of his hand, motioned for me to sit too.

"All right, what is it you want to ask me, Mr. . .?"

"Carver sir, Christopher Carver. We're doing a story about the murder of Elihu Martin, one of your fellow trustees at the Social Library." I let that sit for a moment to see how he reacted.

Since I didn't say any more, he finally said, "I don't see why you're talking to me about this. You should be looking for the killer."

"We are, sir. We are, but we need any help others can give us."

"If I were you I'd be talking to Constable Gray. He must have some idea who did this. Now that I think about it, I find it odd that Sam even assigned you to this story, since many believe it's you and your friends behind this killing."

Jesus, the man wasn't even trying to hide his feelings. "Mr. Ellis, I'd be careful about who you accuse of murder if I were you."

"No one else in this town can perform the black magic you and your friends perform. Why shouldn't I accuse you? I'm surprised Sam keeps you and the others on his payroll. You've obviously fooled him." I ignored this. What could I say?

Instead I said, "Black magic hurts people. What we showed you at the Social Library helps people. You should know better, and I think you do. I think you're accusing us to deflect attention away from the real killer."

Ellis's face grew red. "And who do you claim that is?"

"We have our suspicions, but we're not going to reveal anything to Constable Gray until we have proof. I was going to ask you, but you accused me and my friends, so I doubt if you will be any help in finding the real killer. One thing we do know it could only be one of a very small group."

"And what group is that, if I may ask?"

"Only the people who knew about where we came from. The library board, the librarian and Sam Hall. Oh, and the schoolteacher from Lynn."

"Well, that excludes me because I don't know where you came from. Oh, I've been told you came from the future, but clearly that's witch mumbo-jumbo. Nobody in their right mind would believe that."

"As a board member you would have seen us recover our spaceship from the ocean a few months ago."

"I was not on that silly little expedition. Neither was poor Elihu. I have no idea how my fellow trustees got taken in, but I can only attribute it to the cleverness of you and your fellow witches."

"May I quote you in the article accusing us of being witches?" His answer to this would be interesting.

He didn't answer immediately. He was obviously considering the ramifications of going on record with his accusation.

"You may not. Oh by the way. Your reasoning is flawed. When you say the killer had to be one of that small group you mentioned, you left out another obvious group."

"What group is that?"

"Yourselves. As the new people with the clever magic tricks, you are certainly the most obvious ones."

I didn't like the guy, but he was no dope. In 2019 he'd sound like an idiot, but in the year 1775 many people would buy into his reasoning. This interview was not going well.

"I'm obviously going to disagree with you, Mr. Ellis. I suppose I should leave now, but before I do, you should know that we have good reason to believe that the murder of Elihu Martin involved more than one person. We believe that one person carried out the actual attack, but he did it because he was persuaded to do it by another person. . . an influential person here in Salem. Between Constable Gray and us at the *Gazette*, we'll find both of those people because both of them are murderers."

"You have a vivid imagination, Mr. Carver, but so do I. You should know that those of us in Salem who recognize the Evil One when he takes possession of otherwise normal citizens are not going to submit. We will conquer evil just as our grandparents did 80 years ago. Those among us who are possessed must consider their days numbered. Good day, Mr. Carver."

Chapter 40

July 30

I LEFT ELLIS'S OFFICE with a shudder. I felt dirty. I couldn't wait to get outside into the fresh air. Talk about evil. It was as if I'd been carrying on a conversation with the Devil. First of all, I couldn't believe that a man of his apparent prominence in the community would speak so recklessly to someone from a local newspaper. He had to know that he was taking a risk with his wild accusations. Then again, it was 1775. . . only a few decades after the Salem Witch Trials. Maybe the things he said would resonate with the *Gazette's* audience.

I knew that the British Parliament had passed a law in 1735 that made it a crime to claim that a human being had magical powers or was guilty of practicing witchcraft. That would apply to the American colonies too. Still, it's not likely that a new law would automatically change the thinking of every citizen in Massachusetts. Maybe they couldn't legally press charges in a court of law, but an appeal to public sentiment might not fall on deaf ears. If a prominent citizen accused us of witchcraft, no doubt some people would believe that we were indeed possessed. At the very least we could be ostracized from the community. At the worst we could be spat upon and abused. Certainly, we'd have a hard time holding onto our jobs. Who would want to be interviewed by a person who'd been condemned as a witch by one some of the most respected people in town?

When I got back to the *Gazette*, I pulled Gil aside and gave him a capsulized version of my conversation with Nathaniel Ellis. I finished by telling him my fears that the *Gazette* audience might actually side with Ellis. I told him that my first impression had been that using Ellis's own words against him would bring about close scrutiny of the man, and if he was behind the killing of Martin, that truth would come out. I then began to wonder. Maybe my story in the *Gazette* would backfire on me and my friends.

Gil grinned. "You're taking all of this on your own shoulders. You don't have to. You should talk to Sam. He'll have a better understanding of the prevailing sentiment in Salem and Massachusetts in general. You'll know for sure how he feels about this when he either tells you to run with the story or kill it."

"I'm afraid he'll kill it."

"Well it is a hot subject. Doesn't Sam have to approve your stories before they go to print anyway?"

"Yes, of course. Usually he just rubber stamps them. Sometimes he'll make a few suggestions, but he's never killed one of my stories. If he kills it, Ellis will get away with murder."

"Not necessarily. I assume Constable Gray is working the case. Besides, maybe Ellis is innocent."

"I don't think so."

"Can you prove he's guilty?"

"No, I can't. I'm hoping the story will put so much pressure and scrutiny on him that it'll come out or he'll confess."

"That's a lot to hope for my friend. I hate to say it, but aren't you being a little naïve about this? Why would he confess?"

"If he gets enough support in the community, the man is so arrogant that he might openly brag about it just assuming that people will applaud him, not condemn him."

"Even if he does get some support, I think it's illegal now to accuse someone of witchcraft."

I said, "Yes, it has been for 40 years. But even if they prosecute against him he might get off with a wink and a slap on the wrist."

"I never knew you were such a worrier, Chris. Talk to Sam and let him sort this thing out."

One of his ship captains had just returned from Charlestown, South Carolina, with a big grin on his face. It had been an extremely profitable trip. He should be happy. Business had been good this year. He couldn't enjoy it, though. Not yet. Not until this Martin business was behind him. That visit from that Carver fellow from the *Gazette* had not gone well. He'd allowed his emotions to betray him. He should have played the humble, concerned citizen and sympathized with the man's desire to find the real killer. Yes, it would have been risky to encourage the young man, but it was probably riskier to reveal his true feelings about demonic possession and witches in general. It was almost certain that Carver and his three friends were possessed, but he should have remembered that possession didn't render them senseless. To the contrary, it made them all the more wary and clever. By practically accusing Carver of witchcraft, he opened himself to all manner of risks.

Yes, he, Nathaniel Ellis, had set in motion the killing of Elihu Martin so as to bring attention to the four young men who'd descended on Salem from God knows where. The whole idea was to force the community to see what evil lived in their very midst. So far his plan had not worked. So far his plan had brought attention to his own doorstep. He had to find a way to salvage the situation before things got out of hand. He knew that a good number of his fellow Salemites still recognized the very real threat of witchcraft. He just had to find some way to make them see just how close the threat was.

He had to hope that when the *Gazette* published the story enough people would rally to his side to embarrass Sam Hall and his resident mini-coven of warlocks. He also had to hope that Constable Gray was secretly sympathetic to his views on the ever-present threat of witchcraft. A lot to wish for, but his cause was just. It was God's will that the possessed among us be eliminated before they can do any harm to the community. The *Gazette* was a weekly and the next issue would come out the day after tomorrow. He wouldn't be able to relax until he knew how the community was going to react to the story.

He had one other hope and that was that Sam Hall decided the story shouldn't be published at all. If that happened, he had nothing to fear.

Chapter 41

August 1

SAM HALL HAD BECOME convinced that any story I wrote was usually solid and would not put the *Gazette* in a bad spot. That did not mean that he didn't offer suggestions, because he did. He was a hands-on editor and a damn good one. He was respected throughout all of Massachusetts and even the rest of New England.

When he read my story he pursed his lips and shook his head from side to side slowly. Ever so slowly. I held my breath. I was afraid of what he was going to say.

"Marvelous piece of work, Christopher. Marvelous. It does give one pause though. You say things about a well-known shipping merchant that will at best be considered controversial. If we run the piece as is, it will sell a lot of copies. However, I don't want to tarnish the reputation of the man unless we're certain of our facts. You know I believe you, but I'm certain that you can see that when we put your words against a long-standing member of the community like Nathaniel Ellis, he and his defenders will claim bias. They will say you put words in his mouth as a means of getting back at a man who was a friend of Elihu Martin, not someone who may have set in motion his death. Your story doesn't exactly accuse him of murder, but you give the impression you think he's behind it. If only we could point to something that suggests that he is behind it."

I smiled for the first time in days. "As a matter of fact, I might just have something that does that." I pulled out my cell phone and clicked on my voice recorder app. The voice of Ellis was loud and clear as he accused my friends and me of being witches.

"Good Lord, Christopher. I won't ask how you did that because I've already seen what that little device can do. Then the elation drained from his face. Something was clearly bothering him. "As remarkable as that is, it still doesn't capture him admitting to the murder of Elihu Martin. Even if it did, I fear that demonstrating it with your cell phone as you call it could work against you as much as for you. Those obsessed with witchcraft would see it as another example of Satan's work. I think you must delete any hint that he might be the killer. Keep the part about where he accuses you and your friends of witchcraft. He would probably not deny that anyway. I'm afraid we're going to need more facts if we're going to name anyone as being the instrument behind young Talbot's assault. We shall see what the story elicits from the community."

I had to agree that he was right. Now I wondered whether we should run the story at all. If the community turned on us instead of Ellis, our time in Salem could become rather uncomfortable.

"What do you think, Sam? Should we run it or not?"

"I would like to run it, but I'm sure you realize that if public opinion turns against you, things could become rather unpleasant for you and your friends. This time I'm going to leave it to you."

I bit my lower lip. My decision would not only affect me, but Gil, Tom and Matt as well. "I think we should run it after I make those changes. I hope I'm making the right decision."

"I do, too, Christopher. I do, too."

Chapter 42

THE DAY FOLLOWING THE publication of my story about the shocking death of Elihu Martin we began to get reactions from the community. I hadn't actually identified Jedediah Talbot as the killer because he hadn't confessed to me, but I had said that a young schoolteacher in a neighboring town was believed to have stabbed Martin. The article suggested that the murder was the killer's way of pointing the finger at the new people in Salem that he believed were conjuring up black magic. The article also said that there was reason to believe that a prominent merchant in Salem had talked the young schoolteacher into committing the crime.

Some people who came into our offices said that the story had their interest, but were disappointed that it had not been more specific. They needed to know who these terrible sinners were. We understood those complaints and frankly agreed with them. We told the complainants that we were working on finding more facts to support what we'd discovered so far.

Then there was a smaller, but more vociferous group of folks who viewed the story as my way of getting back at people who had discovered the evil truth about us, the four new residents of Salem. Some of the complainants demanded that Sam fire Gil, Tom and me. They didn't mention Matt. Guess they didn't know he worked at the other paper in town. Some of these complainants threatened to stop advertising in the *Gazette* if we weren't fired. Now our problems were becoming Sam's problems.

Sam assured us that he wasn't going to give in to these threats, but the three of us felt bad about the whole situation. If we didn't go, it would cost Sam money. Sam was a trooper, though. He said the way to deal with these threats was to learn the truth about the killing and find something tangible that pointed to the two suspects. He had no intention of letting us go, but he was going to make us work hard. He was depending on us to find something solid to support our beliefs that Talbot and Ellis were behind the murder of Elihu Martin.

That night the four of us from the 21st century met at Pierce's Tavern to discuss our situation. Matt had seen the article in the *Essex Gazette* and discussed it with his boss, the publisher of the *Salem Gazette*, Ezekial Russell. So far his customers and advertisers had not complained to Russell about Matt because they hadn't connected him to us yet. Russell told Matt that his job was still good. He wasn't emphatic about it, but he didn't seem ready to get rid of Matt. At least not yet. The four of us knew that things were probably going to get worse in the coming days as more people in the community became aware of the controversy.

When the young barmaid came to our booth, she had her usual ready smile. Then, when she realized who we were, her demeanor changed. The smile was gone, and I could see that she was nervous. "What can I get for you gentlemen?"

We ordered and she left as quickly as she could. When she returned to the bar, I noticed that she said something quietly to the other barmaid, who then gave a furtive glance our way before she went back to her customers at the bar. After we got our beer and our food was served we became aware that some of the customers were casting stares in our direction.

Matt said, "What the hell do you think these people are talking about? I know it's based on your story, Chris, but you didn't actually name anybody, so nobody should be taking offense."

I said, "It has to be us. The article says that this un-named man accused us of being possessed. Obviously some people still believe in possession and the Devil and witchcraft. If they think we're possessed, they're going to treat us a lot differently."

Gil said, "This is going to be interesting. Will people treat us differently from now on?"

"Will they avoid us all together?" asked Tom.

Nathaniel Ellis was not happy about the way things were going. His plan was not working out as he had strategized it. Constable Gray had not arrested any of the four young Satanic newcomers. Not only that, one of the newcomers, this Christopher Carver, had somehow earned the trust of Sam Hall and had the gall to ask questions about the death of the unfortunate but deserving Elihu Martin. This Carver person had the audacity to question him, a respected citizen from an old and well-regarded family. That article in the *Gazette* didn't name him, but the way it was written could easily lead people to think that Carver was referring to him. Maybe it was just his imagination, but that's the way he read it. No, it wasn't his imagination because one of his fellow merchants on the wharf had come up to him today and said something to the effect that he shouldn't worry. His friends will stick with him. The man had added, *"If it really was you, I'm glad you did it. I never liked Martin and I'd love to see someone bring these newcomers down. I haven't seen their magic, but I hear it's so amazing that only a witch or warlock could perform such wizardry."* He hadn't acknowledged his part in the killing, but he hadn't denied it either. He kind of enjoyed the approval of this particular competitor.

He had to do something to take the attention away from him and put it on the four Satanic newcomers. At the very least he had to stop that Carver person from continuing to probe into the Martin matter. He had the feeling that the man wasn't going to stop until he found some way to prove that he, Nathaniel Ellis, was the one behind Martin's death. There was no way in Hell he was going to let the Satanic troublemaker disrupt his life and the thriving business he'd worked for decades to build. He was desperate now. Whatever he did, he had to do it soon or it could be too late. Carver had said that he was going to continue to investigate the murder. It was only a matter of time before he came up with something to prove what he was now just hinting at. Even if Carver failed to get proof, young Talbot might weaken under pressure. No, he couldn't relax. He had to do something very soon.

Chapter 43

August 10

COLONEL DAVID MASON was at home in Salem. Obadiah Taliaferro had just ridden in from Amesbury to confer with him.

"What brings you in from Amesbury today, Obadiah? I assume it's about what happened up in Gloucester yesterday."

"I've heard nothing about anything in Gloucester. What happened, David?"

"A messenger just came less than an hour ago. A British warship attacked two schooners out of Gloucester that were returning from the Caribbean. The British boarded one of the schooners, but the other one made it into port to avoid capture. Ironically the British ship was the sloop-of-war *HMS Falcon*, one of the ships that lay siege on our men at Bunker Hill. British troops from the *Falcon* were sent into town to seize the other schooner, but they were captured and held prisoner by the local militia. The *Falcon* captain then attempted to set the town on fire by cannon fire as a diversion in order to retrieve his men. The attempt failed, so he sent more men in. They, too, were captured. The captured schooner was taken back by the Americans and the captain was forced to return to Boston and report his failure to Graves. A job well done by our fellow patriots."

"Yes, very well done, but this means that things are heating up. Our British brethren are not going to let up on their aggressions."

"Obadiah, did you really think they were going accept what we did to them at Bunker Hill. They claim victory but they lost twice as many men as we did, and they know they almost lost in the end. They've suffered one humiliation after another. Don't forget their humiliation after Leslie's retreat here in Salem back in February. First that, then Lexington and Concord, then Bunker Hill and now Gloucester. They're going to want to teach us a lesson. They can't afford to accept more embarrassments. Pretty soon we Americans will think we don't need them." He smiled. "Little do they know, we already think that."

Taliaferro said, "Then we must continue to build our military forces, because we're going to need them."

"I'm afraid we are. Fortunately, since General Washington arrived in Cambridge after Bunker Hill, enlistments have grown dramatically. That was even before he called for more enlistments. I think that now that we have a Continental Army, men see this as a fight on behalf of all the English colonies here in North America, not just Massachusetts."

"As soon as we announced the new Continental Army in our town, recruitments began to increase rapidly. How has it been going here in Salem?"

"The same. Bunker Hill prompted the increase," said Mason. "Even though we lost, everyone knows we would have won had we had more ammunition and more cannons. On top of that, the reputation of Washington was an added incentive. Every militia in the area has enlisted new men. Most of those militias are being folded into the new army. The only negative reaction I've heard was the resentment that Washington was chosen over Artemas Ward." The Continental Congress had placed Washington in charge of the newly created Continental Army and made Ward second in command.

"I can understand that. Ward's on a pedestal here in New England, but probably the Continental Congress knew what they were doing in choosing Washington. As a Virginia man, he'll have better luck recruiting in all the colonies. I think many in the southern colonies would have resented having the top general a Massachusetts man."

"After embarrassing the Crown up in Gloucester yesterday, I expect a new upsurge in recruitments."

"We've avoided the obvious question, David. What's going to happen to our militias and what role will you and I have in the future?"

"Ward has already notified me that the state militias will be needed to supplement the Continental Army. Men can choose which they wish to be part of. The Continental Army will pay privates 50 acres of land in God knows what part of the colonies. Captains will be promised 300. That's rather attractive if the land isn't too far away. Word is it's out west, but who knows what that means? Could be western Massachusetts. Could be as far away as western Pennsylvania. We pay our militiamen six dollars a month. And they usually get paid, but if the Continental Congress can come through on their promise, the acreage is a lot more attractive to most men."

"I've heard that the recruits are given a choice. Dollars or land."

"Yes, I've heard that, too. It's early days. We'll know soon enough. The problem is not all colonies want to provide financial support for the Continental Army. They have no control over it as they do with their own militia. I predict Washington is going to have trouble paying his troops."

Massachusetts PATRIOTS, AND
ALL INTREPID ABLE-BODIED
HEROES

Who are willing to ferve in the CONTINENTAL ARMY under the command of GENERAL WASHINGTON for the defence of the Liberties and Security of the AMERICAN COLONIES will have an Opportunity to manifeſt their Spirit by affiſting in defeating the forces of a tyrannical King and acquiring the polite accomplishements of a soldier by serving only two Years or during the time it takes to defeat the forces under the arbitrary usurpations of the British King.

Such spirited fellows who are willing to engage will be rewarded at the End of the War. Besides their laurels they will be granted 50 acres of land where every gallant Hero may retire and enjoy his Bottle and Laſs.

Each Volunteer will receive as a Bounty FIVE DOLLARS besides Arms, Clothing and Accoutrements and every other Requisite proper to accommodate a Gentleman Soldier by applying to Lieutenant Colonel JONES or Captain MARSHALL at Army Headquarters, Cambridge.

Recruitment Poster

Chapter 44

August 11

I LIVED ONLY A HALF MILE from the *Gazette* offices, so I usually walked to work. I kept my horse at a livery stable under the care of an ostler who took good care of her. Even though I didn't need my horse every day, I tried to ride her at least once every other day. Horses need exercise just as much as humans. It was raining when I left work and so cloudy that it was almost as dark as night.

As I neared the house where I was renting two rooms, a smart-looking landau pulled up beside me and the driver got my attention by saying, "Mr. Carver, I'd like to give you a ride. The voice sounded familiar, but I couldn't tell what the driver looked like as he was covered with rain gear.

I yelled back, "Thank you, sir. That's very kind of you, but my house is only a hundred yards away."

"Yes, I know. I want to show you something. It's on the edge of town. I think I owe it to you. I wasn't very pleasant the other day when we met. I think we got off on the wrong foot. I believe if I show you what I want you to see, you'll see that I'm not at all the kind of person you think I am."

Of course. It was Ellis. What could he possibly have in mind? I was almost home now. Did I want to ride to the outskirts of town with this man on such a lousy night? On the other hand, if he really could somehow demonstrate that I was wrong about him, I owed it to him to at least check it out. After all, he was driving, and the coach looked rather comfortable.

"Mr. Ellis. You've aroused my curiosity. Yes, I'm curious. I assume you'll bring me back when you've finished showing me whatever it is you want to show me?"

"Of course. Of course. Get in. The carriage is pleasantly dry. I think you'll find what I have to show you quite interesting. Where we're going is only a little over a mile from here. Sit back and enjoy the ride."

I got into the carriage and was surprised just how comfortable it was. I'd never ridden in a landau or, for that matter, any horse-drawn carriage before. I suppose I'd just assumed it would be bumpy and uncomfortable, but I quickly discovered that the carriage was suspended on elliptical springs that absorbed much of the shock from the unpaved road. Some of the streets in downtown Salem were paved with cobblestones, but they were not any smoother than the dirt roads. In some ways they were bumpier. As we made our way south down Essex Street, one of the man streets in Salem, we gradually encountered fewer and fewer houses. I knew that we were heading toward Lynn and I wondered just how far Ellis was taking me. In order to be heard I poked my head out the window and yelled, "How much further?"

"Only a few minutes and we'll be there."

"Are we going into Lynn?" It suddenly occurred to me that maybe this wasn't such a well-intended trip. Maybe Ellis had something nasty in mind. Maybe he and Talbot had devised some sick plot to do away with me in Lynn.

"No. We're not going that far. We're almost there."

"We must have gone a lot farther than a mile."

"I may have misjudged slightly, Mr. Carver, but not that much. Just enjoy the ride. Be glad you're not still walking in the rain. Be glad you're riding in comfort. You're in for a big surprise when we arrive at our destination."

I had no idea what the hell the man had in mind, but the farther we went, the more nervous I got. What could he possibly want to show me that would require a ride out into the countryside? I'd had a lot of time to think and my mind was considering all sorts of possibilities. One thought that was eating away at me was, *Why would a gentleman be driving a carriage?* Anyone who could afford a fancy carriage like this would have a driver. The owner would sit comfortably inside—especially on a rainy day like this.

The carriage started turning as we left the southern extension of Essex Street and entered a narrow country road that was overhung by trees that must have been very old. The roadway became a dark tunnel through the overhanging branches.

"Where in God's name are you taking me, Ellis?"

"Just a few more yards and we'll be there." As he said this, he pulled off the road into a small clearing. There was nothing but trees as far as the eye could see.

"I don't like this, Ellis. There's nothing here. What in God's name are you going to show me?"

"See that trail running off to your right. We're going to take that. Just a couple minutes and then you'll see what I have in store for you."

"It better be good. I was looking forward to dinner and you have me out in the middle of nowhere."

As Ellis got down from his seat at the front of the carriage, he opened the door for me. He had a smile on his face that seemed a bit forced.

"Go ahead. Take the path. I'm right behind you. It's only a minute or two now."

"I'll let you lead the way," I said, not wanting him behind me.

"Here, I'll join you. We can walk together." The path ahead began to narrow. The cloud cover had grown ominous. It was difficult to see on the densely forested trail. There was no way we could walk side-by-side much further. As we hit the narrow part of the trail, Ellis again fell behind me. I didn't like it. Just didn't feel comfortable with him walking behind me, knowing what I thought I knew about the man. I stepped to my right side to let him reach my left side. I was going to make it clear that he would walk ahead of me. As I stepped to the side, I felt something pierce my coat and enter my left side. The son-of-a-bitch had stabbed me. I grabbed his arm and twisted it behind his back. I gave it a good wrenching in the process. He screamed in pain as the knife fell to the ground. He tried to wriggle away, but I was stronger than Ellis and I wasn't letting go. I'd been a marine in my other life, and dealt with tougher customers than Ellis. You have to be fit to become a chrononaut, too. Still, I was bleeding on my left side, so I knew he'd done some damage. I just didn't know how much, and I wasn't going to give him the satisfaction of knowing that he'd hurt me.

"You brought me here to kill me you bastard." Then I added, "Only you're not as effective as your lackey, Jedediah Talbot."

It was almost dark, but I could still see fear in his eyes. "I had to shut you up. You ask too many questions and you have this uncanny ability to know what people are thinking. Only a witch could have such powers. You are a threat to the community."

"I'm a threat? You're the one who killed Elihu Martin."

He looked defeated. "What are you going to do now?"

"You're going to get back up in that driver's seat and take us back into town. I'm going to sit next to you with your knife in my hand. When we get back in town you're going to head for the constable's station. You just played right into my hands Mr. Ellis. You made it easy for me."

As we headed into town, I felt my side, and my hand felt wet. When I looked at my hand I saw blood. A lot of blood. I needed to have someone look at me before I lost too much.

When we neared the constable's station, I noticed Gray was just leaving. Probably on his way home after a long day. When Ellis saw him, he whipped the horses. He obviously wanted to take the carriage past the constable as quickly as he could.

I grabbed the reins and steadied the horses until they came to an uneasy halt just a few yards past the station. Needless to say, Constable Gray had noticed this little disturbance and came over when the carriage finally came to a complete stop. Ellis tried to get down on the street side of the carriage. I suppose he hoped to slink away before the constable recognized him. It was a stupid move because I was onto him and yanked him in the direction of the constable.

Gray immediately recognized both of us and said, "What in tarnation is going on here?"

Before I could get a word out, Ellis said, "This young man has threatened me with a knife. Fortunately, I was able to wrestle the knife away from him before he could do me harm."

The man may have been slow with a knife, but he thought on his feet. I'll give him that.

I yelled, "The man is lying, constable. He tried to kill me. Here, look. I'm bleeding where he stabbed me."

Gray shook his head. This was all he needed at the end of the day. He was probably looking forward to getting home and have an ale with his dinner. "I think you'd both better come into the station and sit down so I can get a clearer understanding of what's happening here. Inside there were two other men who were just about to go about their rounds as town criers. The constable asked them to stay until he was finished with us. Smart move.

"All right, Mr. Carver, let me see that wound you have there. I see you're still bleeding."

When I lifted my shirt I could see that the knife had pierced the skin just below my ribs for about three inches parallel to the surface, so it hadn't penetrated any internal organs. The constable studied it carefully and then barked an order to one of the men. "James, go fetch Doc Felson. Tell him someone here is losing a lot of blood from a knife wound."

Then he turned to me and said, "I doubt that you did that to yourself. What in blazes is going on here Nathaniel? Why did you attack this man?"

"I told you, William. The man attacked me first. The man is possessed. I had to defend myself from the Evil One."

"Constable Gray, to you, sir. We have never been on first-name terms, and I am not all-of-a- sudden your friend. I'm trying to understand the facts, and one fact I observed with my own eyes is that you tried to run when Mr. Carver pulled the carriage to a stop in front of the station."

"I . . I was confused."

"The man who runs ships up and down the coast was confused. I doubt that very much. Are you also confused about why you stabbed this young man in the side?"

"When he attacked me, I took the knife from him and stabbed him in self-defense."

"I'm finding that a little hard to believe, Mr. Ellis. If you're the victim here, why did you try to run when the carriage came to a stop?"

"Because this man is possessed. He's dangerous. I didn't want to be near him."

"Yet you sat next to him in the driver's seat."

"He threatened to kill me if I tried to get away. I keep telling you, the man is possessed. You'll see when you get to know him. He's driven by the Evil One. He and his three friends. They're all . . ."

"Hold on there, my friend. Let's not go calling people witches. We don't want to stir up that old business again. Too many people died the last time someone started accusing people. I know you and your little circle of friends see witches everywhere you go, but I have yet to see one. I don't know anyone who has."

"So they've got you in their power, too. I see I have no chance against you now."

"I have never locked up a merchant before and don't want to lock one up now, but you leave me no choice, Mr. Ellis. He turned to the other deputy crier and said, "Robert, you've heard all this I assume? And you saw the man try to run away?"

Robert nodded and said, "I did, sir. I always thought Mr. Ellis was a man to admire, but I have to say, I'm shocked at what I've heard here."

Gray then said, "Remember exactly what was said here today. You may have to testify in court someday." At this, Ellis's face went white. It was no longer his word against that of the constable.

Just then a man in his late sixties came shuffling into the station with deputy James trailing behind him.

Constable Gray turned to me and said, "Mr. Carver, this is Dr. Felson."

"Good Lord," said Felson, "what happened to you young man?"

I pulled my shirt up and showed him. I then pointed to Ellis and said, "Thanks to Mr. Ellis here. He tried to kill me."

He looked at Ellis and recognized him. "Why would you do that?"

Ellis said, "I was defending myself."

Felson shook his head in disbelief. "Don't tell me anymore." Then he said to me, "Here, let me look at this." He examined me carefully and said, "Looks nasty, but it's actually very superficial. I'll dress it and if you keep it clean it should heal in a few weeks."

Gray then said to deputy James, "Lock Mr. Ellis up."

Ellis then demanded of Gray, "Get Simon Fields down here."

I remembered that Fields was Elihu Martin's law partner. All these guys hung together. No pun intended. I wondered if Fields was part of the local Anti-Witch society.

Gray said, "I'll have one of my men run over there in the morning."

"You can't leave me in here all night," yelled Ellis angrily. "This warlock gets to go home, and a respected member of the community is treated like a common criminal. I'll have your job for this, William."

"I didn't see any respectable behavior tonight, Nathaniel. Respectable people don't try to kill people, and they don't recklessly call

---

people warlocks and witches. Oh, by the way. I don't take kindly to being threatened. You'll be well advised to hold your tongue."

Then Gray took me aside and said, "I read your article in the *Gazette*. I have a feeling the prominent merchant you were talking about is Mr. Ellis. His conscience must have brought him to the same conclusion. It was a good article and now that Ellis has shown his hand tonight, I think we may be able to bring this to a close a lot sooner than I at first thought.

A half hour later I left the constable station with the frantic voice of Nathaniel Ellis still echoing in my ears. I didn't know how much influence he wielded in Salem, but I supposed we'd find out soon enough. I certainly had a lot of respect for Constable Gray. The constable had made me write down my version of what had happened before he let me go. I still wasn't good at writing with a quill, but I was gradually getting the hang of it. He'd had Ellis do the same, though the man had protested vehemently. I really didn't like Nathaniel Ellis. And not just because he'd tried to kill me. Even before that I'd gotten bad vibes from the man every moment I was in his presence. If he was a typical example of the Anti-Witch society, I feared Salem was in for a lot of trouble.

———

Chapter 45

August 12

AT TEN THE NEXT MORNING, Sam Hall asked me into his office.

"I had a visit from an attorney this morning. He said his client was threatening to sue the *Gazette* unless we printed a retraction of your article.

"Was the lawyer a Simon Fields?"

"You already know."

"I didn't know his client planned to sue, but I'm not surprised. I assume he told you his client was Nathaniel Ellis?"

"Of course. He said you wrote the article with a personal bias and had no facts to back it up. By doing so you sullied the reputation of an upstanding citizen who's been serving the community for decades. Said his client was not only on the board of trustees of the Social Library, but also had served on numerous other local boards. Not only that, his growing shipping business employed a number of Salem residents providing them with a good living."

"All that may be true, but he's also a member of some kind of secret society that wants to punish witches in the community. He's just as much a witch hater as was Elihu Martin."

"We have to use caution with that, Christopher. Many people believe in witches. They may not openly accuse folks of witchcraft, but I can tell you from conversations I've had with people over the years, that many secretly accuse some of their fellow citizens of being possessed. They're just not as open about it as they were back in the last century. Our defense can be that Ellis recklessly accuses people of witchcraft when he has no evidence to support his accusations. People will sympathize with that, but they won't take our side if we deny the very existence of witches."

"We shouldn't need a defense, Sam. Ellis is the murderer. Ellis is the one calling people witches."

"Yes, I know, but I also know Simon Fields. Litigious is his middle name. He's known for filing charges against anyone who accuses his clients of the least little thing. It's a strategy that often works for him. By putting legal pressure on the accuser it sometimes costs him so much that he drops the charges because it's costing him too much to continue. Fields is a clever rascal. I don't like him, but I have to admit that he's very effective."

"Are you saying that if he files charges against the *Gazette*, you won't fight it?"

"That's not what I'm saying. What I'm saying is that this won't be easy. It would help us if we could come up with some proof that he was behind the Martin killing."

"Won't the fact that he tried to kill me be enough to convict him?"

"I would hope so, but I don't know. I think Ellis is friendly with most of the local magistrates. Your case against him will have to be so clear and obvious that the judge will have no alternative but to convict Nathaniel Ellis."

"Won't there be a jury?"

"I would think so. If there is, the judge or magistrate has enormous power to direct their conclusions in the direction he thinks they should be."

"When do you think the case will be heard?"

"There'll be a lot of pressure to bring Ellis before a jury soon. He and Fields will want to resolve it soon and the constable will, too. I hope the constable has a good lawyer to press his case."

Chapter 46

September 4

ESSEX COUNTY MAGISTRATE Henry Hubbard called the court to order. Hubbard was 77 years old. He was born in 1698, only six years after the Witch Trials. He was a grizzled veteran of the court system, with white hair down to his shoulders.

There was a buzz the judge rarely heard in his courts because this was the first time he'd tried a murder in several years. On top of that, the defendant was a prominent member of the community who was rumored to be a member of a clandestine witch-hunting society. Usually the only people in the audience in his courts were relatives of the accuser and the defendant. Today, the courtroom was packed.

Hubbard now addressed my lawyer, Thomas Gregson, a man Sam had recommended, since I knew very few attorneys in Salem or anywhere else, for that matter. Gregson was a short compact man of about 50. His black hair was graying around the temples and you got the impression that he was always trying to restrain a smile. Curious. I had no idea what that signified, but Sam said he was honest and competent. What else could I ask for. Hubbard cleared his throat to get Gregson's attention and then said, "Mr. Gregson, please tell the court what it is that you allege the defendant is guilty of."

I'd been told that the plaintiff's statement had to be brief. Gregson rose and looked over toward the jury to be sure they were paying attention. Then he faced the judge and said, "The plaintiff, Mr. Christopher Carver, maintains that on the night of August 11 the defendant, Nathaniel Ellis plunged a sharp knife into the plaintiff's body in an attempt to kill him. The plaintiff maintains that he is alive today only because he was able to deflect the defendant's attack sufficiently enough so that the knife missed important internal organs.

Hubbard banged his gavel. "Thank you Mr. Gregson. You may examine the defendant."

Nathaniel Ellis made his way slowly to the front of the courtroom. When he was seated, Gregson began.

"Good morning, Mr. Ellis."

"What's so good about it?"

"Very well. Then we shall proceed. Why did you try to kill Mr. Carver?" My lawyer didn't waste any time getting down to business. I'll give him that.

"I was not trying to kill him. I was defending myself against his attack."

"Please describe this alleged attack?"

"We were walking along a path through the woods when he turned on me and stabbed at me with a knife. I was too quick for him and turned it against him. I didn't want to, but it was him or me. What choice did I have?"

"Why were the two of you walking in the woods?"

"He told me he had something to show me. I didn't like the man, but he implied that it was something that would please me. I had the impression that he was trying to make peace with me, but I soon found out it was a cunning trick to get me alone so he could kill me. It was the kind of trick someone possessed by the Devil would attempt. This time good won out over evil." As he said this, words could be heard from a dozen or so men sitting in the audience: *God be praised. Satan be damned. Hang the sinners.*

The judge rose and roared, "Silence in the back there."

"Let me get this straight. He was in a landau and approached you with this scheme that was intended to kill you?"

"No, no. It was my landau."

"So he talked you into taking your landau out to the edge of town to a secluded woody area so he could kill you. Is that right?"

"Yes. That is precisely what happened."

"And you expect the court to believe that Mr. Carver, a new resident who has only been in Salem a few months, would know about some secluded place in the woods several miles out of town?"

"It's possible. I mean isn't it obvious that he did know about it?"

"No, I don't think it's obvious. Why would he have any reason to know about a secluded spot in the woods far from the center of town? He barely knows his way around the town itself. It's also hard to believe that you would go to such a secluded place with a man you obviously suspect of being possessed by the Devil. I don't believe any man of sound mind would go alone with someone he believed to be possessed. It would be a suicide mission. I don't think you're a stupid man, Mr. Ellis. Are you that stupid?" Hisses could be heard from the rear of the audience.

The question took Ellis by surprise. Gregson waited some time and then said, "I asked you a question, Mr. Ellis?"

"It was a momentary lapse in judgement. I shouldn't have gone with him."

"Why did you attempt to run away when Mr. Carver brought you to the constable station?"

"That's a lie. I never attempted to run away."

"That is not what the constable said. Are you saying that Constable Gray is a liar?"

"No, I'm not saying that. What I'm saying is that I was just getting down from the carriage and Constable Gray misinterpreted my stepping down as an attempt to run away. It was an understandable mistake on his part."

"That's curious, Mr. Ellis, as I have sworn testimony from one Robert Cobb that he saw you attempting run away from the constable station."

"I have no idea who this Robert Cobb is."

"He is a deputy crier who is an experienced observer of the behavior of lawbreakers. He is convinced that you were running away."

"Objection!" It was the voice of Simon Fields, Ellis's attorney. Fields was maybe 55. He was a man of average height and slightly heavier than average. He moved slowly, as if every step was a great effort. His face was white. I know, all of the faces in the courtroom were white, but his was nearly as white as snow that had fallen a few days ago. There was a gray, sickly tinge to it. Looking at him I expected a weak, sickly defense, but I soon found out that I was wrong.

Judge Hubbard demanded, "On what grounds?"

"On the grounds that it was impossible for an observer to know what was in the mind of Mr. Ellis. How did this Robert Cobb know what Mr. Ellis was doing?"

"A response, Your Honor?" It was Gregson speaking.

The judge said, "Yes, what is it?"

"A trained observer knows the difference between someone who is getting down from a carriage and someone who is running away from that carriage. Nay, it doesn't take a trained observer. Any normal person knows the difference. What does it matter what was in the runner's mind? The fact is, he was running. It doesn't take a trained observer to know that someone who runs from the constable station is attempting to avoid the law."

Ellis then said, "Would you not run from a man possessed? A man who made a contract with the Devil. A man who performs a kind of magic never before seen on this Earth?"

"In truth, in truth. He must be stopped," could be heard from the cluster of men at the rear of the room.

"Silence in the back of the room or I shall have you removed." Judge Hubbard was not happy. Hubbard then said, "It has not been established that Mr. Carver is possessed. Besides, according to the Witchcraft Act of 1735 it is a criminal act to accuse a person of having magical powers or of practicing witchcraft. If you persist in this accusation, I will be obliged to add another charge to what you are already accused of." More hissing from the back of the room.

"Constable, have your men remove those people from the courtroom."

When the troublemakers were removed and things had settled down, Judge Hubbard said, "I think it is time for Mr. Fields to examine the defendant." He looked at Fields and said, "Mr. Fields."

"Thank you, Your Honor." Then Fields addressed Ellis. "Mr. Ellis, have you ever been accused of using violence against another human being?"

"Never. I'm a peace-loving person."

"Why do you suppose Mr. Carver attacked you?"

"Objection!" It was my man Gregson.

"On what grounds?" said Hubbard.

"It has not been established that my client attacked Mr. Ellis. The fact is, it is he, Nathaniel Ellis, who attacked my client."

"Let me rephrase my question. Why, Mr. Ellis, do you claim that Mr. Carver attacked you?"

"He suggested in a commentary in the *Essex Gazette* that I murdered Elihu Martin."

I leaned over and whispered to Gregson, "The article never even mentioned his name."

Gregson then said, "If you believed the article was referring to you, sir, you must have a guilty conscience because the article does not mention your name once."

"Ask a question, Mr. Gregson, snapped the judge. "This not an oration."

"Yes, your honor." Gregson turned to Ellis and said, "Since your name is not mentioned in the article even once, how do you conclude that it suggests that you murdered Mr. Martin?"

"The article said that a prominent Salem merchant had encouraged the young Lynn schoolteacher to kill Elihu Martin. I'm a fairly prominent Salem merchant. That alone didn't convince me though. The fact that Mr. Carver had come to my office to interview me before he wrote the article convinced me that he had me in mind."

"I can understand that, sir. Let me ask you another question. Why do you think Mr. Carver is making these wild accusations against you?"

"Because he and his three friends who descended upon us in the last few months know that I question what they are doing here in Salem. They know that I suspect them of dealing with the Evil One. Nay, more than that. I suspect them of having a contract with the Evil One."

Judge Hubbard banged his gavel. "Watch yourself, Mr. Ellis. You're on shaky ground."

"I know. I know, Your Honor. The Witchcraft Act. Do we really have to adhere to that now? We are defending ourselves against the British now. Why must we follow their laws anymore? Especially when their laws don't protect us from threats in our very midst?"

I could see that Judge Hubbard was giving this matter serious consideration. After maybe 30 seconds he said, "I understand how you must feel, sir, but we are still guided by British Common Law. This court will abide by it. However, even if we were to put British law aside and consider what you are contending, I must tell you that you have not made a case for your contention that Mr. Carver is possessed by the Devil in any of his forms."

The trial adjourned at four p.m. and resumed the next morning at nine. The lawyers went back and forth with no attorney striking a decisive blow. At 11:30 a.m. the judge sent the jury to the jury room to deliberate. At 1:30 p.m. Hubbard brought the jury back into the courtroom and asked the foreman for the jury's decision. A crusty old fellow slowly pulled himself up from his seat and said, "Your Honor, the jury could not agree on why Mr. Ellis stabbed Mr. Carver. All jury members believed that if evidence of bodily possession and examples of magic were introduced, we would have been better guided in our decision. Because we lacked sufficient evidence on which to make our decision, we must conclude that Mr. Ellis is not guilty."

Chapter 47

September 9

THE ANTI-WITCH SOCIETY met at the home of Nathaniel Ellis at the request of three of the most active members. Ellis had sent his wife over to their son's house for a couple hours, as he wasn't entirely comfortable with her knowing what transpired at these meetings. She was a bit squeamish about some of the types of things they discussed. All 15 members of the group had attended the two-day trial of Ellis and wanted to celebrate his not-guilty verdict. All but two of the 15 were over the age of 50. About half of them were in their 60s. Ellis and his fellow society members had noted that younger people, unfortunately, were not so concerned about demonic possession.

Most of Ellis's fellow society members were pleased that the judge had ruled in his favor about the alleged attack on young Carver. Carver was a threat to the community, and some even believed that it would have been God's work if someone had eliminated him. If Ellis had made the attempt on Carver's life, it would have been a just act. Ellis had told some of them that Carver had accused him of persuading the Lynn schoolteacher to kill Elihu Martin. Many of Ellis's fellow members weren't quite sure if he had actually set in motion the Martin killing, but they were delighted that neither the constable nor any magistrate had pressed charges against him. Ellis was perhaps the most valuable member of the society. It was critical that he remain free to carry on the good work against Satan and his disciples. Even if Ellis were behind the killing, some members believed it was a bold move in an era of laxness and neglect regarding the ever-present danger of the Evil One who never missed an opportunity to take possession of otherwise normal human beings. They understood that whoever persuaded the schoolteacher to do it had done so to bring attention to the growing presence of the possessed ones in Salem. If people believed that a person possessed had actually killed someone they would take the threat seriously.

The Witch Trials had rid the community of the Evil One's presence for decades, but now he was trying again to make his presence known. It was no secret that the four newcomers to Salem were almost certainly where the Evil One was making his presence known. Since the Witch Trials, Massachusetts residents had let down their guard. The deniers had discouraged and intimidated those who still recognized the presence of the Evil One in their midst. The members of the society knew that, just because you deny it doesn't mean the threat doesn't exist. The deniers simply make it easier for Satan to take possession of defenseless people.

People make contracts with the Devil when the Devil masquerades as something else. The society members knew this and believed it was their duty to protect the guileless deniers from their own naïveté.

Ellis welcomed them all to his home and said, "I am glad to be sleeping in my own bed now, but I cannot completely relax until the threat has been stopped. I hope between all of us we can come up with a way to put a stop to this very real danger. Since I failed to deal with Carver successfully, I fear that he and his three fellow warlocks will be on the lookout for me. He may very well want to silence me. I hope we can put our heads together and end this infestation of our community once and for all before it's too late."

Ebenezer Purdy spoke up. "You say this Carver fellow is possessed and we believe you, brother Nathaniel. It would be helpful to the rest of us to know in what form this possession manifests itself. If we know something about that we may be able to come up with something to counteract that manifestation."

"They carry a small device with them that by some black magic captures images so accurately you would think they were real. Some of these images actually move. In God's honest truth, they are pictures that actually move. Some of these moving pictures show something this Carver fellow called a spaceship. It appears to be leaving Earth and heading up into the sky. It is most amazing, but that very amazement is scarifying. I ask you, where did they get these devices?"

Before anyone could voice an opinion, Ellis went on. "You can speak to this magic machine using English and it can translate your words into French or any language you can imagine. This device of the Devil can tell you the meaning of any word you can think of. It even has words that none of us has ever heard of." He let all this sink in for a moment.

Purdy took advantage of the pause and said, "Where did this Carver person say he got this magic device?"

A contemptuous smile distorted Ellis's face. "Listen carefully to what I say next. He claimed he got it in the year 2019. He says that he and his friends are visiting us from the future. Do I need say anymore?"

"Good Lord," said a man with a florid face and short-cut hair. I agree with you, Nathaniel. These men are possessed."

Purdy interjected, "Is it not strange, though, that these men openly make such outrageous claims? Would we expect a witch or warlock to be so bold?"

"I agree," said a large man with a jowly face. "That is not typical of someone possessed. In my experience they try to hide the fact that they have made a pact with the Devil. These men are bold. It's almost as if they are challenging us to see what they can get away with."

"That is not what I meant," said Ebenezer Purdy. "Could it be that these men are telling the truth?"

Every man in the room turned to face Purdy. They glared at him as if he were out of his mind. "You don't mean that, Ebenezer?" said Ellis incredulously.

"I . . .I . .What I mean is that it makes little sense that someone possessed by the evil one would announce that fact. In the past such a confession would have led to death for that person. Today, at the very least, it would make him a pariah in the community. From what you've told us, these men openly spoke of their magic. They did so without hesitation. There has to be another explanation for why they would take that chance."

"Like they really do come from the future," said Ellis with a sneer.

"You can't believe that, Ebenezer."

"When you heard them say this, did they sound sincere?"

"Of course they sounded sincere," he snapped. "The Evil One may be evil, but he's wickedly clever. When he takes possession of you, he makes your speech sound engaging and inviting. This is what the Devil is so good at. This is how he deceives us so often."

"How did your fellow trustees at the Social Library react to these men? Did they believe them to be from the future, or did they see them as a small coven of possessed individuals put in Salem to hurt our people?"

"That is a very good question, Ebenezer," said Ellis. "Other than Elihu, most of the others seemed to believe the lies coming out of the mouths of these servants of Satan." He let some time pass for the significance of this to hit home with his audience. Then he said gravely,

"That very fact should prove to you just how dangerous Carver and his friends are."

"I hesitate to say this, Nathaniel, as I am a guest in your house, but your very words belie what you seem to have concluded. If your colleagues at the library were convinced that these young men were telling the truth, then how do you conclude they are possessed?"

"Aha!" Ellis's eye dark eyes burned with fire in them. "I just told you. The very fact that these intelligent men were taken in by the silken words of these young men proves just how clever the Evil One is. The evil master has total control of his four young servants, and he has made them his living poppets on this Earth. They do his bidding and they do it effectively." He stared at his audience victoriously. He was certain that he had cast aside all doubts. How could they not see the truth he had put before their very eyes? No one said anything, so he went on.

"Now that I'm sure you all understand what we're up against, I think we should put our heads together and come up with a way to combat this evil presence that is thriving in our Christian community."

A man who had thus far said nothing stood up to make a point. "As we all know, when Parliament passed the Witchcraft Act 40 years ago it became much more difficult to fight Satan when he took possession of our human brothers and sisters. The act made it a criminal offense to accuse anyone of witchcraft or of being possessed. I'm sure that very act of Parliament was itself the work of Satan, for it tied the hands of good Christians who want to fight against such evil. Gentlemen, Satan is winning. We must find a way to stop him."

"Yes," said Ellis. "We all agree with you. Conditions have never been more dire. We need to combat our local threat, and we need to do it now. We all know the problem we face. What we need now are strategies we can use to thwart the evil that infests our community. Please, dear friends, offer us some ideas. I don't want you to leave here knowing that we failed to accomplish anything."

A tall man with a cane stood up. It was Ezra Crane. All eyes turned to him. He was recognized as a man who only spoke when he had something significant to say. He spoke in a deep resonant voice. "Gentlemen, I think we all owe Nathaniel a debt of gratitude for all he has done for our cause. If it weren't for him, there would be no society dedicated to fighting the Evil One. I doubt if any of us know how much work and effort he has devoted to this most honorable cause. Let us all give Nathaniel a hearty round of applause." At this the room broke into a round of enthusiastic applause. Ellis beamed at this passionate show of support. As Crane sat down, Ellis rose. He waited for the room to quiet down before he spoke. He had never felt more confident or more certain of his mission than he did at this moment.

"Friends," he said, his heart swelling on a surge of hubris, "You have warmed my heart with your demonstration of support for my efforts. To show my appreciation for that support and to show how strongly I feel about all of this, you deserve to know just how far I've already gone in the fight against the Evil One and his four new Satanic disciples." The room fell even quieter. "If you have wondered whether I urged young Talbot to sacrifice brother Martin for the cause, I did. I did not make him do it. I merely planted the seed in his very receptive head. I regret that brother Martin had to be sacrificed, but he was the logical choice, as he had accused the four young newcomers of being possessed, and it made sense that they would seek revenge on him. As all of us in this room know, the community still treats these four men with the respect and common decency that they do not deserve. While my strategy was not as effective as I'd hoped, I think it demonstrates how strongly I feel about our mission and how far I'm willing to go to defeat the Devil. We cannot allow Him to triumph in Salem." It was clear that Ellis was finished. The men in the room struggled to know how to respond appropriately. After a full minute Ezra Crane rose again and started to clap his hands together. Slowly the others in the room responded with half-hearted applause. This weak show of approval petered out after only a few seconds.

Ebenezer Purdy rose and said, "We appreciate how much you put into our mutual cause, Nathaniel, but I think I speak for all of us when I say that we'd appreciate your discussing it with us before you think it necessary to actually take someone else's life. Some of us were acquainted with Elihu, so we take his death, sacrifice as it may have been, as a loss that we might not have condoned had we been consulted."

Ellis then rose and said, "When I seek support for an idea, someone will always find a reason to defer or postpone or dissuade me altogether. Through long experience I have found that it's better to take an action and apologize later if it offends someone. Yes, I had a passing acquaintance with Elihu myself, and I'm not happy that he had to be sacrificed, but this is a war we're fighting against an evil force that never lets up. We have to fight fire with fire."

"Perhaps we might try something like this." It was a weak, almost timid-sounding voice from a slender, frail-looking man in his early 50s. All eyes turned to the man who was known by the members of this group as never having anything to say in any of the meetings they attended. He invariably voted with them, but he had never been known to verbalize anything but good evening or good-bye. Tonight the man had obviously summoned up his courage as he said, "Perhaps we should display posters or some form of public notice all over town warning of the danger that these four men present to the community?" He waited to see what kind of reaction he was getting. Seeing nods of agreement, he continued. "As the good citizens of Salem become aware of these warnings, they will begin to treat these four outsiders for what they are. At the very least life will become so difficult for them that they will no doubt lose their employment and find it difficult to continue living in Salem. With any luck good citizens may punish them physically."

"Yes, yes," said several members of the society voicing their approval.

Ellis then said, "An excellent suggestion, brother Walcott. Mr. Purdy, you own a print shop. If we give you the words, can we depend on you to produce some of these posters? Let's say 100 or so."

"It would be an honor. Just tell me what you want to say."

"What did you have in mind, Mr. Walcott?"

"I can think of two or three different messages. Give me a day or two and I'll deliver what I have in mind to Mr. Purdy's print shop."

"I would be obliged if you'd let me see what you have in mind before you deliver it to Mr. Purdy."

"Of course."

Ellis rose to say something more to the group. As he scanned the room, he gave thought to how he had escaped the long arm of the law. For one brief moment when he was sitting in that cold, damp, filthy cell, he had questioned the morality of what he had done. How would God look upon him after causing the death of another human being? Especially an innocent human being. For a few brief seconds he had imagined how others might have viewed the act. He had almost felt a pang of remorse. Now, among allies, he discarded any feelings of self-condemnation. Martin was a necessary sacrifice in the war against Satan.

He said with moral conviction, "This is a good plan. Each of us can help by making subtle hints when meeting good people. For example, we can mention that we have heard that so-and-so performed this act of magic or that. Or we can mention that so-and-so claims to have come to Salem from the future. If we don't make an official complaint to a magistrate or to the constable, I think we're on legal safe ground. Just be sure to make it sound as if you heard this rumor from someone else. If you're careful you can do this safely, but effectively. The combined effect of our posters and the spreading of rumors should be most effective. With your dedicated efforts, these four men possessed by the Devil himself will be punished one way or another. If not punished, they will be forced out of Salem. Go out and fight the valiant fight on behalf of all good Christians.

AVOID THESE MEN:

Christopher Carver

Matthew Blair

Gilbert Lee

Thomas Howard

These men masquerade as normal, law-abiding members of the community, but the Evil One has taken possession of their bodies and their minds. Avoid them for your own safety. They can do you harm

Chapter 48

September 22

I DIDN'T WANT TO DO THIS, but I felt in good conscience I had to. I'd discussed it at length with Gil, Tom and Matt, and we'd all agreed it was the right thing to do, despite the problems it would cause for the four of us.

As soon as I got to work this morning I'd entered Sam's office and closed the door behind me.

Sam studied me for a minute before he said, "What's troubling you, Christopher?"

"These postings around town have gotten to me. They've gotten to Gil and Tom, too. Between the posters and the rumors that seem to be going around town, we're being treated like lepers. It's harder and harder for me to interview people for a news story. They don't want to be seen near me. The shopkeepers who used to wish us a good morning are now either saying they don't want our business, or simply taking our money without even a *good morning*. Our friend Matt is experiencing the same thing over at the *Salem Gazette*. Our landlords are saying they want us to come and go as quietly as possible, as their other tenants don't want people to know that they live with a witch. They don't say it, but I get the feeling that my landlady would be happy if I moved out. Two weeks ago she treated me as if I were part of her family."

Sam said, "This has to be extremely difficult for you and your friends. These posters must be illegal. I would hope that some magistrate would have them removed soon."

"The problem is, no one is claiming responsibility for them."

"There are only two print shops in town. It shouldn't be too difficult to find out who ordered the printing of these vile little posters."

"I could check on that myself, Sam, but I'm afraid no one would give me the time of day. I'm now *persona non grata* in Salem."

"I'll ask the constable to look into that."

"Why do you suppose he hasn't already tracked down the person behind this?"

"A very good question. One has to wonder, doesn't one?" We sat for a couple of minutes as we considered this and other questions related to this campaign blitz against us. Then Sam said, "I'm honored that you felt you could confide in me about your concerns, Christopher. I only wish I could do more."

"I didn't drop in on you just for consolation, Sam. I came in to offer my resignation. Gil and Tom also are willing to leave if our departure will take pressure off you. This rumor campaign has to be hurting your business."

"I won't hear of it, my boy. Not another word on that subject."

"But Sam, this isn't getting any better."

"We're going to get to the bottom of this. That's what newspapers do. We need to clear your name and the names of the others, too. We are also going to find out who's doing this vile thing."

"I have my ideas, but I can't prove them."

"You mean Nathaniel Ellis?"

I said, "Yes, but he's too smart to reveal it's him. I also think he has help. There's no way he could post dozens of these sheets without being seen. He must have help and even they must be posting the posters in the wee hours of the morning when the criers are not around."

"It wouldn't take much to avoid the criers. Everyone knows their routes and the times they come by.

"This Anti-Witch society must really exist, and Ellis must be part of it. His fellow members could be posting these notices. Or they could hire young boys to do it."

"Well," said Hall, "we're still under British law and the law says that accusing someone of witchcraft is a crime. Both the posters and the rumors are therefore crimes, yet these people seem emboldened to spread both posters and rumors. If we can't catch these people in the act, we'll need to conduct our own campaign against these lies. I have some ideas."

The next edition of the *Essex Gazette* contained an editorial by Sam Hall:

Scurrilous lies are being spread around the community about four young men who have come to Salem in recent months. The perpetrators of these lies hide their identity, a clear indication of their cowardice. In spreading these lies via both posters and vicious rumor, these cowering perpetrators of untruth and innuendo violate both the civil law and the law of common decency. By attacking defenseless young men who have already made numerous contributions to their new community, these vicious lie spreaders are to be scorned by ever decent person in Salem.

All four of these young men have fought valiantly for the Patriot cause. Two fought at Bunker Hill and the other two at Lexington and Concord as well as Bunker Hill.

The motive of the perpetrators is clear. They accuse these four good men of being possessed by Satan only because these men speak of wonders that may yet come in the years ahead. These men have great imaginations and bring hope of good things in the future. That does not mean they work for Lucifer.

The posters and rumors offer no proof of what they say. Rather they recklessly and cruelly spread hurtful lies that redound to the detriment of the accusers. This writer challenges the spreaders of these lies to come forth with proof of their callous accusations or immediately cease and desist in this toxic campaign of libelous indecency. In the meantime this writer urges the good citizens of Salem to be on the alert for anyone posting these posters or spreading these rumors. Please report the names of such offenders to either the constable station or the Essex Gazette. The names of anyone providing such information will be kept in confidence.

Two days after the editorial came out, Sam Hall visited Colonel Mason.

"Sam, what a pleasant surprise," said Mason. "I don't think you've ever been to my house before. It must be important."

"It is, David. It is. It's about these foul posters that are appearing all over Salem. I'm sure you've seen them."

"I have and I find them most disturbing. Something has to be done about it. Do you have any idea what vicious soul is responsible for this libelous display? Why someone would malign four of the finest young men I have had the pleasure of working with in my entire life is a mystery to me."

"I do have a good idea, but I can't prove it. Until I do have proof, something has to be done about these posters and these rumors. Have you heard any of the rumors?"

"As a matter of fact I have heard one. Somebody I respect told me he heard from a neighbor that this young chap who works for Sam Hall at the *Gazette* practices all kinds of amazing magic. He was almost certainly referring to Christopher Carver. According to this person, this young chap practices a kind of magic that far exceeds the magic practiced by some of the folks accused of witchcraft back in '92. He said he didn't know if it was true, but thought I should be aware of it. Is that the kind of rumor you're talking about, Sam?"

"Yes, that's exactly the kind I'm talking about. Rumors of that ilk and similar to that have been reported all over town. Some mention the other young men who've come to town recently."

"Sam, how can I help?"

"I have at least one idea, if you're willing."

Chapter 49

September 29

COLONEL DAVID MASON'S editorial in the latest edition of the *Essex Gazette* gave a strong defense of the four of us newcomers. He described in vivid detail how all four of us had fought valiantly as he put it in both the battles of Lexington and Concord and more recently the bloody battle at Bunker Hill. Mason's editorial asked, "Would men possessed by the Devil risk their lives fighting side by side with Provincial patriots if the Evil One intended them to do harm to their fellow citizens? Would these same young men go to the aid of injured soldiers if the Devil wanted them to hurt good people?" His editorial went on to say that he had made judgments about hundreds of men in his military career and these four men ranked among the finest of any he'd ever seen.

In the same issue of the *Gazette*, Sam had published a letter from Obadiah Taliaferro, the leader of the Amesbury Committee of Safety saying fine things about Matt and me. Taliaferro's letter and Mason's editorial both said they were shocked and appalled at the scurrilous attacks on us by the cowardly men attacking us. If these scandalmongers truly believed what they were saying they should have the courage to come forward and defend their attacks in person. If they were unwilling to make their identities known, the public should ignore them and God should punish them.

Ebenezer Purdy asked Ellis to call an emergency meeting of the Anti-Witch Society. He urged Ellis to call the meeting for the following day even though that gave them very little time to reach all the members. Purdy felt it was so important that he said, "Even if everyone cannot attend, it's important that some of us meet because things have gotten serious, Nathaniel. We have to make some decisions."

The next day ten Society members found themselves in Ellis's parlor. It had been inconvenient for some of them to make it, but they all realized just how important it was that they get together and discuss things.

Ellis called the meeting to order. Meeting on such short notice had been an inconvenience for him, too, as his wife was growing tired of being shunted out of the house for these gatherings of Society members. She was not enthusiastic about his involvement in the Society anyway, as she was not convinced that witches were as commonplace as her husband so fervently believed. Many of the people he claimed to be witches or otherwise possessed she wrote off as just being a bit odd. She had said on more than one occasion that you couldn't go around accusing people of being witches just because they had odd habits or a personality you disapproved of. He loved his wife, but she found good in everyone. It was the sort of naïeveté that allowed Satan to flourish. He surveyed the room. He had to shake off these thoughts. The members were eager to begin.

"My friends, it is unfortunate that I had to ask you back to my parlor on so little notice, but brother Purdy has deemed it necessary. I suppose I agree with him." He then directed his attention to Purdy and said, "Ebenezer, why don't you tell us your concerns."

"For a few days our efforts went ahead as planned. And they were effective. I have it on good authority that all four of the warlocks we directed our efforts against were suffering directly as a result of the poster campaign and the rumors we initiated in the community. These men have been under pressure to leave their jobs. The owners of their lodgings wanted them out. They are snubbed on the street. They are not welcome in many shops. It was only a matter of time when they would be forced from the community if not physically attacked by some Salemites who could no longer abide them." He saw from the nods that his fellow Society members agreed with him so far. Would they have an answer to the problem that now faced them? He would find out now.

"I'm sure most of you now know that a fierce counterattack has been waged against us by Sam Hall's *Essex Gazette*. It's a respected paper and people take it seriously. Sam has apparently dug up support from Colonel Mason, a well-known and highly respected Salem citizen and leader of the Salem Militia. Editorials and letters in the *Gazette* have challenged us to come forth with proof of what we have been saying about these four men. My question to you is how do we respond to this challenge? Or do we respond?"

Ellis rose with all the gravity of a superior court judge. "Friends, the only way to meet this challenge is for one of us to come forth and state our case openly. Until this counterattack by the *Gazette* and Colonel Mason, our plan was effective. They have called us on our approach and only a coward would hide behind anonymity under these circumstances. One of us should come forth and I believe it should be yours truly."

Ezra Crane stood up abruptly and said, "No, Nathaniel. It is too risky. They could take away your freedom. It's not worth it."

"Thank you for your concern Ezra, but I believe this is one of those times in a man's life where he has to take risks. God gives me no choice." Then the seriousness left his face and a smug smirk transformed it as he said, "Besides, I believe people in this town respect me so much that I could kill one of these tools of Satan in the middle of Essex Street and citizens would applaud me. Not only that, I believe that if people in Salem learned of our existence, they would applaud what we are trying to do."

Purdy rose with a concerned look on his face. "Nathaniel we know that you are well respected in the community, but not as many people view witches and witchcraft as a major threat these days as they did in 1692. A few still do, but I'm not so sure that in 1775 a majority of the citizens here in Massachusetts would agree with our thinking. All I'm saying, Nathaniel, is that if you openly declare that we are behind this campaign against these four men, it may go wrong, and you may regret it. We may all regret it. I urge you to reconsider what you just said."

"I'm surprised at you, Ebenezer. I took you to be one of the strongest advocates of what we are trying to do. You're a good church-going member of the community. God is on our side. How can we have doubts at a time when the Evil One is testing our faith? Now, is the time to remain stalwart. Now is not the time for the faint of heart."

"All well and good," said Crane, "but we should not forget that much of what we do is in direct defiance of the civil law. We may be able to defend ourselves in the eyes of the Lord, but civil law now takes precedence over the law of the church when the two come in conflict. Civil magistrates now determine what is lawful and what isn't. Sad to say, but it's true."

"That may be true in Boston or New York, but this is Salem. Folks in Salem still place God above secular concerns. Don't forget, one of the first Protestant churches in the 13 English colonies was established in Salem. Salem is the birthplace of Puritanism in America. Have faith, my brothers. If this becomes a matter for the civil authorities, our local magistrates will honor us, not condemn us."

Another member rose slowly. When all eyes turned to him he said, "Your confidence in how our actions will be viewed is admirable, Nathaniel, but if you are wrong it is not just you who will suffer the consequences. All of us will be held accountable by the civil law. Do you feel that you should be putting us all at risk?"

"Frankly, my brethren, I am becoming tired of this timidity among our noble society. I had thought we were all stronger than what I am hearing. We formed this Society to fight against evil. Are we unwilling to continue that fight when we meet with the slightest resistance?"
Purdy said, "When we formed this society seven years ago we agreed tha it was best to make it a secret society. Not because we were too cowardly to make it a public society, but because we knew even then that our views wouldn't be accepted by everyone in the community. Nothing has changed in those seven years. I think we should remain a secret society in that it will be true to our founding principles. Even if I agreed with

you, Nathaniel, that we should break with that seven-year tradition in order to set the record straight about these four men we suspect as being warlocks, we don't have enough proof of our accusations to convince people that we are right. If we go public we put ourselves at risk, yet accomplish nothing."

Ellis's temper was at the point of erupting. How could these people keep questioning his judgment? "Then how in the name of God do we expect to take the pressure off ourselves if we don't at least attempt to show that it is these four men who should go to the gallows, not us?"

"Dear God, Nathaniel," said Purdy, "You don't really believe that we would be hanged if we cannot support our allegations? If you even think that's even a possibility, then we should not go public." The others in the room echoed his sentiments with "Agreed, agreed."

"Good Lord, Ebenezer, get a hold of yourself. The maximum penalty for violating the Witch Act is one year in prison. So far no one has ever been sentenced to even that . . . . as far as I know. Let's try to concentrate our thinking on coming up with some kind of evidence to justify our campaign against these warlocks. If we do that we won't have to worry about a thing. It'll be Christopher Carver and his Devil-loving friends who'll do the worrying."

The meeting was going on longer than Ellis had expected. He heard his wife as she returned from the neighbor he had suggested she visit.

He faced the group and said, "Excuse me for a moment. My wife has returned from visiting with a neighbor. I just want to tell her that we'll be finishing up shortly. Be right back."

When he left the room Ebenezer Purdy rose and addressed his fellow members.

"I think we're all in agreement that we cannot afford to go public as the organization behind the campaign against these four men. We know in our hearts that we are right, but we don't have enough evidence to support our claims. The risk is too great. We must be firm about this when Nathaniel returns. Do I have your agreement?"

To a man they all uttered their support. Just as Purdy sat down, Ellis re-entered the room offering a nervous smile. "Gentlemen, I think it best that we call it a night. My wife is about to go to bed and I fear that our conversation will disturb her. She has not been feeling well lately, so I want her to get her sleep. Before you go, though, I hope we can agree that it is best that I go public with this tomorrow. I have every confidence that the majority of folks in Salem will agree with what we have been doing, despite the disappointing behavior of Sam Hall and his *Gazette*."

A look of exasperation transfigured Ebenezer Purdy's face as he rose to respond.

"Nathaniel, much as it pains us, we don't agree. In your brief absence we discussed this and concluded that we are all against any such disclosure. Please do not go public with our involvement."

Ellis was fuming, but he couldn't allow the discussion to get out of hand. He didn't want his wife knowing anything about what the Society discussed. Yes, she knew that they were in principle against witchcraft and yes, she knew that some of them wished for the days when witches were punished, but as far as he knew she had no idea that they were actually taking action against men who were allegedly possessed by the Evil One.

He didn't fear his wife. She took orders from him, and she obeyed him dutifully as a good wife should. What he did fear was that she had a wide circle of female friends she met with frequently. If she were to share with them any of the plans or actions taken by the Society, it could give support or warning to the very people he was trying to punish.

The members were still waiting for his response. He had to be careful with his words.

"My good friends, I appreciate the thought that has gone into your heartfelt request. I want you all to know that I will not do anything that I believe to be wrong."

Purdy jumped up. "That is not exactly saying that you will comply with our wishes."

The impertinence of these men had gotten out of hand. He was the founder of the Anti-Witch Society. Without him, nothing would happen. Who in God's realm did they think they were?

"It is not my role to comply with your wishes. Without me you would be nothing. I will do what I want, and I'll thank you to remember that. This is my Society, not yours. I gave you the benefit of my thinking on the subject and you rejected it. That is your right, but my right as leader and founder of this group is to make the final decision. Now I think it best that you all leave. Good night."

Chapter 50

September 30
NATHANIEL ELLIS presented himself to Ezekial Russell, the publisher of the *Salem Gazette*, Salem's other newspaper and the place where Chris Carver's fellow chrononaut, Matthew Blair, worked.

"What can I do for you Mr. Ellis," asked Russell hesitantly. Ellis was known for not being overly friendly. He seldom greeted people unless he had a complaint. Russell, on the other hand, was a big teddy bear of a man in his late sixties with a jovial nature. Sometimes people misread his friendly, outgoing manner as weakness. He was far more serious about journalism than his cordial manner suggested.

"I was hoping you could help me."

"And how might I be of help to you, sir?"

"I suppose you have heard about the poster campaign around town . . . the one accusing four young men of being possessed?"

"Of course. Who hasn't? Do you know something about that?"

"I know that your competitor, the *Essex Gazette*, has launched a retaliative strike against the campaign."

"Yes, I know that. I read the competition. You have to know what they're saying. Again I ask, how might I be of help to you?"

"I was hoping that your excellent paper might put the lie to what the *Essex Gazette* has been saying about the campaign. After all, all the campaign has been doing is warning our good citizens of the very real danger in their midst. Journalists should be praising the campaign, not attacking it."

Russell did his best to keep from smiling. "You feel rather strongly about this, Mr. Ellis. What is your interest in this campaign?"

"I'm just a public-spirited citizen who cares about his community."

"And you have no other connection to the campaign?"

"As a matter of fact I belong to a group of citizens who share my views on this. I speak on behalf of all of them. It's important that you know that many in the community believe that something has to be done about these four warlocks. The *Essex Gazette* has taken the side of Satan on this issue. I was certain that you and your paper would take the side of Christ and combat the Evil One before he takes control of all of Salem."

"I see. Yes, I think this could be an interesting story for our paper. It's important that our readers become as well informed as possible. Hopefully with your knowledge of this campaign you could tell me who I would talk to if I wanted more information about it?"

Encouraged by Russell's interest in the campaign, Ellis said, "I can give you all the information you need. I fashioned the idea myself." He said this proudly.

"You did. That's very interesting. No one helped you? That's an ambitious campaign for just one person."

"Oh I had help. As I said, there's this modest group of good citizens who worked with me on this project. It was much too much for one person."

"If we do a story on this it would be only fair to give as much credit to your friends as possible. If you could give me some of their names, I'll try to include them. Why don't we go into my office so I can take some notes. I don't want to trust this to my memory. It's too important."

Ellis was pleased that he'd thought of going to see Russell. This could work out better than he and his fellow Society members could have hoped. To have the other respected newspaper on his side could turn the tide against the four disciples of Satan. At the very least it would take the pressure off him.

As he leaned back in his chair in Russell's office, he began to relax. Things were going better than he'd expected after last night's disappointing meeting with his spineless fellow members. He gave Russell several names and leaned back confidently. "Anything else I can tell you? "

"How did you know these four men were possessed by the Evil One? You and your other fellow citizens wouldn't have created this poster campaign if you didn't have a reason."

"I witnessed with my own eyes some of their black magic at a meeting at the Social Library."

"Aha. You actually witnessed this black magic. That's interesting. Frankly I'm surprised at their boldness. I wouldn't expect someone who was possessed to actually demonstrate it at a meeting of respected citizens. Why do you suppose they took that chance?"

Ellis broke into a smug grin. "When I tell you, you will see what we're up against here in Salem. The Evil One has infused these men with such arrogance that they don't realize how they insult our intelligence."

"I'm afraid, sir, that I don't follow you."

"They claim to have come to Salem from the future. The year 2019 to be precise." He waited a few seconds for this to sink in, then said, "I see by your expression that you're beginning to understand what the community is up against. Believe me, I was there. These four young men said they had come here by means of something they called a spaceship— a ship that flies through the air. I wish you had been there. It was one outlandish claim after another. At first I thought they were making these claims in jest, but it soon became clear that they were deadly serious."

Russell was thrown by what he'd just heard. Up until now he'd been convinced that Ellis was a throwback to the nineties—someone who suspected almost any eccentric person of being possessed by the Devil. Now, if what Ellis was telling him was true, he had to examine the whole issue more carefully. Clearly, if Ellis's account was accurate, these men were at the very least not of sound mind. Yet this made no sense. One of them perhaps, but not all four of them could be out of their mind at the same time. He found it hard to believe that anyone would openly declare something so ridiculous. There had to be more to this. He would press Ellis for more details and then have one of his people talk with one or two of the trustees at the Social Library to get their version of what Ellis had told him. His head was spinning.

"I have a few more questions if you don't mind?"

"Not at all. What else can I tell you?"

"What reason did these four men have for speaking before you people at the Social Library in the first place. I can't believe the library would give an audience to such men without good reason."

"Apparently several months back two of these young men came to the library with a request to place a sealed document in their archives so that some of their colleagues in the 21st century could retrieve them in order to learn about their experiences in our century." Ellis noted the doubtful expression on Russell's face and said, "I know. Preposterous, but hear me out. It gets better. Naturally the trustees were skeptical and turned them down. The young men were persistent and asked for a chance to prove to the trustees that they were not lying . . . that they were telling the truth about where they came from. Now here's where it got really interesting. I was not present, but apparently several of the trustees went out to Great Misery Island to see them attempt to salvage this spaceship that was now underwater. My fellow trustees told me that they had actually witnessed the spaceship when it was brought up from the depths."

"Are you telling me that these young men were telling the truth . . . that there actually was a spaceship?"

"They maintain that they saw this spaceship. They claim that it was brought up on the shore of Great Misery Island, yet if you go there as I did, it cannot be found."

"Surely you're not saying that your fellow trustees were lying?"

"No, they are all good men. Don't you see, the two young warlocks worked their magic on the minds of these good men. If ever there was evidence of the power of the Evil One when he takes possession of human souls, this is it. My Social Library colleagues believe that they saw this so-called spaceship because black magic made them believe it. It is perhaps the most powerful example of what possessed individuals can do that I have ever heard of."

"I see. That is truly remarkable," said Russell.

"Then the *Salem Gazette* will write a story about what I've told you?"

"Good Lord, sir. We would be remiss in our duty to our readers if we did not."

|

An hour later, Russell asked Matt to come into his office. "Matthew, I need to talk with you about something. I just had a visit from one Nathaniel Ellis. Mr. Ellis is a prominent shipping merchant in Salem."

"Yessir. I know who he is."

"Well Mr. Ellis has taken responsibility for this poster campaign against you and your three mates. He claims to represent a group here in Salem who are behind it and he wants us here at the *Salem Gazette* to write a story setting the record straight. By that he means showing how Sam Hall and his paper are on the wrong side of the issue."

Matt pursed his lips. He couldn't believe what he was hearing. "You mean to tell me, sir, that he is proud of this campaign?"

"Very definitively. At first I was ready to write a story endorsing the position that Sam Hall has taken." He smiled. "Believe me, that doesn't happen often. Then Ellis told me something that has me confused. If what he told me is right, then I'm not sure how we should handle our story and I'm not sure how I should handle you."

Matt didn't get rattled easily, but this set him back. "My God, sir, what could he have told you that would make you say that?"

"He told a story of how your mates, Gilbert and Thomas, I believe, showed the trustees of the Social Library something called a spaceship that they salvaged from the sea off Great Misery Island. They did this to prove that they had come to Salem from the future. Matthew, what kind of poppycock is this? Wait, don't answer me yet. Let me finish with what Ellis told me. He then said that when he went to investigate for himself, there was no so-called spaceship to be found. Big surprise there. Ellis takes that as proof that your mates Gilbert and Thomas were possessed and that the Evil One who possessed them had clouded the minds of the trustees into thinking they had seen this spaceship, thereby believing your mates and granting them permission to leave some sort of document to be opened by their colleagues in the year 2015. There. I think that sums it up fairly well. Now, Matthew, what can you tell me about all this because I don't mind telling you that I don't know where to begin. All of this is so outlandish I'm hoping you can shed some light on it. Is Ellis telling the truth or is he fabricating this ridiculous story?"

Matt had no choice but to come clean about his own background if he was going to explain the situation to his boss. He'd lied to Russell when he was hired when he told him that he had come from Halifax. He'd done it because he and his three friends from the future wanted to keep the awareness of their actual origin limited to a very few people. He now realized that it had been a mistake to keep the truth from the man he was asking to give him a chance by giving him a job. Now he had to deal with that mistake.

"Sir, Ellis is telling the truth. My friends did come to Salem in a spaceship . . ."

Russell, who was known for his temper, was livid. "I should show you the door right now." he roared.

Chapter 51

September 30
"**WHAT IN GOD'S NAME** do you take me for, Matthew?"

"Please, sir, let me explain. My friends did in fact come from the future. The truth is, I did, too." Russell started to object, but Matt held up his hand and said, "I was afraid to tell you because my friends and I felt it best to limit the truth to a very few people. You should have been one of those people since you were good enough to give me employment. I'm very sorry for that."

Russell looked dumbstruck, as if he didn't know whether to fire Matt or throw up his hands in disbelief at what he'd been hearing. "Matthew, this is no time for tomfoolery. I called you in here because I had a serious question to talk about. I expect you to take this seriously."

Matt pulled out his cell phone and said, "I am taking this very seriously, sir. If I may, I'd like to show you something. Hopefully this will convince you that what I'm telling you is true, as amazing as it must seem to you. This device I'm holding is what we call a cell phone in the 21st century." Matt held out the phone and took a photo of his boss's desk. He then showed the photo to Russell, whose eyes popped at what he was seeing.

"This is truly remarkable, Matthew. How did you do that?"

"Technology has advanced tremendously by the 21st century. We call that a photograph. Here, let me show you another photograph. I think this might help you understand what a spaceship is. I then showed him a photo of our spaceship on the launch site back in Nevada."

"My God," that is truly amazing. That thing actually flies through the air?"

"Yes sir. It flew through the air of our atmosphere here on Earth. Then, when it left our atmosphere, it flew through outer space where there is no atmosphere. No air at all. These photographs, or photos as we call them, are taken by what we call a camera, which is part of the cell phone. If you've heard of the *camera obscura*, you'll understand the scientific principle behind the camera, which applies that principle to a much smaller device and through science is able to record the image that the camera sees. I can take a picture of anything you can imagine."

"You use a strange terminology when you say, 'take a picture.' You are not exactly taking anything, are you?"

"No, I suppose not. Somehow we've come to say that when we use a camera. The cell phone does other things, too. It can take pictures of things that are moving and record what we say. Here, let me show you.

Would you walk from behind your desk to the door and say something while you're doing it?"

Russell did as Matthew asked and said, "I feel foolish doing this."

When Matt showed him the short video and his boss heard himself talk while walking the few feet to the door, he shook his head from side to side in awe. "That is truly an amazing device you have, Matthew. Who has such things in the 21st century that you claim to have come from?"

"Most people, sir. They are quite common. What I've shown you is not the principal use of a cell phone. People use them most to communicate with one another. Even with people many miles away. In 2015 people talk into their cell phones and communicate with people on the other side of the world. People in Boston can talk to people in London, for example."

"Show me how you do that?"

Matt was afraid he'd ask. "Unfortunately, I can't do that in the 18th century because someone else has to have a cell phone too. Even if someone did, it still wouldn't work because there are no cell towers." As soon as he said this, Russell's blank look told him he would have to explain further, which he did. It wasn't easy to do, either. How do you explain radio waves and cell towers to someone in 1775? Even an educated person. Matt did the best he could and when he was through the expression on Ezekiel Russell's face told him that his boss didn't know what to make of what he'd been told. Matt waited for Russell to say something.

After what seemed like an eternity, his boss said, "Matthew, I'm not sure I quite fathom everything you've told me, but you've been an excellent employee in the short time you've been with me. You've also been a good influence on my other employees. I have no reason to believe what's being spread by these posters. Quite honestly, I'm not sure there are as many witches among us as Mr. Ellis seems to think. My grandparents told me that one of our relatives was accused of witchcraft back in '92. Fortunately, the trials were terminated before she was hanged, but my grandparents believed she was far from being a witch. She was a good neighbor to all and a very fine woman. If there are witches, they are few and far between. Certainly it is an evil in itself to wantonly accuse people of being possessed when there is no evidence of anything of the sort. Matthew, we are going to fight this poster campaign. Sam Hall will be shocked when he learns that we're fighting for the same thing."

Then Matt remembered something. "Oh, by the way, sir, Ellis wasn't lying about everything. The reason he couldn't see the spaceship that his fellow trustees had seen, is that the ship was designed to rust away at a very fast rate once it had arrived in the 18ths century. It was designed that way so as not to leave evidence of our arrival for too many people to see. Again we didn't want our presence to be known by many so that our presence wouldn't alter the course of history."

215

Chapter 52

October 6

AS A RESULT OF two very effective articles supported by persuasive editorials written by respected members of the community, pressure mounted on Nathaniel Ellis and his Anti-Witch Society. People began to scoff at the posters and started to snub Ellis on the rare occasions he was seen about town. He wasn't liked anyway and now he was becoming a virtual outcast. More importantly, a number of community leaders pressured Constable Gray into arresting Ellis on the charge of violating the Witch Act. Ellis's lawyer, Simon Fields, defended Ellis on the grounds that Ellis himself did not actually accuse anyone of practicing witchcraft. It was the posters, not him. That was, of course, ridiculous, but Gray's town attorney botched the job and somehow the jury sided with Ellis. Maybe this indicated that more people believed in witches than we'd thought. In any event, Ellis walked away smugly, more confident than ever that he was right. He was, however, furious that we and our supporters had gone after him. Since I was the one of the four newcomers he knew best, he made it clear that I would rue the day I ever questioned his integrity.

I was well aware of his feelings, as friends and even new supporters kept me informed. Sam Hall said I should be careful, since Ellis was clearly a vindictive, mean-spirited man. I knew that, but what could I do? I certainly wasn't going to hide from him. I would go about my business and hope he would do the same. The man obviously had nine lives. He should be in the Salem Jail now, but he wasn't. He was responsible for the death of one person and he tried to kill me, yet he was still a free man. Of course, his reputation was now so tarnished that most people avoided him unless they absolutely had to do business with him, but he was still a free man. An embittered man, but still free.

After dinner and a couple ales at Pierce's Tavern, I was on my way home on foot. I lived about three quarters of a mile from the Tavern, so it was a good way to burn off a few of the calories I'd consumed at dinner. I'd gotten into the habit of eating at Pierce's several times a week. That way I got to meet up with some of my new friends and acquaintances. It was also much easier than preparing a meal in my little apartment on Essex Street. It had no kitchen. The building I lived in had a central kitchen, which was shared by all the tenants. It made it very difficult to put together a meal for yourself. It wasn't easy to prepare meals in 1775 anyway. You couldn't just pick up some things at the local supermarket, as there were no supermarkets or convenience stores. There were greengrocers and meat markets, but you had to prepare everything from scratch. I didn't feel like plucking a chicken after working at the *Gazette* all day. Neither did I want to roast coffee beans or soak and blanch hams to make them edible. And I certainly didn't feel like firing up a wood stove so that I could cook my meal. If I did eat at home it was usually bread and cheese and maybe an apple. It cost more to eat at Pierce's, but it was easier and frankly, a lot more sociable.

This particular night, after an especially tasty beef stew at Pierce's, I was enjoying the clear, crisp air on my walk home. As I approached my building, I saw a man standing in front of the door staring at me. When I drew closer it became clear that it was Nathaniel Ellis, the last person I wanted to see.

"Aren't you a long way from home?" I said.

"Yes, I don't normally find myself in this part of town, but I wanted to warn you."

"Warn me about what?"

That you should expect to be killed at any time. The reason I'm warning you now is that part of the joy I'll get from your departure from this Earth will be knowing that before that fatal moment you will always be looking over your shoulder. You will constantly be fearing that you could be fallen upon at any moment."

"You're actually threatening me?"

"Yes I am. And enjoying every delightful minute of that threat."

"So you intend to attack me when I least expect it. That's sick."

"It may not be me. There are others who would see you dead. Don't you see, that's the beauty of the threat. It could be anyone at any time. Oh, in case you were thinking of reporting this visit to the constable, don't bother. I'll deny it, and you will have no proof that I was even here."

The next morning I told Sam what had happened the night before. I didn't tell him because I was looking for sympathy. I told him because I thought he should know in case Ellis tried to make good on his promise. I figured there was a good chance he would, as he was self-deluded and filled with hatred. Sam took the news seriously and said that it should be reported to Constable Gray right away. I told him I would, but wasn't sure what the constable could do about it because it would be Ellis's word against mine. As far as I knew, there were no witnesses to our conversation last night. On my way to the constable station I was thinking that it was probably a waste of time. Ellis was as slippery as an eel. He constantly evaded justice no matter how serious the crime. Without a witness Constable Gray was going to shake his head and say there was nothing he could do. At least that's what I expected.

I entered the station and asked one of his deputies if I could see the constable. The deputy recognized me and said, "It's good that you're here. Constable Gray wants to see you."

That was a surprise. Things couldn't get worse, or could they?

A minute later Gray emerged from the rear of the station and said, "Glad you're here, Carver. Let's go back to my office."

His office couldn't have been much more than 8 by 10 feet. When we were seated in the tiny rough-hewn room, he said, "What did you want to see me about?"

I told him about how Ellis had confronted me the night before and how he'd threatened me repeatedly. I volunteered that as far as I knew there were no witnesses."

He smiled when I finished and I couldn't help thinking he must be treating the threats as a joke. It gets pretty discouraging when the chief law enforcement officer in town doesn't take death threats seriously. He finally spoke. "Mr. Carver, less than an hour ago a gentleman was in here claiming to be a witness to a confession of guilt on the part of Nathaniel Ellis."

"Guilty of what, sir?"

"Inciting to murder. I shouldn't be telling you this, but Ellis has put you and your friends through so much torment that I thought you should know."

"Who is this witness, if I may ask?"

"I doubt if you know him. It doesn't matter anyway. He's a member of something called the Anti-Witch Society. Ellis is the leader of this group. They formed a few years ago with the express purpose of making life miserable for anyone they suspected of being possessed. Being witches, in other words. Apparently in a moment of hubris Ellis boasted of this to the members of this group. He said he had persuaded a young schoolteacher in Lynn to take the life of Elihu Martin."

"Why would he admit that?"

"Apparently to demonstrate to his sycophants that he was extremely serious about the mission of this misguided group."

"By coming to you wasn't the witness admitting to sharing that guilt?"

"He claims that their secret society was dedicated to making life uncomfortable for those they suspected, but not to killing anyone. He said most of his fellow society members were shocked by Ellis's admission, but are afraid to challenge him. Said his conscience finally got to him and he felt he had to take the risk to stop Ellis from killing someone else. He said that over the years Ellis has gradually become more suspicious of people in the community and more violent."

"I see. I assume you're going to arrest him?"

"Yes. I hesitated at first because the man seems to lead a charmed life. He's hard to convict, but now that I have one good witness. . . oh by the way, he thinks at least two others will come forth now that he has taken that first step. At any rate, I'm sure we can send Ellis to the gallows this time. If not that, at least he'll spend the rest of his life in jail. I don't know if you've seen the inside of the Salem jail, but you wouldn't want to spend one day there, much less a lifetime. Oh, and Mr. Carver, it'll help if you'll also testify. I assume I can count on you."

"Very definitely."

"I expected you'd say that. I haven't known you very long, but in the short time that we've been acquainted I've come to respect you and your three friends. Quite honestly, when I first met you I had the feeling that you were holding something back. I was suspicious of you and your intentions. Since then, too many respectable folks have had good things to say about you. Don't disappoint me."

When I left the station I wondered whether we should have told the constable about where we came from. He deserved to know. Still, too many people knew now. We couldn't afford to let things get completely out of hand. Things were turning our way now. We should leave it that way.

Chapter 53

October 31, 1775

THE TRIAL OF NATHANIEL ELLIS had gone well. Well for Salem. Not so well for Ellis. His lawyer kept Ellis from the gallows. He'd argued that his client may have said things that Talbot interpreted as being directives to kill Elihu Martin, but that was not their intent. Talbot was sick in the head and misread Ellis. Afterward, some of the jurors said that they believed Ellis tried to persuade Talbot, but the judge stated that the law said the intent had to be clear. Since Ellis's words were subject to interpretation, the jury concluded that he contributed to the death of Martin and that Ellis should spend at least 30 years in the Salem jail. I was happy with that. It seemed as close to justice as one could expect in a community where many people still believed in witches and possession. Talbot's fate was not at all subject to interpretation. Under pressure he admitted to dispatching Martin and was sentenced to hang. I frankly thought the penalties should have been reversed, but at least both men paid dearly for their transgressions.

When the trial ended, Matt, Gil and Tom, over a few brews in the Tavern, said it might be time to send a summary of my journal to our team back in 2019. We were sure they'd be eager for some word as to how things were going. We agreed that a recapitulation of our experience in the Battle of Bunker Hill and the threats from Nathaniel Ellis would be stressed, but we knew they would also want to read about our everyday experiences. So far, leaving a log or journal with the Social Library was the only way we knew of communicating with our people back in the 21st century. We knew that they would go to the Salem Athenaeum periodically and ask them to look for it in their archives. Gil and Tom had done that, and we intended to do it also. Actually, it didn't matter when we placed the journal in the Social Library. No matter when we did it, it would be there in 2019. Still, it was a good idea to place it soon while our memories were strong. We could always update it in the future as we experienced more.

There was a remote chance that someday we would be able to return to Nevada, but we weren't counting on it. It was a longshot. When we left Nevada, the engineers and other brass were already working on a larger ship for a third mission. The larger ship would have the ability to pick up one or more of the four of us and take us back to the 21st century. The plan was complicated by the need to keep people in 1775 unaware of the ship because awareness of it would definitely change the course of history. In order to send such a ship, yet make 18th century people unaware of it, the engineers would have to put the ship into orbit around Earth and send a smaller ship down to Earth. Even that presented enormous problems, because even a small ship had to remain undetected. How to do that was the biggest problem of all for Mission 3. You also had to know when to pick up your return-trip passenger. You couldn't phone for obvious reasons. You could, however, use radio. The engineers said they thought they could orbit the mother ship at about 250 miles above the Earth. Radio waves should work fine. They'd provided Matt and me with very sensitive pocket radios that were solar powered. Our instructions were to keep our radios on during daylight hours every day starting one year after we arrived in Salem. They couldn't narrow it down more than that. They hoped they could lift off from Nevada sometime during that second year, but that's all they could promise. If we didn't hear from the mother ship the first year, we should keep listening. There was no guarantee they could ever pull this off, but it gave us something to hold onto. It wasn't that any of us were desperate to return.

The fact of the matter was that all of us had adapted. Actually, that's not fair. It was more than mere adaptation. All four of us liked our new lives. Some of us had met someone with whom we'd become attached. As a matter of fact, I recently met a young woman that I was spending more and more time with. Enough time that I wasn't eager to leave her. Still, all four of us knew that at least one of us should return to the 21st century if we got the opportunity. It was too important to the time-travel program for all of us to turn down the opportunity. Jason Farnsworth, the government and the other people behind the program deserved as much first-hand return on their financial, intellectual and emotional investment in the program as we could give them. Most likely returning to Nevada wouldn't be as much of a sacrifice as it would at first appear to be. The movers and shakers behind the program said that if one or more of us are able to return, they could go back to the 18th century on the fourth mission if they wanted to. If all that can be pulled off, it's likely a fourth mission will be approved.

Chapter 54

October 20, 2019

AS MADISON HALLIDAY ENTERED THE Salem Athenaeum the young woman behind the desk looked up and smiled.

"How may I help you?"

Halliday did a quick scan of the warm, tasteful wood-paneled room with its rows of old books from floor to ceiling. At the moment it appeared that she was the only visitor.

"I'm Madison Halliday from the Center for Advance Exploration in Nevada. Are you Trish?"

"Yes. I remember the first time capsule you people retrieved a few years ago."

"Are you the one who contacted us about another time capsule that you have here at the Athenaeum? I understand it's addressed to me and two of my colleagues."

"Yes I contacted your organization. This is the second time capsule that we've found in our archives. Someone claimed the first one back in 2015, I think it was. That was very exciting. I'm assuming this one is just as exciting. The package itself is quite old. Much like the first one. It says on the wrapping that it should be given to the Center for Advanced Exploration on October 20, 2019. I remember that first package was from the year 1775. Is this another time capsule from the same year?"

"Yes, I think it is, though I can't be sure. I certainly hope it is, or close to 1775 anyway. The first one came from 1775, and you probably know that we were surprised. Shocked would be more accurate because the plan for the mission had been to send the two men two years into the future. You can imagine the surprise when we found they'd gone back in time about 240 years."

Trish smiled at this.

"I know, it sounds pretty incompetent, but believe me, it's not easy to control your destination in time travel. The last time we did this was the first successful time travel ever in the history of the world. We'll get better at it. As you can see by the date on the package, we are already getting better at it.

Trish looked puzzled. Halliday realized why. "The fact that it says 1775 is really reassuring to us, because it means our second mission landed in exactly the time period we were shooting for. That is an amazing accomplishment. When we open the time capsule and see what our chrononauts say about the trip, we'll see just how successful the second mission was."

"You said chrononauts. I think I know what you mean by that, though it's the first time I've ever heard anyone speak it."

Halliday knew that Trish and the Trustees had seen the first time capsule four years ago. At that time the library had said they wouldn't let it out of their hands until they'd at least had a chance to view it. They'd vowed to keep what they'd seen secret. So far Halliday had no reason to believe they had violated what they'd agreed to. She hadn't known whether they would keep the existence of the time capsule secret or not, but she had no choice. She had to retrieve Chris's journal. This time once again the CAE had to let the library see the new time capsule.

You might wonder why the Social Library would agree to keep the original time capsule in their archives in the first place. Gil and Tom had promised them that when it was opened in the 21st century, the CAE would give the library a fairly large sum of money . . . 100-times the amount Gil and Tom had given the Social Library at the time.

Trish said, "Before I give it to you I must let the trustees know. Of course they're aware that we have the time capsule. They asked me to notify them as soon as you arrived. They're as eager to see it as you are. I can try to round them up for tonight if you don't mind waiting a few hours."

Halliday knew she could have demanded to see it immediately, but the Athenaeum had played such an important role in the CAE's ability to communicate with the past that they had agreed to allow them to be part of the little ritual of turning over the capsule to the organization.

"That's fine. What time shall I plan to come back this evening?"

"Let's say seven. I think I can get them all here by that time. I can't wait to see what's in there. You can't imagine what it's like to have something like this in your hands and know you can't open it."

"Oh I think I can."

At seven o'clock the chairs were assembled around a large table in one fairly large room in the Athenaeum. In all Madison Halliday counted 11 people including herself, Trish and the trustees. She was told that the trustees hadn't changed in the last four years so nobody new would be privy to what they were all going to witness that evening.

Trish introduced Halliday and then turned the meeting over to Carlotta Robb, the president of the board of trustees. Halliday estimated Robb to be in her late fifties. The woman had short, stylishly cut graying hair and a pleasant face. She was about five-six and carried herself as if she was used to having responsibility. She waited until the room fell silent, then began by saying, "I want to welcome Madison Halliday who's come all the way from Nevada to be here with us. I remember vividly the last time we opened a time capsule for the Center for Advanced Exploration. We were all overwhelmed by what we saw. I expect tonight we're in for a similar surprise. I must stress that we've agreed with the Center for Advanced Exploration that whatever we view here tonight will be held in strict confidence until the CAE decides to go public with their explorations. Most people find explorers exciting and admirable. We're privileged to be in on humankind's first time-travel explorations, something that only a few years ago was only discussed in science fiction. It's imperative that all of us honor our agreement about keeping this project secret. Premature release of this information could create all sorts of problems for the CAE, the Athenaeum and perhaps even the human race. With that said, I'm going to turn this over to Madison Halliday."

"Good evening. Believe me, I'm as excited as you are. This is an historic moment for science and for the world. I wish it could be made public, but we're not quite ready for that at this point. This is what we're all eager to open." She held up a package that was perhaps just under two inches thick and about 10 by 12 inches in size. It was wrapped in brown paper that looked quite old. It was obvious that the paper was hand made because it was rough around the edges and you could actually see the fibers in it. It occurred to her that her small audience could not see the package very well from their seats so she said, "Why don't you come up here and form a rough circle around me so you can all see better." This brought a sigh of appreciation from the others and they moved quickly to get a better view.

As Halliday carefully removed the wrapping it revealed what appeared to be a manuscript or document of well over a hundred pages. The pages themselves were an off white and also appeared to be handmade and quite old.

The top sheet was handwritten in block letters and said,
An Accounting of our trip Through Time. By Christopher Carver and Matthew Blair. Salem, Massachusetts, 1775. Halliday held it up so everyone could see it.

She grinned and said, "I know these guys. We were colleagues back in Nevada. Chris Carver was the one who came here four years ago." A murmur of recognition emanated from the group. "You can imagine how weird this feels knowing I'm reading something from them written in 1775." She then turned to the first page of the document. It, too, was handwritten, though it was in cursive writing. Fortunately, Chris Carver's handwriting, while not beautiful, was fairly clear and easy to read. Halliday had expected this, as the only printing available in 1775 was from printing presses, and Carver and Blair could not have been expected to be allowed to use a printer's facilities to set a couple hundred pages of type. Typesetting in those days was a slow and tedious process and any time available would have been dedicated to the jobs a printer was paid to produce.

As the evening proceeded, Madison read excerpts from various parts of the document. At first, they excerpts were from their trip in space. Then she read from their experiences in Salem after their arrival there. The most exciting excerpts were of their personal involvement in the Battle of Bunker Hill. A surprise element discussed the murder of Elihu Martin and the role a former Social Library trustee, Nathaniel Ellis, played in that killing. When this latter matter was read aloud, the current trustees of the successor to that old and respected library gasped. They had no idea that a murder was in the Athenaeum's past.

As the evening approached the witching hour, pun intended, Halliday told the audience she thought she should end the session, as tempting as it was for everybody to hear more juicy and fascinating tidbits from the past being reported by two men from the present. Carlotta Robb said they understood that it needed to come to an end, but asked Halliday if the Athenaeum could make a copy for their archives so they'd at least have a vestige of the real thing. She also asked that whenever the CAE went public with its project they would mention the important role the Athenaeum had played in making the project a success. The CAE had anticipated both of these requests as they had been granted four years earlier after the first mission. Halliday said yes to both requests and delivered a check as a tangible show of appreciation for what the library and its predecessor had done on behalf of the first two missions. When asked about a third mission, Madison told them that the lab back in Nevada was working on it and it was an even more ambitious mission than the first two.

End

Sources

History of Bunker Hill Battle, By S. Swett. Munroe and Francis, 1826

For statements in Chapter 22 attributed to Major John Pitcairn and General Gage critical of American Patriots see:
The Spirit of 74 by Ray and Marie Raphael, The New Press, 2015
Ray Raphael is a senior research fellow at Humboldt State University in California.
  and
TheHistoryJunkie.com

Richard Scott is a retired editor, writer, and publisher, having been president and publisher of the David McKay Company and president and publisher of Fodor's Travel Publications. He's also been director of the Reader's Digest Educational Division and managing editor of American Bookseller and Bookselling this Week. In the 70s Mr. Scott was co-host with Isaac Asimov, Brendan Gill and Nat Hentoff of a nationally syndicated radio talk show called In Conversation. Mr. Scott has written 13 books. He lives with his wife Jeanne in Peabody, Massachusetts.

For a sample of Richard Scott's book, **_Jefferson and the Barbary Pirates_**, read on.

JEFFERSON
and the Barbary Pirates
RICHARD SCOTT

Jefferson and the Barbary Pirates

Part 1

Chapter 1
The Atlantic, May 1784

The 300-ton merchant ship *Betsey* was within sighting distance of Tenerife, the capital of the Canary Islands. The Canaries, an

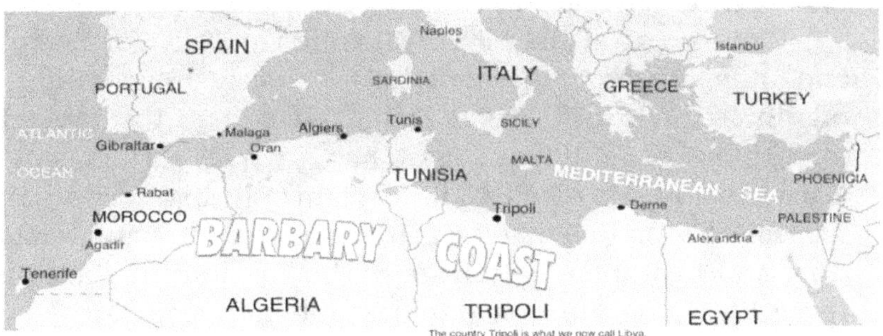

The country Tripoli is what we now call Libya.

archipelago conquered by Spain in the 15th century and roughly 100 miles west of Morocco's Atlantic coast, had been a profitable port of call for British North American merchant ships for decades. The *Betsey* was one of the first vessels to fly under the flag of the United States.

Up to this point the *Betsey* had enjoyed a swift and uneventful crossing, having left Boston just 28 days earlier. One of the ship's crew pointed to another ship less than a mile off to their starboard. The vessel appeared to be minding its own business, as they were. It was not unusual to see ships as you neared land.

William Proctor, the *Betsey's* first mate, was looking forward to arriving in the colorful island capital. This was his first voyage as a first mate, having been promoted just two months ago at the age of 19. As far as he knew, he was one of the youngest first mates out of Boston. He'd been a seaman for two years and had distinguished himself with competence and maturity beyond his years.

As a seaman, William Proctor had had very little time or money to spend pursuing his own interests when arriving at a foreign port. This time, as first mate, he hoped to enjoy Tenerife more. He'd been there on a previous trip and found it to be a pleasant, welcoming place. He couldn't wait to explore it.

Captain Henry Orne, a man in his early forties, balding and of average height, looked more like a schoolteacher than a veteran sea captain. Proctor knew from personal observation that Orne's stern, scholarly manner and less than robust appearance was deceptive. The man was strong, forceful and commanding when the occasion called for it.

Orne stood at the helm watching carefully for reefs, shoals and other hazards that can turn a successful crossing into a nightmare. Proctor, several inches taller than the captain, with long, blond, slightly unkempt hair, was at Orne's side. He'd learned on the trip over that the captain only appeared stern at first glance. He soon saw that the man made an effort to understand his crew and treat them with respect. Proctor, in turn, found himself respecting Orne. He looked to the captain as a mentor.

Now, at the helm with the captain, he was keeping a watchful eye out for things that Orne might miss. So far, everything had gone more smoothly than any seafarer could have hoped for. Even the weather had cooperated. The captain appeared relaxed and even exchanged a joke or two with young Proctor.

A few minutes later Proctor called his attention to the ship off in the distance.

"Looks like a Mediterranean sloop," said the captain. "Probably Spanish or Portuguese. Seems to be heading our way."

"You think she's on her way to America?"

"Doubt it. These cargo sloops tend to run up and down the coast of Africa or along the northern coast of the Med. Mostly trade in sugar, coffee, bananas and other fruit."

Proctor nodded his understanding, but something didn't make sense to him.

"Doesn't it seem a bit strange, captain, that she'd be heading our way if she was plying the coastal trade? She's heading almost due west."

"Aye, I see your point, William. 'Tis a bit strange. If they come close enough we'll ask 'em where they're off to. In the meantime best you talk to Cathcart about landing."

William left the helm and met with James Cathcart, bosun of the *Betsey*, and told him it was time to ready the crew for landing in Tenerife.

"Aye, sir," said Cathcart, who was five years Proctor's senior. At first he'd found it difficult to take orders from someone so much younger. Gradually, though, Proctor had won him over as he demonstrated a competence beyond his years. "What do we do about that sloop approaching us?"

"Probably nothing but say hello as she passes us. Looks innocent enough."

"I suppose so, sir, but why do you thinks she's heading our way?"

"She must be on her way to America, though the captain says most of these sloops stay on this side of the Atlantic. She's not that big for a crossing, so it would be strange if she really was on her way to the New World. We'll know soon enough when she's closer."

"I can see her flag now, sir," said Cathcart. "Spanish, I think?"

"She's heading directly toward us, so we should be able to hail her and find out her destination. Continue on, James. I'd best be getting back to the helm with the captain."
Cathcart nodded.

Back at the helm Captain Orne said, "Fast-moving vessel. We'll be able to talk to them in a minute or two. Take in some sail, William, and be prepared to hail them as they pull close. I'm assuming they'll trim a sail or two so we can exchange a few words."

"Aye, sir," said Proctor. "They should pass our port side. I'll go down there to hail them. Will you be joining me?"

"If they want to come aboard, I'll be glad to welcome their captain so we can chat."

As the trim ship neared the *Betsey* someone aboard the sloop waved, and Proctor waved back. Now the sloop was within 50 yards and parallel to the *Betsey*. She obviously intended to come alongside. Proctor smiled. He hadn't seen anyone but the crew in 28 days. He always enjoyed meeting folks from other parts of the world.

What he saw next made his heart stop. The Spanish flag was being lowered. As soon as it was down a new flag was raised—yellow crescent with a yellow star on a red background—one of the many flags used by the Barbary pirates. The Barbary pirates were known maritime predators based in four North African countries: Morocco, Algeria, Tunisia and Tripoli. The four countries were known as the Barbary Coast.

"Alert the crew!," yelled the captain. "Raise sail for as much speed as we can muster. We'll see if we can outrun them, but I'm not optimistic. If they come alongside, we'll have to deal with 'em. In that event tell the lads not to resist, as these bastards can be ruthless, and we're mostly unarmed."

Minutes later Proctor said, "They're gaining on us, cap'n. Should be abreast shortly. Nothing we can do. They're faster, and they maneuver better."

As he said this one of the pirates on the attacking ship raised what appeared to be a cutlass and bellowed in a heavily accented English, "I'm Captain Habib of the *Jabbar*. We are coming aboard to claim your cargo. Do not try to stop us, or you will not survive." Habib's jet black facial hair and piercing fiery black eyes lent a fierceness to his appearance that couldn't be ignored. Orne had no doubt that the man meant business. Still, he was not about to roll over without a show of resistance.

"You have no business on this ship," roared Captain Orne.

"We are in international waters."

"You are in Moroccan waters, captain, and subject to the authority of Mohammed Ben Abdallah, Sultan of Morocco. As such, you must submit to our demands. We demand your cargo." The Barbary corsair paused to let that sink in before continuing. "If you resist, you will perish."

Captain Orne turned to Proctor with a look of desperation on his face. "Do we have any choice, William? Most of our men are unarmed. If we resist we are all doomed." It was not as if Orne was afraid to fight. He'd fought nobly as a foot soldier in the war of independence, but now he was captain of a merchant vessel. His crew were not soldiers or naval seamen. They were not trained or equipped to fight.

"No, Captain, I don't think we have any choice. We will lose the cargo, but at least we shall have our ship and our lives."

"Aye, lad, go ahead and tell them. 'Tis a terrible choice, but what else can we do? Hopefully it will be quick so we can be done with them."

"Yes, Cap'n. God willing we can at least pick up a cargo in Tenerife so our trip won't be a total loss."

"Won't be much lad, as we won't have the coin from the sale of this cargo."

They were interrupted by a cry from the pirate on the Moroccan sloop. "What's your decision? Will you comply or do you wish to die? This is the last time I ask."

Captain Orne, looking pale and beaten, said, "Tell him to come aboard, Will. Let's get this over with."

Proctor walked to the rail of the ship and yelled, "The captain says to come aboard. We will hold you to your word that you will not harm the crew or take the ship."

"Yes, yes. We're coming aboard."

As the sloop pulled alongside the *Betsey*, two pirate sailors threw lines around the *Betsey's* bollards, securing the two ships so that there was no space between them. With that, a dozen or more pirates with cutlasses raised, led by Captain Habib, scrambled over the gunwales of the two ships, landing on the deck of the *Betsey*. As they landed they pushed several of the *Betsey's* crew members aside brusquely. Captain Habib cried, "Take me to your hold. The rest of you stay clear."

Will Proctor noted that he could barely understand the man as his English was heavily accented with what Will assumed was Arabic.

No one stood forward to lead the pirates to the hold. Will realized that no one wanted to be the person who cooperated with the attackers.

"I said take me to your cargo hold," roared the pirate leader. "Show me, or we will start throwing men overboard. Do not make me wait."

With this, Will stepped forward. He was not going to sacrifice lives to save cargo. Before he'd gone more than one step, bosun Cathcart strode forward, saying, "I'll take you there. Follow me."

With that the pirate captain said, "That's better. Show us the way."

As Cathcart started toward the hold, one of the pirates accompanying the pirate captain shoved Cathcart forward impatiently, forcing him to struggle to maintain his balance. In a rage Cathcart roared, "You bloody bastard!" and struck the pirate on the chin, stunning him and nearly knocking him to the deck.

On seeing this, Captain Habib drew his cutlass, and with a forward thrust, ran it through Cathcart's abdomen just below the sternum. As he withdrew the bloody sword he smiled and said, "Now I expect your cooperation, or the rest of you infidels will enjoy a watery grave."

"My God!" cried Captain Orne. "You've killed him."

Habib motioned to two of his men and said, "Throw his body overboard." Then he turned to Orne and said, "That is the fate of you and your crew if you defy me again. Do you understand?"

Orne swallowed and said, "Yes, we understand." Then he shouted to his crew, "Stand down men. Do as the captain says."

Habib told his crew that he was going below to inspect the cargo. While he was down there he expected them to keep an eye on the *Betsey's* crew. If they gave them any trouble, kill them all.

Minutes later the pirate captain emerged from the dark hold and spoke to Captain Orne. "I see that you have a much larger cargo than I expected. It is far too much to bring aboard my smaller vessel. I have decided that we shall take the cargo and the ship."

"But how will my crew and I return to America?"

Habib grinned cruelly. "You will not be returning to America. At least not now. I declare you my slaves. During the trip to Agadir, you and your crew shall be secured so that you cannot create any more mischief. I haven't decided yet whether to hold you hostage or to sell you at the slave market. Either way this encounter should be profitable for me and my crew and for His Royal Majesty, the Sultan of Morocco."

"Is there nothing we can do to persuade you otherwise?" pleaded Orne. "Morocco was the first country to recognize the United States back in 1777. At that time your country opened its ports to American ships. Why are you treating us so disrespectfully today? We are not your enemies. Why do you not let us go about our business? Would you and Morocco not be better off if we could trade with you?"

"Very nice words, captain. Very nice, but apparently you are misinformed. That agreement seven years ago quickly came to an end when your man in Paris failed to thank the Sultan for recognizing your little country." He was referring to Benjamin Franklin, one of the five American commissioners sent to Paris to negotiate the treaty officially ending the war of independence against Great Britain.

"There must be some mistake."

"There is no mistake, Captain. The Sultan informed all Moroccan ships of this insult, and because of it, authorized our ships at sea to treat American infidels as enemies. Enough of this, though. We must set sail for Agadir."

Chapter 2
Agadir, Morocco 1784

After five days at sea, the *Jabbar* sailed into the small Moroccan port of Agadir.

Will Proctor was glad to soon be on land, for the voyage from the Canary Islands had been wretched. They hadn't starved, as Captain Habib had said they would always be fed because that would make them more attractive on the slave market. He pointed out that, if he decided to hold them as hostages, he would still need them to be somewhat healthy in order to bring a decent ransom. The diet was barely edible, but sustaining. The men could handle that, but they were miserable because each of them had been tied or shackled to prevent them from interfering with the pirates, or worse, from attempting a reckless attempt at mutiny. While shackled in the dark hold of the ship, each man had been allowed one trip each day to relieve himself. If they could not control themselves beyond that they were forced to defecate or urinate in place where they were tied down. By the end of five days the ship's hold was a stinking, festering cesspool.

At first sight, Will thought that Agadir was a ghost town. Habib's crew pushed the shackled members of the *Betsey* crew through the streets of the dismal town. It looked to Will as if it had once been a thriving small city, but now many of the aging adobe brick dwellings seemed unoccupied. Dust was swirling in the air, and only a few dirty, bedraggled souls could be seen on the town's grimly depressing unpaved streets. Many of the these souls looked as if they could barely move. Those who could move approached the shackled Americans hesitantly, but with obvious curiosity. A small, motionless boy garbed in tattered rags was leaning against a crumbling building with flies crawling all over his face, neck and arms. Will wondered why Habib had brought them here to Agadir if he intended to put them in a slave market. Will couldn't believe that there were people in Agadir wealthy enough to own slaves.

As they were prodded stumbling through the town's streets, Will noticed that they were beginning to attract a crowd of jeering, taunting townspeople. Soon the crowd was quite large and menacing. Obviously, realized Will, Agadir was not quite the ghost town he'd thought it was. As the crowd became more threatening, he almost wished it were a ghost town.

"Where are you taking us?" demanded Orne.

"A place where you will be safe until I decide what to do with you, Captain. As you can see, the local residents do not think kindly of Christian infidels. You will be much safer under my protection."

"We would be much safer back on our ship."

"That's not going to happen, Captain Orne. That's not going to happen."

If you enjoyed this sample of *Jefferson & the Barbary Pirates*, the book is available in paper and ebook at Amazon.
https://amzn.to/2NeVSv1